DIPLOMATIC CORPSE

PHOEBE ATWOOD TAYLOR

DIPLOMATIC CORPSE

An Asey Mayo Cape Cod Mystery

A Foul Play Press Book

THE COUNTRYMAN PRESS
Woodstock, Vermont

DIPLOMATIC CORPSE

i

IF you summed up the whole silly situation in a nutshell, John Orpington decided, he was stripped and living in a pea-green folder. Stripped of his last cent, stripped of all his clothes except the shorts and shirt he stood in, and living in a crazy eight-page folder named *Picturesque Quanomet — the FRIENDLY Cape Cod Town*.

And he'd walked into it all by himself. Nobody shoved him.

"Picturesque Quanomet, the *friendly* octopus," he said aloud with irony as he paused on the sweltering rut lane to wipe the perspiration from his glasses. "Picturesque Quanomet, I didn't know it was loaded. Yah!"

In a sudden gesture of irritation, he jerked the pea-green folder from his pocket and pitched it toward the roadside grove of scrub pines. But the flimsy pamphlet only flapped two feet away to dangle on a bayberry bush, with the picture of View Number One, his immediate objective, face up and leering at him.

It certainly looked innocent enough, Orpington thought resentfully. When that folder was thrust into his hand last night as he stepped off the bus on Main Street, he'd accepted it as a pleasant gesture. He'd even felt flattered by the accompanying greeting from Quanomet's one-woman Welcoming Committee, a fragile-looking, white-haired, definitely lavender-and-old-lace type. No town in his previous experience ever bothered to welcome chance visitors with what amounted to a Whistler's Mother character!

He was touched when she insisted on reading him the folder's subtitles. "Quanomet — Where Old-Time Hospitality Abounds." "Quanomet — Where Home Folks Take a REAL Interest in *You*." He was moved to the core by her dismayed tongue-cluckings on learning that he had no advance room reservation. And he'd poured forth heartfelt gratitude when she generously proffered her best spare room, the last available bed in town.

Congratulating himself on his good luck, rejoicing in the cool salty air after New York's unmitigated August heat, he'd strolled down the moonlit street with Whistler's Mother pattering along beside him. He'd grinned and said "With pleasure," when she suggested he call her Aunt Thamozene instead of Mrs. Sturdy. He'd nodded in complete agreement at her assurance that he'd enjoy his Quanomet vacation.

But his genial glow began to wane a few minutes later when they arrived at the square, white-frame Sturdy home on Church Street. For the first time it dawned on him that Aunt Thamozene's sole aim in life was to prove that every word of the pea-green publicity folder was true, if not a downright understatement. Within half an hour, he had a sense of being swamped by Picturesque Quanomet, and folksy interest, and old-time hospitality.

Over his vain protests, she personally unpacked his suitcase, viewing with mounting horror each successive garment she unearthed. Before he could grasp her intention, his entire wardrobe had been whisked away to be darned or mended or washed or sent to the cleaner's. His wallet was whipped into the sanctuary of Grandfather Sturdy's safe, and the iron door banged shut. Somehow, as he'd followed her around the house in bewilderment, she'd managed to extract from him a variety of pertinent data, like his college, his war record, his mother's maiden name, and his age. He looked lots older than twenty-eight, she announced, but charitably ascribed his tired appearance to the bus trip and his bachelorhood. Then she'd made him drink a nice glass of hot milk, and returned to tuck him into Captain Obed Sturdy's canopied bed after he'd fled to it in desperation.

At seven this morning he'd been roused and forced to face a breakfast of oatmeal, fishcakes, fried potatoes, waffles and hot doughnuts. When he refused pie, Aunt Thamozene had commented tartly on his queasy appetite. A couple of weeks of good home care, she said in ominous tones, and she'd have him eating more like a man and less like a sick canary.

Whereupon she'd bundled him off to see View Number One, referred to in the pea-green folder as a "First Must" for every new Quanomet visitor. To prevent his confusing it with other and lesser views, she pointed out the illustration and kindly read him the descriptive paragraph underneath.

"Just drink in that scene for a few hours," she added briskly as she held open the screen door for him. "It'll rest you, like the folder says. And be home at noon sharp for dinner."

Of course he'd protested. At least, he told himself defensively, he'd tried to. On three triumphant occasions he'd got as far as "See here, Aunt Thamo —" before she interrupted him with more facts and anecdotes of Old Historic Quanomet.

Reaching gingerly across a patch of poison ivy, Orpington removed the folder from the bayberry bush and replaced it in his pocket. He might as well face this idiotic situation with calm and detachment. Short of knocking out Aunt Thamozene and blowing up Grandfather Sturdy's iron safe, there was no easy way of retrieving his wallet and his clothes. Until he recovered them, he was stuck.

"Quanomet Gives You Sports and Games." He quoted the first page from memory as he trudged up the lane. "A Veritable Hiker's Paradise. Terrific Scenic Views and Vistas. *This* Vacation Will Be the Jolliest Ever! Fun. Fun! *FUN!*"

When he rounded the curve at the top of the hill ahead, he stopped short and whistled softly.

View Number One wasn't bad at all! Even though the panorama of Quanomet Bay had been so often reproduced in photographs and paintings that little element of novelty or surprise remained, View Number One was actually something to look at. Below and in front of him stretched the vivid blue water of the harbor, with marshmallow clouds billowing against the pale, postcard-blue sky. Everything duly noted in the folder was present, too — the glistening sand dunes, the white strips of beach, the scallop boats anchored off the old whaling wharf, the weatherbeaten fish houses, the cluster of tiny sailboats racing out against the horizon.

There was even an artist at hand, Orpington discovered with considerable amusement as he concluded his survey and glanced around him. Not just an ordinary fellow with a paintbrush, either, but a bearded artist wearing yellow slacks and a pink shirt, daubing paint with a palette knife at what would probably turn out to be a somewhat frenzied version of View One.

"Hired by the Board of Trade?" he said conversationally.

The artist never turned his head.

"Because the Quanomet folder," Orpington raised his voice, "says there's rarely a time when some artist isn't painting this spectacular view from this specific vantage point. So I wondered if they'd hired you to provide general atmosphere and local color."

The artist continued both to ignore him and to slap away at his canvas as if he had some deep-rooted grudge against it.

Orpington grinned, and sauntered over toward the easel with the intention of kibitzing until he achieved some sort of response. He hardly expected to find any conventional rendering of the scene. Neither did he expect that his first sight of the canvas would stop him, as it did, cold in his tracks.

For the fellow wasn't working on another interpretation of View One. He was painting what appeared to be a swarm of infuriated ants running excitedly over a splotch of spilled molasses. He seemed, furthermore, to be painting something he actually saw, because he paused every few seconds to peer anxiously down the hill.

Following the line of his intent gaze, Orpington located what he'd previously overlooked — a baseball park in the meadow below, and a throng of people milling around it.

"I think," he said judicially, after watching a moment, "you've got something here. That's exactly what they do look like, ants on molasses. And I admire your conception of the sun as an enlarged fried egg. Truly a terrific vista!"

Without waiting for an answer, he strolled on along the lane. Part way down the hill, he stifled an impulse to return and inform Pink Shirt that from a lower angle the crowd ceased being ants and looked more like a small, dispossessed Balkan nation.

Down on the meadow, Orpington leaned against the boundary railing of the ball park and stared at the scene before him, fully conscious of the fact that his eyes were popping and his mouth gaping idiotically.

At least, he told himself, he clearly was no longer living in the pea-green folder.

At this point he had departed from Picturesque Quanomet and was out of the world entirely.

It wasn't the fault of his glasses. He'd wiped them again, put them back on, and found he was seeing the same thing. It wasn't a touch of sun. This was no mirage.

Slowly, because he was almost afraid to hurry, he hoisted himself up on the rail and proceeded to devote himself to a close, incredulous appraisal.

He began negatively, since it seemed easier to figure out what it couldn't be. It wasn't a circus, although there were a couple of circuslike tents in center field. Nor a carnival, although someone was selling balloons over by first base. Nor the folder's Quanomet Indians gathering for a reunion — or possibly a massacre — although there were half a dozen assorted braves in war paint sitting on a tier of the small grandstand. Nor gypsies, although every now and then a stray gypsy emerged from the miniature mob clustered around home plate.

"Okay," Orpington said. "Okay. Now tackle a positive approach. What the hell *is* it?"

It was a quartet of women in absurdly bustled skirts and perky Victorian bonnets — and strapless bras. It was a WAC in uniform, with two rows of campaign ribbons — and a pair of oars over her shoulder. A man in antsy-pants and a stovepipe hat. Three girls in hoopskirted crinolines and lace mitts — bearing among them an orange-striped beach umbrella and an assortment of collapsed camp chairs.

It was an elderly man wholly Pilgrim from his leather belt to his brown knee breeches and buckled shoes, but wearing a Hawaiian shirt stenciled with hula girls. It was a trio of Revolutionary War redcoats, one of them pushing a wheeled golf-club cart filled with muskets. It was George Washington, bewigged and tricorned, carrying a clam hoe. And General Grant with a bashed-in forage cap and a brass-buttoned blue frock coat — and gray flannel Bermuda shorts. It was a Red Cross nurse of World War One vintage. A pantalooned and helmeted fireman toting a bass drum. A black-garbed, beaver-hatted preacher with a long white beard in his hand.

And it was children. Children of all ages and all sizes, dressed and undressed in every conceivable costume. It was sunburned children, tanned children, parboiled-looking children. Screaming children, laughing children, sulky children, and every last one of them in constant and perpetual motion.

Just about all this terrific vista lacked, Orpington decided, was a Pied Piper.

Suddenly, and somewhat to his own critical dismay, he found his attention focusing once again on a plump, middle-aged matron dressed in a trailing pink lace gown with leg-of-mutton sleeves, and a picture hat as wide as a cartwheel. He'd noticed her several times before as the center of a huddle near third base, but now she had abruptly detached herself from the group and was scurrying toward the crowded parking space to his left.

There was almost a sense of flight in her hasty retreat, Orpington thought reflectively, and wondered what there was about this Madame-President-of-the-Thursday-Club character which should rouse such interest on his part. He didn't know her, after all. He didn't know anyone in Quanomet except Aunt Thamozene. And to the best of his recollection, the trailing lace dress and the feathery picture hat didn't conjure up any tender or nostalgic memories.

Why should he be completely unable to take his eyes off this plump matron who was trying so unsuccessfully to spring from the scene in high-heeled pink satin slippers?

"Mrs. Henning! Mrs. Henning!"

After a quick, nervous glance over her shoulder at the sound of what was obviously her own name being called out, the Pink Lady put on a very creditable last-lap spurt.

"Mrs. *Henning!*"

Another woman, a very much younger woman, emerged from the third-base huddle and headed in a beeline for the Pink Lady. To judge from the beaded moccasins on her feet, the tall feather sticking bolt upright in her brown hair, and the strings of Woolworth glass beads draped around her thin neck, she had probably hoped to achieve the general effect of an Indian Maiden. Without those overt clews, Orpington decided, he would unhesitatingly have described her costume as something unfortunately compiled in haste from a couple of old fringed burlap bags.

What with her brandishing a scroll of paper in her right hand, and hanging onto the nose bridge of her shell-rimmed glasses with her left hand, her pursuit wasn't too graceful or too efficient. What she lacked in speed, however, she made up for in sheer tone volume and persistency.

At the sixth piercingly shrill repetition of her name, Mrs. Henning gave up, and Orpington heard her unhappy sigh as she paused a few feet away from his perch on the railing. Yet the smile which she summoned up to greet Indian Suit was the proper and traditional clubwoman smile that could be seen a thousand times a day in the newspapers. Probably any senator would have been warmed and mollified by that smile, and responded in kind.

Indian Suit wasn't, and didn't.

"Look, Mrs. Henning!" Completely out of breath and curiously tense, she continued to brandish the scroll. One of the braids coiled around her ears had fallen down, and her head-feather was unattractively askew. "Mrs. Henning, look here!"

"Yes, Muriel dear?"

It was a most conciliatory coo, but dear Muriel wasn't being placated.

"Mrs. Henning, *if* you want posterity to think that the Reverend Phineas Winter was blond, all right! But *my* records and all the other records prove definitely and beyond any peradventure of a doubt that he was *not* — "

A trumpet flourishing in a badly executed fanfare and a ruffle of assorted and off-beat drums drowned out the rest of the conversation. When the tumult subsided, dear Muriel had a firm grasp on Mrs. Henning's leg-of-mutton sleeve, and was propelling her back toward third base.

Then a slim girl in blue shorts and a blue denim shirt strolled into view from behind the grandstand, and at the sight of her, John Orpington teetered on the railing. By the time she passed in front of him, the collar of his shirt had been jerked neatly into place, and he was smoking a cigarette with great calm.

"No guards," he said, in a voice pitched just loud enough for her to hear.

It was Kay Pouter, all right. She swung around and recognized him immediately.

On the whole, it wasn't as bad a moment as he'd anticipated. She said quickly it had been good of him to write when Bob was killed. "And how are you, Buff?"

He said quickly that he'd meant to write her again only it had been a busy war, and how was she? "And the baby?"

"The baby's seven," Kay said, "and will probably come as something of a shock to you. He's temporarily mislaid in this shuffle, and I'm hunting him — he has a strong tendency to sample box lunches if he knows they're in the car. Whatever did you mean, no guards?"

"This can't be the annual outing of a madhouse," he said. "No guards. No strait jackets. Kay, what *is* it? What goes on here?"

Before she could speak, a small, black-haired boy in dungarees and red sneakers came rushing up to her.

"Mother, can I have a portable Geiger counter for my birthday? Why *not?*"

"Because" — her composure didn't appear to be shaken in the least by the request — "you can't. Bobby, this is Mr. Orpington — no, this is the time you don't shake hands, you're much too greasy. Mr. Orpington was a friend of your father's. They did their flight training together."

"How do you do. I know," Bobby said. "I know him. He's in the wedding picture. You said he was best man. But Mother, if someone finds a uranium deposit around Quanomet, I'm going to look dumb! And Miss Babcock wants to know where Gramp is, and Auntie Maude says what did you do with that flintlock?"

"I gave it to her half an hour ago, tell her," Kay said. "And I couldn't guess where your grandfather is. When I last saw him, he was teaching what he claimed was a sea chantey to those teen-age Benson girls. Go find your group, they were yelling for you."

"Mother, can I have a Popsicle first? A raspberry Popsicle? Why *not?*"

"Because from the evidence smeared around your mouth, you've already had at least three Popsicles — "

"Only two!"

"Then," Kay said, "you don't need any more for a while. Hop along to your group." She watched him as he raced away, and then turned back to Orpington. "What're you doing here, Buff?"

He didn't bother with any of the elaborate explanations he'd concocted during the bitterness of that long train and bus trip. The truth came out quite naturally. "Pettingill,

Watrous and Company fired me yesterday morning because I'd irked their favorite pet-food account — I went into advertising when I came back, you know. So I decided to take a vacation, and told the man at the window to pick a town, any town. The ticket said Quanomet — Kay, what *is* this?"

"This? Oh, you mean all this mess. This is the Quanomet Associates."

"Associates what?" He offered her a cigarette and she perched on the rail beside him.

"Well, originally there was the Quanomet Neighborhood Association, but a great schism divided it into the Quanomet Summer Residents Club and the Quanomet All-Year-Rounders — sounds raffish, doesn't it? I've never been able to find out why the split occurred. Maybe it had something to do with Roosevelt's trying to pack the Supreme Court, maybe it was just someone's ordering banana instead of peach ice cream for refreshments. Anyway, those two limbs withered and died, and out of the dust and ashes came the Quanomet Associates. We're just one big happy family of summer people and natives, currently bound together by a vicious interest in zoning, and no more overnight cabins, and where is the new, *new* state highway going?"

"I see," Orpington said. "The Quanomet Associates. Yes. Uh-huh. But what's all this?"

She stared at him. "Buff, it isn't humanly possible for you to have walked ten feet through the streets of Quanomet without seeing the posters — I know, I helped put 'em up! You couldn't have got here without *tripping* over posters!"

"I came," he pointed, "by that thar hill. By quaint rut lane — and I quote from the pea-green folder — and through scented pine grove. There was an artist, there were green-head flies. But no posters. Now break down and tell me — what is it?"

"Why, this is the pre-dress rehearsal for the Quanomet Associates Annual Pageant. 'Quanomet Through the Ages.' Auntie Maude — see her over there, in pink lace, trying to get out of the clutches of the Squaw Woman, alias our Miss Babcock? Auntie Maude's the moving factor of this show. She's chairman. Oh, you know Auntie Maude, Buff! She was at the wedding, and she's always spoken very highly of you because you found her a chair to sit on when her feet hurt."

He nodded slowly. "She's in that group picture — I remember now. So that's the reason why she's been haunting me! I couldn't figure out — "

"Mrs. Pouter!"

The thin little man in the neat, sand-colored Palm Beach suit had approached so quietly that neither of them was aware of his presence until he somewhat apologetically spoke Kay's name. Buff's first impression, as he automatically turned around toward the newcomer, was of being spied upon by a small tan bird.

"Mrs. Pouter, I'm so sorry to interrupt your conversation — but I find to my dismay that the programs haven't come! I checked with the Tonset printer by telephone, and he assures me that he's never even *heard* about the pageant programs! Er — as the Program Committee, do you — er — I mean, have you *any* inkling what — er — "

"I'm not programs, Father is," Kay said. "But I looked after everything. Relax. The Weesit Press man swore he'd have them done today, and he's delivering them in person to Mrs.

Oakes, who's in charge of selling and general distribution. I just forgot to tell Father that I'd made a number of improvements on his original plans. It would have been so silly to print the things earlier. I knew there'd be a million last-minute changes. Mr. Bird," the look of warning she flashed at Buff effectively squelched his half-audible reaction to the little man's name, "this is Mr. Orpington. If Miss Babcock's brother doesn't arrive in time tomorrow night, we'll use Buff for that 1812 scene of the British being repulsed on Quanomet Point. He's tall enough to make an admiral you can see from a distance, and the costume'll fit him."

"Mrs. Pouter, you are unique!" Clasping his hands together as if he were congratulating himself, Mr. Bird surveyed her with undisguised admiration. "You think of everything! You even give me the courage to think that this affair *may* run smoothly, after all!"

"Has there been more trouble?" Kay asked quickly.

The faintest of shadows seemed to flit across Mr. Bird's face. "Er — trouble, Mrs. Pouter?"

"Trouble. Not mishaps or accidents or minor casualties. Trouble."

"You refer, I assume, to the rowdy element. No." Mr. Bird's smile was practically the equivalent of a pitying pat on the back, Buff thought. He further decided that it angered Kay, although her expression of curious concern didn't change. "No, dear Mrs. Pouter, I feel that the rowdy element has shot its bolt."

"Oh?" Kay looked past Mr. Bird in the direction of third base, where Mrs. Henning was still in conversation with Indian Suit. "Oh?"

"I really do, Mrs. Pouter! I've had the carpenter go over the grandstand, and that's all right — nothing else has been sawed through."

Buff found himself blinking at the casual manner in which the little man tossed out that provocative item.

"I'm having all the wiring checked — but I *do* feel," Mr. Bird continued earnestly, "that last night's wiring fiasco resulted solely from the Harriman boy's ineptitude. In his youthful enthusiasm to assist, he permitted us to presume him an electrical expert when such was far from the truth."

"The Harriman boy," Kay returned, "was probably God's most innocent bystander. Those wires had already been crossed and tampered with when he flipped the switch. If Aunt Maude had been in her proper place instead of on the side lines conferring with you — well, we gnawed all that to the bone last night, didn't we, Mr. Bird?"

"Er — yes." Mr. Bird didn't exactly wince, but he sounded as if he wanted to. "Yes, indeed we did!"

"And I like to think," Kay went on, "that you're having the parking space watched to see that no one drives any *more* nails into Aunt Maude's tires?"

"I mean to inspect her tires myself, very soon." Mr. Bird paused, and then drew a long breath. "Actually, I'm convinced that Mrs. Henning is, and always has been, perfectly safe. I most strenuously doubt if anyone really intended to harm her. Those acts of vandalism were committed by the rowdy element. I'm positive that there's no other answer."

"My father is equally positive," Kay said, "that these acts of vandalism were committed in the name of jealousy. He calls it activated sour grapes from someone who got left out of the show, or got only a little part. I can only say you're both a lot more sanguine than I am! I can still remember what's happened in the past when Aunt Maude's run other pageants in other places."

"Mrs. Henning is so zealous," Mr. Bird murmured. "Your father mentioned some of those other incidents. But there's absolutely no similar rivalry between the natives and the summer people here in Quanomet! I know, since I belong to both groups now I've become a year-round resident. Truly, I'm sure that some of the rowdy element were carried away in a sort of — oh, call it a carnival spirit, a Hallowe'en spirit, if you will. Just thoughtless boys — "

"Being boys." An acidulous note had crept into Kay's voice. "Let's hope you're right, Mr. Bird, or that Father's right. But let's keep checking up on things, constantly, just the same."

"I promise you that I will. At the moment, I feel that we have to face only one *real* problem." Mr. Bird cleared his throat. "That is Miss Babcock."

"Muriel Babcock has her faults," Kay said, "but she doesn't saw through grandstands or drive nails in tires or contrive lethal short circuits. Muriel's utterly devoid of what you like to call the carnival spirit."

Her irony was wasted on Mr. Bird, who said hurriedly that wasn't at all, not at all what he'd meant by Miss Babcock's being a problem.

"I referred to her overwhelming passion for accuracy, Mrs. Pouter. If only we could tone that down in the interests of harmony! I've repeatedly tried to impress on her that an occasional lapse in minor detail — like the color of a wig or the cut of a collar — is quite unimportant in relation to the smooth running of the whole affair. But she is obdurate. She will not tolerate errors. She is obstinately resolved that every last detail shall be, to coin a phrase, one hundred per cent correct."

Kay smiled.

"Whenever Bobby's persistency tries me, I think of Muriel, and Bobby becomes a pliant piece of putty in comparison. And of course since she's been writing the definitive history of Quanomet for the last ten years, she does know all the details — that's the most completely irritating thing about her, I suppose, she's always so damned right! And she's certainly pestered Aunt Maude to the bone. Make her count, Mr. Bird."

"Er — count?"

"Put her to work counting things. Father kept her quiet for hours yesterday counting stars on flags to make sure they were historically proper. He faithfully promised he'd keep her counting things at a distance from Aunt Maude today, but he apparently got sidetracked."

Mr. Bird brightened. "She can count costumes and check the firearms list," he said. "A splendid suggestion! And I'm so happy to be reassured about the programs."

He bowed rather formally, and walked away with short, quick steps.

"I keep wondering," Kay remarked almost absently, "*would* he remind me of a sparrow if his name was something else, like Shark, or Lyon? As you probably gathered, he's Aunt Maude's chief assistant — vice-chairman, it says on the program. He checks and correlates. He holds things. He smooths over. He pours oil on."

"What I primarily gathered," Buff said, "was that something's sour, and that you don't begin to string along with the jealousy or the rowdy element angle. What's the matter, anyway? Sabotage?"

"Someone," Kay said, "is trying to kill Aunt Maude, that's all."

As he stared at her, Buff came to the conclusion that she really meant it.

"You heard," she said. "Someone's trying to kill her. Kill, as murder. And don't pat me on the back and say probably I'm tired, and Bobby's such an active little fellow, *is*n't he, and goodness this heat has been enough to make anyone upset, hasn't it! Spare me that. Someone's trying very hard to murder Aunt Maude. They're working at it."

Buff teetered back on the railing, and grinned at her.

"Yesterday," he said cheerfully, "I might actually have raised an eyebrow or two at that calm utterance. But not today. Not in Picturesque Quanomet! After all, I'm the man who waked up this morning in a canopied bed with swallows."

"With *what*?"

"Swallows," Buff said. "First they swooped around the canopy and then they swooped into their fireplace nest — my landlady keeps one window unscreened for their benefit. Her ancestor who fought at Bunker Hill brought the first English swallow back to Quanomet, see?"

"Look here, Buff! You — "

"Look here yourself! At least, listen here!"

Briefly, he summed up his life from the advent of the pea-green folder to the ant-and-molasses painting of the artist on the hill.

"So now," he concluded, "I fall into 'Quanomet Through the Ages.' D'you think anything can stagger me at this point? D'you think you can throw me by quietly announcing that Auntie Maude's going to be killed? Don't be foolish! Sure, she's going to be murdered. Shortly we'll hear a loud bang — and Auntie Maude will suddenly topple into a heap of pink lace, with that cartwheel hat sitting on top like the cap of a feathery mushroom — "

There was suddenly a loud report, and Aunt Maude toppled.

ii

BUFF leaped from the railing, and Kay followed suit.

Then they both stopped short and looked questioningly at each other.

"Car backfire," Buff said. "There it goes again — it's the red truck over by the big tent. But damn it, she *toppled!*"

Kay put a restraining hand on his arm as he started forward.

"She's fainted. Wait — don't rush off and get mixed up in all that crowd yet. I want to talk to you — "

"But how do you know it's only a faint, Kay? What makes you so sure?"

"I've been waiting for it and watching for it," she said, "for roughly half an hour. When anyone backs Aunt Maude into a corner the way Muriel Babcock's been backing her, she always faints. She belongs to the tag end of the last generation that learned to faint in self-defense — look, Buff, she's already starting to sit up."

The crowd that had been clustered around Mrs. Henning was now being shooed away and dispersed, and he could view her evident and unmistakable recovery.

"Besides," Kay went on, "I noticed she toppled very carefully so that she wouldn't hurt her dress. She adores that pink lace. She wore it at her graduation ball the night she first met Marcus Henning, and she wouldn't tear that gown for worlds."

"I quote in a weak voice," Buff said, "from the folder. 'Fun. Fun! *FUN!*' Kay, are you really serious about this attempted murder business?"

"I'm so deadly serious that if I let myself raise my voice, I'd scream and never stop! Listen, that grandstand was sawed through in the exact place where Aunt Maude's been standing to direct the mob scenes. Bobby was wriggling around underneath and discovered it, and mercifully came and told me. I can't explain to you just how the wiring was tampered with — I've never understood anything more about electricity than how to replace a burned-out light bulb. I don't know what sort of lethal device was planned. But *some*thing blew up with a lot of smoke and flame in the exact place where Aunt Maude stands to make her opening speech of welcome. Now that's not just sheer coincidence — that's placement of a high order, and you know it is!"

Buff conceded that she had a point. "What about this tire situation?"

"I accidentally spilled the coins out of my change purse yesterday morning, and while I was grubbing around to pick 'em up, I noticed the nails driven into her front tire. And — "

"That's really something less than attempted murder, isn't it?" Buff inquired.

"It certainly wasn't the work of any well-wisher!" Kay retorted. "Obviously someone hoped she'd have a blowout and an accident! But because they're those self-sealing tubes that won't blow out if you drive a million nails into 'em, Father brushed that episode off with a blithe wave of his hand — if it couldn't work, it doesn't count, in his estimation! Father — d'you remember him, by the way?"

"Owing to the festivities that preceded your wedding," Buff told her with honesty, "my memory of it has certain very dim areas. Seems to me he's a large man, and he writes. Ezio Pinza type, isn't he? Iron-gray hair and a lot of charm?"

"Definitely," Kay said. "Definitely. He's lousy with charm. He's one of the most delightful people I know, but he doesn't like to face things. He likes everything to seem to be running smoothly, and he's perfectly willing to thrust his head deep into the sand and hold it there forever, if that'll maintain the illusion. He's been such an ostrich about all this that I've abandoned hope of trying to make him take it seriously."

"You told Bird there'd been other trouble in other pageants, or words to that effect," Buff said. "I didn't understand — does Auntie Maude make a hobby of running pageants, or just of running into trouble?"

"Aunt Maude — look!" Kay pointed. "They've got her up on her feet now, and she's being gently steered toward the girls' dressing tent. Aunt Maude is simply a sucker for pageants. Wherever we've spent summers, she's always thrown a pageant if she possibly could. At the drop of a hat. Once she fixes her eyes on a suitable site, she digs up some worthy purpose for giving a pageant, and the community's licked. In passing, this show's basically to raise money for the Quanomet Associates Fund. We have some benevolent intention of painting the Town Hall. Two coats."

"But where does the trouble enter in?" Buff persisted. "Or troubles?"

"Well," Kay said, "that isn't too easy to sum up in any grand sweeping statement. Things go sour in so many different ways. Ordinarily there's a pitched battle between the town natives and the summer people, with Aunt Maude in the middle, taking it on the chin from both sides."

"That isn't true of Quanomet, though, according to Bird —"

"Like Father," Kay broke in, "Mr. Bird enjoys thinking that everything is running smoothly. I regaled you with the history of the Quanomet Associates and all its past schisms, didn't I? And did that sound particularly peaceful? Why, Mrs. Sturdy — your folksy Aunt Thamozene — left the pageant in a huff ten days ago. She and her friends now cross the street to avoid speaking to Aunt Maude. Or me. The librarian tells me that they're even boycotting the inscribed gift copy of Father's newest book!"

"So that's why Aunt Tham never muttered one word about all this," Buff remarked thoughtfully. "I've been wondering. She briefed me so exhaustively on so much else. But would this little village spite brigade run to grandstand-sawing and the like?"

Kay shook her head.

"I can't think so. I'm just pointing out that this sort of ill-feeling usually exists in these affairs, and sometimes it's led to some very trying problems. Then there are always top-brass troubles — squabbles and heartburn from the vice-chairmen who yearned to run things themselves. I'm sure that Bird would have adored being head man, for example, and I know that Muriel Babcock would have given her front teeth to be head girl. Not," she added critically, "that anyone would want those teeth."

"Mr. Bird and Miss Babcock," Buff said, "seem to me hardly the saboteur type. Or do I do 'em a grave and underestimating wrong?"

"No, you most certainly don't! So the only other angle I can think of — "

"Is?" Buff prompted as she hesitated.

"Well, the only other thing," Kay said slowly, "is that Aunt Maude always gets to chewing on underlying purposes. She always feels constrained to *prove* something with her pageants if she can. Then — bang!"

Almost automatically, Buff looked over his shoulder.

"Don't go banging around like that," he said. "It has a tendency to unnerve me. What d'you mean? How could you inject any purpose into this mad romp?"

"Well, 'Quanomet Through the Ages' was originally and primarily fun for all. But then Aunt Maude began to invest it with a holy purpose. You know — 'This Is What We Stand For.' All that sort of thing."

"From where *I* stand," Buff returned, "it still looks like a mad romp for kiddies and adults alike."

"But it isn't any more. It hasn't been for several weeks. It's a patriotic issue. It's the grass roots of America pushing onward and upward. If you display the glories of our past, and the wealth of our traditions and heritages, why nobody'll bore from within and undermine us, see?"

Buff looked at her quizzically. "That a quote from Aunt Maude?"

"Not a quote, just the gist of the informal lectures she's been giving to the pageant cast. 'Why I Believe in Quanomet,' and all about our role in the conflict of ideologies, and so on."

"Good God," Buff said.

"Uh-huh. And the cast seemed to eat it up. I've come to the sad conclusion that pageant casts really enjoy holy purposes. Only — it was just about that time that things started to sour. I could feel 'em curdling."

"Now look," Buff said, "you're not seriously suggesting that Aunt Maude's got subversive elements out against her, are you?"

"Oh, dear, I can't put my finger on what went sour, or exactly when it soured, or why! I only know it's sour, good and sour, right now! And it *is* serious — I haven't told you about last night, Buff. That really terrified me. It still terrifies me."

She paused to light a cigarette, and then moved back and braced one hand against the railing, as if she felt the urgent need of some solid support.

Watching her, Buff's sense of perplexity continued to mount. In a fine effort at detachment and objectivity, he asked himself if it were that frightened, groping gesture of hers that sent such a sudden, ominous chill running up and down his spine. Or was it the anguish in her voice, or the anxiety written on her face?

Probably none of them, he decided as he looked across the ball park. He was just letting himself get carried away. If he'd actually felt any chill, nature was providing an entirely legitimate excuse for it. He'd just been too deeply engrossed in Kay's recital not to notice before that those marshmallow clouds had been spreading until, for the moment, they'd blotted out the bright hot glare of the sun.

Somehow it gave the effect of footlights and spotlights being turned off a stage, and of theater house lights coming on. The scene looked real and rational for a change. True, everyone was still milling around, but the milling seemed more orderly and less chaotic. The bright colors of the costumes were dimmed. People looked like people, not grotesque hybrids. This was a pageant rehearsal. The fate of nations wasn't hanging in the balance. Mrs. Henning wasn't in any danger.

Of course she wasn't!

It simply had become cooler. That was all. As he'd told himself during yesterday's torrid journey, even being booted out of a job would probably make sense when the heat finally abated for ten consecutive minutes. Everything always made sense when it cooled off.

"Bobby," Kay said, "called me around three o'clock this morning, and when I went into his room I heard the rustle of someone moving on the balcony outside — the balcony leads to Aunt Maude's room, too. She was snoring serenely. So was Father. The rustling stopped when I turned on Bobby's light, but I could feel someone out there, someone staring in. You can laugh if you want to, but it was something so evil that it paralyzed me. I had an awful feeling that I was going to be sick. Actively sick."

She glanced up for a second at the darkening sky.

"I didn't know what to do," she went on. "I hadn't any gun or any weapon. I wouldn't have known what to do with one if I had! I knew I never could arouse Father quietly. So instead of getting Bobby his drink of water and ordering him to go back to sleep, I sat on the side of his bed and told him stories until I heard the person rustling away. Even then I couldn't bring myself to leave Bobby's room. I sat there until daybreak. I didn't know what was going on. What anyone meant to do. But I'm still terrified!"

Buff told himself that it really was cooler, and that you had to be objective about this sort of thing. There was always someone who drove nails in tires, pageants or no pageants. Wiring went haywire. Kids got hold of a stray saw and hacked away at the first available piece of wood they could find.

"I know what you're thinking," Kay said. "I didn't see anyone. I just heard something. There's a wide margin of doubt and error, if you want to be brutally logical. All these things I think are focused against Aunt Maude can be unfocused incidents, entirely without purpose or meaning. They *can* be. But they aren't. After last night, I know better!"

"Did you break the news of this to her?" Buff asked.

"Of course. The instant I heard her stirring this morning. She laughed that tinkling laugh of hers," Kay said, "and told me she thought I should leave Bobby with her and Father, after this show is over, and take a nice cruise somewhere by myself. She thinks what I need is a nice rest. Buff, what can you do when nobody'll believe — " She broke off. "Oh! Hullo, Muriel. I hardly recognized you in your war paint. What's gone wrong now?"

Miss Babcock's other braid had fallen down and was dangling over her shoulder, and her head-feather trailed off into space from the nape of her neck — rather, Buff thought, like the tail of an unhappy cat. The left side of her face had obviously been used as a field for make-up experimentations, and was shaded from a rich plum color to the brown of a melted chocolate bar. Awesome streaks of yellow ochre wandered from her nose to her ear, and across her forehead.

"Kay," she said tensely, "it's the ball team!"

"Ball team? What ball team?" Kay returned. "Is this some new development? I didn't know we had any ball team scene — and don't tell me someone's written one in at this late date, not when I've finally for once got the programs printed without one single schedule error! Don't tell me Father felt inspired to write in a ball team scene — I can't take it!"

"No, no, no, it's the Weesit ball team! They want to hold batting practice. Something about next week's game. I don't want to bother your aunt — she fainted, you know! — but what shall I say?"

"If I were you," Kay said, "I'd point out that batting practice at this time was highly inadvisable and impractical. In other words, no."

"I *said* no!"

"Then say it again at the top of your lungs. Yell it. Frankly, if you yelled at me in all that war paint, I'd fall down dead. Just be firm, Muriel."

Buff continued to look after her with surprise as she hurried away in the direction of the grandstand.

"Why, she's young!" he said. "I mean, I thought she was a contemporary of Aunt Maude's!"

"She's twenty-eight — and I can't guess why she looks so frightfully lumpy," Kay said. "Practically portly. Perhaps her researches prove that local Indian women were padded, and she's being authentic, or something. Actually she's a bony little person. Her family are old, old summer settlers here, and they feel their aristocratic position very keenly — they hardly ever notice anyone who hasn't come here regularly for fifteen or twenty years. They — d'you know, I told Father the dress rehearsal would probably bring on a deluge, and from the looks of that black sky, I suspect the two-month drought's about to turn into a two-month downpour! Buff, why do you seem so utterly baffled all of a sudden?"

"I'm brooding about our Miss Babcock," he said. "She's set up a strange train of thought — is she always that tense?"

Kay pursed her lips and considered his question.

"More or less, I'd say. And always about Quanomet — Quanomet's her lifework. I told you she was writing the town history. She's also an authority on old and quaint sayings and customs — if you ever got her and Aunt Thamozene together, you'd be drowned in a tidal wave of local color! She knows every last thing about this town, and she cares about it, furiously!"

"Go on," Buff said.

"On? On about what, Muriel?" It was Kay's turn to seem baffled. "Oh, she knows where the early town settlements were," she said with a casual wave of her hand. "And who lived in what house. And she's pumped the oldest inhabitants dry. Turns up panting at their deathbeds to make sure they haven't kept any details from her. In her spare moments, she even rubs tombstones — well, to get back to the point, nobody'll believe me about all this mess, Buff! The only bright spot — let's see if I can locate her. I had her a minute ago. Yes, there she is. See that pioneer woman in the calico print and sunbonnet, over between second and third?"

"The short, wide lady?" Buff said. "The one that's bustling so?"

Kay nodded.

"Her appearance is just about as deceptive as Aunt Maude's. Don't let *her* girth mislead you, either. She may resemble a large pumpkin, and Aunt Maude may look like an oversize cream puff, but I'd personally hate to tangle seriously with either of 'em. If she'd flourished in pioneer days, that short wide woman would have scalped the Indians first, and doubtless have pulled the covered wagon along with her bare teeth when the oxen gave out. *That's* Jennie Mayo!"

She obviously took it for granted that the mere mention of the name would suffice for Buff's instant recognition.

"Mayo," he said, trying to remember if Aunt Thamozene had briefed him on any such person. "Mayo. Uh — "

"Oh, you must know the name! She's housekeeper — and a cousin, I think — of Asey Mayo, that incredible man over in Wellfleet. You know. You've certainly heard of Asey Mayo!"

"Sure," Buff said. "He's the one they refer to in the headlines and the rotogravures as the Codfish Sherlock. Tall, lean, salty Asey Mayo. The Hayseed Sleuth. And he's somehow connected with Porter automobiles."

"That's right. He started out in life as a cabin boy or something, and got to be yacht captain for the Porter family, and wound up being chairman of the board of the Porter

Motor Car Company. Well, it dawned on me at breakfast this morning that Asey Mayo was my solution!"

Buff patted her on the shoulder with approval.

"That," he said, "is it! He's your boy! He can ferret out the truth and — "

"But he can't!" Kay interrupted. "I whipped over to his house, and damn it, he's not home! So I told Jennie Mayo everything. I can't make out," she added thoughtfully, "if she really believes me, or if she just leaped at the chance for some action and excitement. But anyway, she dragged that calico outfit from a sea chest and became a pioneer woman on the spot, and dashed over here — as she said, an extra pioneer would never attract any attention. She's promised to keep her eye on Aunt Maude, and her ear to the ground — oh, here's Muriel again! I'll have to go settle that ball team issue — wait here."

Buff relaxed against the railing and surveyed the throng, divided now into little groups which were apparently engaged in carrying on their own separate rehearsals. They'd have to grope their way around with flashlights if it grew another shade darker, he decided. And when the rain came, the ensuing scramble for the shelter of the dressing tents should be as epic as a land rush.

He knew he ought to be concentrating his full attention on the problem of Aunt Maude, but his mind kept ducking the task of making any decision. He kept wishing instead that he knew what Asey Mayo's cousin thought about Kay's story. He wished he knew what she thought of the tense Miss Babcock, too. It was all very well for Kay to dismiss her so casually as hardly the saboteur type. He'd done the very same thing himself, at first. Of course Kay couldn't consider her a saboteur or even a potential murderer when her thoughts were already crystallized about Miss Babcock. Muriel was to her the Quanomet historian, the old summer settler family, the bear for quaint details. Muriel was the familiar eccentric.

Clearly it hadn't ever occurred to Kay to question Muriel's tenseness or the wild look in her gray eyes. Or to attempt adding them together as a possible answer to all this to-do. Kay would probably be highly amused to learn that when a stranger once began second-thoughting about Muriel, she became a character who should be looked into seriously, if not viewed with some alarm.

Jennie Mayo's sunbonnet bobbled into sight in the vicinity of first base, and Buff suddenly moved away from the railing and started to stride in her direction. After all, there wasn't any valid reason why he couldn't get hold of the great Mayo's cousin and find out her impressions of all this business!

It was Mr. Bird, white-faced and trembling, and standing all by himself near the pitcher's box, who hailed him and brought his pursuit of Jennie Mayo to a most abrupt halt.

"Stop! Stop, Mr. — er — Mr. — uh — "

"Orpington," Buff said, staring at him. "What's the matter with you, man? You look frightened to death! Are you sick?"

Mr. Bird's mouth moved and his lips seemed to be forming words, but no sound emerged. Finally, with what was obviously a superhuman effort at pulling himself together, he held out his hand toward Buff, and displayed something he was holding.

"Er — Mr. — er — it's a *dagger!*"

"So it is." Buff felt that it was an inadequate reply, but he couldn't think of anything else to say.

"In the crowd," Mr. Bird began, and then paused to swallow. "In the crowd, I stepped on a stone and — and stumbled. Something pricked me — pricked my back as I moved forward. Then something *dropped*. It was this!"

"Who dropped it?" Buff demanded. "Where were you? Who was near you?"

"This light — " Mr. Bird's voice failed him once again, but he rallied bravely. "It's so dark, I couldn't tell — I couldn't guess! I don't know who — I was caught between the survivors and — I *think* — the packet."

"Between what?"

"The survivors." Mr. Bird drew a long breath. "The joyous homecoming of the Valley Forge survivors, and the first voyage of the Boston packet, and — oh, everybody was *moving* so! Moving about. Just like this, now! See?"

Buff looked around, and saw. On either side of them, in front of them and behind them, people were in motion. Either briskly marching, or walking in single file, or circling in what apparently was some prearranged pattern.

"You mean," Buff said, "this happened while you were in the wake, so to speak, of a lot of converging groups, the way we are now?"

"Exactly. Just so. Mrs. Pouter," Mr. Bird said unhappily, "had a feeling that someone was trying to — to hurt her aunt, but — uh — now I wonder if perhaps *I* was not the individual being discriminated against! I mean to say, nails were driven in *my* tires yesterday morning, too! I disregarded it as just the — the thoughtless work of — of the rowdy element. But now this! I think perhaps I'll go sit down and rest — oh. Oh, my!" His voice rose almost to a squeal as he became aware of someone calling his name. "Er — would you distract Miss Babcock, who's summoning me, until I slip away? I don't feel quite — er — equal to her at this point!"

The little man melted into the crowd so rapidly and so unobtrusively that Buff found himself being pounced upon by Muriel Babcock, and simultaneously addressed by her as "Clifton."

"It's — oh. I'm sorry. I thought you were — where did Mr. Bird go? I saw him right here — he *was* right here! Where did he go? It's perfectly dreadful — where *is* he? I must see Mr. Bird!"

"He had a most important errand," Buff told her blandly.

As a second-thoughter, he decided, he could take a bow. As a second-thoughter, he was good. Because this neurotic, slightly pop-eyed female really looked like someone who just might have been foiled in a quick stab job. The painted side of her mouth was twitching, creating frightful havoc with the streaks of yellow ochre, and she seemed unable to stand still, unable to do anything but crane her neck from side to side, and peer nervously around at the throng.

If anyone asked him to hazard a third thought, Buff reflected, he'd stick his neck out all the way and guess that Muriel was sufficiently keyed up to try taking another lethal whack at Mr. Bird!

"Could I help you?" he asked, and introduced himself formally, convinced the while that she wasn't listening to one syllable he uttered.

"Such a perfectly dreadful thing has happened! I don't know what to do!"

"If you'd tell me," Buff said patiently, "maybe I could help."

"I want everything to run smoothly, I've always wanted everything to run smoothly, I don't want *anyone's* feelings to be hurt!" Her words came out in a rush. "Of course, there's absolutely no sense pretending — I simply couldn't be *true* to myself if I didn't speak up and try to correct all these idiotic errors and inexcusable historical blunders that are being made! When I know what's right and what's accurate — and I *do* know — "

"But what," Buff interrupted, "is the matter?"

She looked up at him as if she really hadn't noticed him before.

"Someone's just made another attempt to murder me." She spoke in the same sort of voice she might have employed to remark on the imminence of the rain. "That's the third time since yesterday morning — oh, there's Clifton, now I see him! There's Mr. Bird — oh, Clif-ton!"

Before Buff could think of stopping her, she had rushed past him and was running pell-mell toward center field.

He started off in pursuit, and then stopped as she was suddenly lost in the whirl of moving groups.

Suddenly lost, and completely lost. He couldn't pick up a trace of her. It was almost as if she'd vanished at a magician's command.

He couldn't locate Mr. Bird, either.

Or Jennie Mayo's bobbling sunbonnet.

Or the slim figure of Kay Pouter.

"'Fun. Fun! *FUN!*'" he muttered sardonically to himself. "What jolly, jolly fun! Kay thinks someone's after Aunt Maude. Bird knows someone's after him. Muriel announces someone's after *her*. What am *I* supposed to do? Damn it, what *can* I do?"

It was now so dark you could hardly see your hand before your face. And while the darkness and the incipient storm didn't appear to have any perceptible effect in decreasing the ever-milling rehearsal groups, some timid souls were beginning to sneak away from the scene. A few cars were starting up over in the parking space, and headlights were being switched on.

"Damn it, *if* all three of 'em are really being hounded! If all three — "

Buff broke off in frustration.

Murders couldn't happen in a setting like this.

They simply couldn't!

But at this point, he couldn't dismiss the possibility of disaster simply because of the more comic aspects of the pageant scene. At this point, he had no choice but to decide that some disaster of some sort was lurking in somebody's offing.

And that he and Kay and Jennie Mayo had to mobilize to avert it.

If he could find them!

He'd have to. That was all.

Squaring his shoulders, he embarked on what he fully intended to be a most thorough and systematic search.

Ten minutes later, after being angrily ordered out of the way by a dozen group heads, unceremoniously shoved out of the way by Indian Chiefs and Pilgrim Fathers and assorted war veterans, after being yelled at and stepped on and jounced and jostled, Buff gave up and walked over toward the grandstand. Perhaps if he just sat quietly and stared into the darkness long enough, Kay and the rest would put in an appearance. They couldn't all have dissolved into the bracing air of Picturesque Quanomet!

On the first tier of the stand, he spotted the small figure of Bobby Pouter sitting forlornly all by himself.

"Old Home Week!" Buff said buoyantly, feeling as if he'd run into an old and long-lost friend. "Bobby, where's your mother?"

"Hi! I think she went off in the car. Do you like thunder? I do. But I don't like lightning, much."

Buff shot a quick, assessing glance at the boy's face. "I hate them both," he said as he sat down. "Particularly lightning. When did your mother leave? What for? Is your Aunt Maude still here?"

"I can't find anybody," Bobby said. "I think Mother went off after Jennie Mayo. Usually she never leaves me, so I guess perhaps she was in a big hurry. Do you like Popsicles?"

"I'm devoted to 'em," Buff said, "but my change purse is over at Aunt Thamozene's. Take a rain check on Popsicles. So you think your mother followed Jennie Mayo? Who was *she* following, anybody?"

"I don't know. Aunt Maude, maybe. They all drove up the beach road, anyway." Bobby pointed toward it, and gave a resigned sigh. "All three. Well, I guess *some*body'll probably remember to come back after me before the storm. I guess *you* probably wouldn't want to bother driving me home. You're

probably in a hurry to get to your house before it lightnings —
I mean, before it rains."

"I haven't got a car, damn it, or I'd take you home in a
minute. I want to find your mother!"

Bobby removed a red Yo-yo from the pocket of his dungarees, gazed at it pensively, and put it back again.

"It's dark enough," he said casually, "so I suppose we could
borrow about any car around, couldn't we? I like being in-
doors in storms."

"Come along." Buff reached out his hand. "We'll take one
last long lingering look about, and then, by — then if we
can't find any of that crowd, we'll just — well, we'll see."

The long lingering look netted no results.

"There's quite a nice car parked over there by the grandstand," Bobby remarked with the same disarming casual-
ness. "We could borrow that, I guess. Then you can bring it
right back after you find Mother. The keys are in it. I know
because Sleepy and me — I mean, I and James — we played
in it a little while ago."

"By all means," Buff said, "if we're snitching cars, leave us
snitch only the best. Leave us snitch a chromium-plated Porter Coupé de Ville. I never saw one in the flesh before."

He didn't know how to start the car, but Bobby expertly
instructed him in the use of the various gadgets, and then
directed him along the beach road.

"You turn by the old cemetery up ahead to go to our house,"
he announced. "Turn off on this next lane — see? This is a
short cut. Nobody ever used it until the new highway opened
last week, but now we always take it, Mother and I — gee,
that's funny!"

"If you're referring to the manner in which I navigated that turn," Buff said, "I can only tell you I never drove a car this length before. It isn't funny. You're lucky I made it."

"I meant that sedan back there. Aunt Maude's sedan," Bobby said. "That's funny."

Buff applied the Porter's brakes with such force that he had to fling his right arm in front of Bobby to prevent his being thrown off the seat.

"*Where?*" he demanded. "Where's Aunt Maude's sedan? I didn't see any car!"

"Beyond those bushes." Bobby pointed. "You can only just see a piece of the top from here, though."

Twisting around, Buff stared back toward the tangle of overgrown shrubs and spindly cedars which didn't quite manage to hide the outlines of a small, weather-beaten building.

"It's beyond that little pump house place. A gray piece of her top," Bobby told him. "If you wanted to back way up, I guess maybe you could see most all of the car. Gee, it's funny for her to be here! Aunt Maude doesn't like cemeteries a bit. They make her cry. She won't ever take this short cut — Oh, listen! There goes the thunder!"

Thunder on the left, Buff thought, and felt butterflies at work in his stomach. Then he sternly admonished himself not to be morbid. He'd been expecting the thunder, waiting for it. There was no reason for his mind to translate those initial rumblings into an ominous tolling of bells.

"I wonder how Aunt Maude *drove* way over there," Bobby went on. "I guess probably she must've turned off to the right, back at the place where you come in. I didn't know anybody drove that way — you almost can't see those old ruts unless you look hard. They're all grown up with grass and bushes and stuff."

Buff looked from the visible patch of gray sedan roof to the child sitting at his side. He could back up, but damn it, he couldn't plow someone's new million-dollar Porter over the sort of terrain Bobby described! Neither could he drive headlong straight across a cemetery, even if that was the quickest way over to the gray sedan. And he didn't wish to leave the youngster here alone with the storm coming up. But inside the coupé, he would at least keep dry.

"Bobby," he spoke with a decisive briskness which he didn't begin to feel, "I think I'll run across and see if there's anything wrong with your aunt's car. Maybe she's got a flat tire or something. You don't mind staying here, do you? I mean, since we borrowed this Porter, I don't think we ought to leave it parked without someone to guard it. So will you look after it for me? I don't expect you'll get anything on the radio now except static, but you could try."

"Gee, can I?" Bobby sounded enraptured. "Sleepy and me didn't dare touch it!"

Buff got out and strode between the rows of old slate tombstones toward the pump house, and the gray car. He didn't let himself speculate very much as he hurried along, making occasional zigzagging detours around the remains of filigreed iron lot-fences in his path. Bobby was a realistic child. Bobby would never accent his Aunt Maude's normal avoidance of cemeteries without having some factual basis for such a comment.

The gray sedan was empty, he found.

But Aunt Maude's pink-feathered cartwheel hat lay on the front seat next to a large pink cloth knitting bag.

As Buff slammed the door shut and turned away, the rain descended. It was timed, he thought, almost like a stage direction. "At the sound of a door slam, rain should fall in cascading torrents."

Uncertainly, he started walking away from the car.

To yell her name around was fruitless. No effort of the human voice would carry an elbow's length in this thundering downpour. To attempt tracking her down was equally futile — Aunt Maude's whereabouts was anyone's guess. Besides, with his glasses on, the world consisted solely of rivulets. With them off, he discovered he couldn't see beyond the nearest row of headstones. There was only a curtain of rain.

If the woman had an ounce of common sense and as much regard for the pink lace dress as Kay had insinuated, Buff guessed that her immediate destination at this moment would be shelter. Perhaps, if she'd been unable to reach her car before the deluge, she might have ducked into the little pump house.

He swung around and began to race toward it. He was already soaked to the bone, but the idea of shelter appealed to him increasingly.

He stumbled, tripped, and suddenly found himself flat on the ground with something hooked around his right ankle, and dragging at it.

The crook of a heavy cane! He hadn't even seen it as he'd raced along.

He disentangled it and arose, and looked about to get his

bearings, still holding the thing in his hand. He ought to be very close to the pump house, but he wasn't. He couldn't even locate its clump of surrounding bushes. Apparently he'd been floundering off in the wrong direction and had arrived at the oldest part of the cemetery — there weren't any iron lot-fences here. Just old slate tombstones, most of them in a sorry state of disrepair. Just —

Buff found he was using the cane as a practical means of self-support.

Not a yard away, in front of a tall tombstone, lay a figure. A lumpy figure of a woman.

If he had the slightest doubt of her identity, it was dispelled when a vicious streak of lightning illuminated the scene with terrifying clarity, pointing up every detail from the weeping willow tree carved on the top of the slate stone to the ghastly streaks of yellow ochre on Muriel Babcock's face.

Buff took a step forward and looked down. He didn't need to wonder if she were alive. Or how she'd been killed.

He never knew how long he stood there, gripping the cane. He never noticed when the rain stopped as abruptly as it had started.

"This is a new trend," a voice behind him remarked conversationally. "Definitely a new trend."

Buff turned so quickly he nearly lost his balance.

Two men were surveying him interestedly. The shorter one removed the stub of a cigar from his mouth and tossed it aside.

"Now here's an obviously recent corpse already *in* a cemetery," the stocky man continued in the same tone. "A heavily clad female, half-made-up as an Indian. And here's the man who bashed her standing on the spot with the lethal weapon still gripped in his hand — Asey, we never ran into the like of *this* before!"

iii

▼▼▼

BUFF felt like an arrant fool standing there facing them, saying nothing and doing nothing.

Not that the stocky man's sardonic comment hadn't got under his skin and bitten. That crack about the basher with his lethal weapon had nearly goaded him into raising the cane and letting the fellow have it as he paused to light a fresh cigar.

Two things restrained him. One was the close, calculating scrutiny of the taller man. The other was the paralyzing impact of his identity.

This tall, lean character in the corduroys and blue denim shirt, with the yachting cap pulled jauntily down over one eye, was Asey Mayo. This was the Codfish Sherlock in person, and Buff thought with some bitterness that the newsreels and the newspaper pictures didn't do the man justice. You had to be on the receiving end of Mayo's appraising eyes to grasp what you were in for. And up against.

"I'm Dr. Cummings of Wellfleet," the stocky man added. "I also happen to be this district's Medical Examiner — that's what other states call a Coroner, in case you don't know. And that's why you've aroused my professional and official interest. My friend here is Asey Mayo. I suspect you may have heard of him. Now, exactly who are you?"

Buff gave his name with less confidence than he'd answered his first school roll call, and watched as Cummings walked past him and knelt down at Muriel Babcock's side.

"What are you doin' here, Mr. Orpington?" Asey Mayo inquired. "I mean, are you stayin' in this town, or passin' through, or just what?"

He spoke in a slightly drawling voice whose Cape Cod accent and inflection were far less pronounced than Aunt Thamozene's. Buff suspected that the man could probably pronounce all those final *g*'s if he wanted to, and conversely that he could turn on dialect and talk with all the salty mannerisms of a stage sea captain if he felt that the occasion required it.

Although he yearned to burst out with the whole story of his chance arrival and subsequent mad sojourn in Picturesque Quanomet, Buff confined himself to a simple statement of where he was staying.

"With *her*?" Cummings turned and stared at him curiously. "Hm. Asey, he killed her very effectively. One quick blow on the base of her skull — reminds me very much of that Whitmore murder we had four or five years ago. Then he lashed out with some vicious blows after she fell. They're what mutilated her, but that first one killed her. Of course Hanson's cops may possibly prove I'm all wrong, only it'll surprise me if they should — Who are you, Orpington? What do you do? What's your business?"

"Advertising," Buff said. "Pettingill, Watrous and Company."

His information ushered in a period of silence that baffled him completely. Both Cummings and Asey seemed to start surveying him all over again from scratch.

"Now see here! Listen!" Buff intended to explode with righteous indignation, and to set all their misconceptions straight once and for all. But under their steady gaze, the explosion soured. Even to himself, he only sounded dismally on the defensive. "Listen, it's just an advertising firm! A perfectly respectable advertising firm! It — look, will you let me tell you what really happened? I think this is a frightful thing that's gone on here, and I regret it, and I'm sorry! But *I* didn't have anything to do with it! It's a mistake!"

"Of course it's a mistake," Cummings returned promptly. "Certainly it's a mistake. It always *is* a mistake — afterwards. Young man, do I really need to point out to you that Asey Mayo and I have seen enough murders to know *most* of the classic comments and answers?"

"Listen here!" Buff protested angrily. "This has gone far enough! Let's sit down and talk this out! I — "

"I suggest," Cummings interrupted, "that you refrain from any sitting. Not here. You couldn't possibly sit anywhere around here without perching on some of Asey's relations, and he's sensitive to that — Asey, did you notice the name on this stone behind Muriel? 'Thamozene Winter.' Who was she?"

"I wouldn't know, Doc. I never heard of her. All that Winter tribe are beyond my genealogical grasp," Asey said. "Maybe Jennie could tell you. What I been wonderin' about is why she rated a weepin' willow cut into the top of her stone instead of a skull an' crossbones, like the rest all have. Probably Jennie'll know the reason for that, too. This's one of her favorite graveyards."

"Thamozene Winter, Thamozene Winter." Cummings rolled the name over his tongue. "If you just heard the sound of that, you'd think it was an antifreeze. Well, Orpington, I never before knew of a murder committed in front of a gravestone named 'Thamozene Winter.' But if you'd —"

"*Will* you listen to me?" Buff demanded. "I didn't kill her! I wasn't even an innocent bystander! I —"

"If," Cummings ignored him, "you'd wanted a really unusual background for your murder, you shouldn't have overlooked Jonathan. You know, Asey, that stone over in the South Pochet cemetery? 'Here Lies The Body Of Jonathan Round, Who Perished At Sea And Never Was Found.' Or possibly Lizzie Thorpe in Weesit. 'This Corpse Is Lizzie Thorpe's.' Or —" He broke off. "All right, Asey. I'll stop."

"I think you better had, Doc," Asey said. "I know your ways, but Orpington don't, an' I think you're makin' him even madder than you mean to. Orpington, if you got a story to tell, tell us brief an' quick, will you?"

"Well," Buff drew a long breath, "I got off the bus last night, and Mrs. Sturdy thrust a pea-green folder into my hand —"

It had been a hilarious recital when he'd told it to Kay. But this account both dragged and sagged. By the time he got to Aunt Maude's gray sedan, and the rain, and his misplaced sense of direction, he began to regret not having hurriedly invented a sensible and credible story. The brutal truth never sounded any zanier. Or untidier. Or less like brutal fact.

The doctor's disbelief was obvious, and expressed itself in

a series of snorts. Buff couldn't guess what Asey was thinking.

"If you've really finished this prize fish story of yours," Cummings said, "I'd like to assure myself on one simple point. *Do* you know who this woman is?"

"Certainly! I told you about her chasing after Mrs. Henning, and talking with Kay, and so on. I *said* I knew who she was!"

"Thank you," Cummings said with ironic politeness. "I'm glad you admit to being aware of her identity. I'm happy to have that one fact established — in the name of heaven, Orpington, d'you expect us to believe all the utter drivel you've been telling us?"

"It's the truth," Buff said. "However crazy it may sound, that's what happened!"

"You begun your story," Asey said, "with your arrivin' on the bus. Somehow I sort of got the impression that you landed in Quanomet by chance. But of course you must've had some reason for comin' here — what was it, anyway?"

Buff hesitated. He'd hoped he wouldn't have to go into that.

"Well," he said, "I'm afraid I didn't have very much of a reason, actually. I gave the man at the station ticket window some money, and told him I wanted to go as far on Cape Cod as that would take me. He looked at a list of fares, and handed me a ticket to Quanomet, and two cents in change. You see, I — well, I didn't care where I went. I just wanted to get away. I'd got fired yesterday morning, and I wasn't in any mood to — "

"Hold it!" Cummings interrupted. "Fired from Pettingill, Watrous and Company?"

"Yes. I —"

"That's all!" Cummings said with finality. "That's more than enough. Asey, I'll admit I've been stumped until now on his motive, but there you have it — simple revenge. He was fired, so he killed Muriel. Now, let's get going and call Hanson and his cops —"

"Doctor," Buff forced himself to speak calmly, "can I manage to make you understand that I never saw this woman until an hour or so ago? I don't know her! I —"

"You admit you were fired from Pettingill's?"

"Yes. But —"

"Pettingill fired you in person, eh?"

"Yes, he did. But —"

"Pettingill," Cummings said, "is Muriel's brother. It's as simple as all that. Oh, you can stammer and look goggle-eyed and bewildered — but you're not fooling us any, and you might as well quit pretending. You can't get away with it."

"She can't be Pettingill's sister!" Buff said. "She can't be!"

"Why not? Eliza Andrews married George Pettingill and had one son, George," Cummings said. "After her husband's death, she married Henry Babcock and had one daughter, Muriel. Muriel's money supports that firm, I suspect — don't you, Asey? Her money usually backs George's enterprises. The Babcocks had all the money. They were rolling. The Pettingills just had family."

"I didn't know that George Pettingill *had* a sister," Buff said. "I didn't know that he had *any* family. Yes, Doctor, George was my boss — but I didn't know George socially. To put it more accurately, George didn't know me socially. He doesn't believe in having any social contacts with his staff outside the office. And he *doesn't* have any. As far as I'm concerned, George Pettingill's personal life is a closed book!"

"Orpington," Cummings said with a touch of weariness in his voice, "give up! Maybe we could have swallowed your being sold a chance ticket to Quanomet. A bit of coincidence always lends veracity to fish stories. But we can't swallow all this! Nobody could. Give up and admit the truth. George fired you, and you were sore. So — "

"He fired me, and I *was* sore," Buff broke in. "I was good and sore about losing my job. I admit it. But I wasn't particularly sore at George. I didn't want to kill him. The thought never entered my head. And I certainly didn't have any desire to kill his unknown sister!"

Cummings shrugged.

"Very well, Orpington," he said. "We've given you your chance. Now have it your way. You don't know anything about anything, including George Pettingill. You're entirely without motives. You were merely standing on the spot with the death-dealing weapon in your hand. We'll let the police take it from here. You can have the dubious pleasure of explaining to them why you just happened to be holding that cane!"

Buff knew that he was being baited, and that he shouldn't bite. But the doctor possessed the most irritating knack of getting under his skin.

"Look, I picked this thing up!" he said. "That's all. I just picked it up!"

"Habit of yours, isn't it?" Cummings inquired. "You just pick up cars, too, don't you? Yes, Orpington, we saw you swipe Asey's car."

Asey's car! Buff told himself he should have known. He should at least have guessed that such a de luxe custom Porter could only belong to Asey Mayo. The newspapers always made a point of playing up his garish super-models. They were practically a trademark.

And something suddenly told him that Bobby had known all the time.

"We frankly didn't suspect what you were up to," Cummings continued. "It's not exactly usual to take a small child along under the circumstances — Asey, I'm going to use your car telephone, if Bobby hasn't demolished it by now, and call Hanson and the state cops. They can notify George Pettingill. I don't see any sense in wasting more time with this fellow. We've got him cold, from start to finish."

As Cummings hurried away, Buff felt a certain kinship with little Mr. Bird. His mouth moved and his lips moved, but no words came.

"I think," Asey said, "that I'll take that cane before you squeeze it to pieces, if you don't mind. Thanks."

"Hey!" Buff regained the use of his voice. "Hey, look! Fingerprints! I just thought — there'll be other prints on that besides mine!"

"If anyone was fool enough to leave 'em in the first place, or if the rain didn't wash 'em off, or if you didn't rub 'em off yourself. By the way, what's Kay Pouter's father's name?"

He dropped the question so casually that it didn't seem in the least out of place.

Buff shook his head. "Damn it, I tried to remember that while I was hunting everybody back at the ball field — I intended to ask if he was around there anywhere. It's right on the tip of my tongue, but I can't catch it. And I've seen it often enough on his books. Something like Davy Crockett. Davis — maybe it's Davis Something."

"Begins with a *W*, don't it?" Asey suggested idly as he continued to examine the cane.

"Williams!" Buff said with triumph. "That's it! Davis Williams! Look, I told you the truth, you know!"

Asey looked thoughtfully at the crook of the cane and at the tarnished silver band on which the name "Davis Williams" was engraved in flowing script. He'd been straining his eyes trying to read that name at a distance without having either Cummings or this fellow notice his interest. Apparently it never had once occurred to Orpington to look at the cane itself. And mercifully, the doctor had been too swept away by his own initial diagnosis to remember that Orpington was caneless when he pinched the Porter with Bobby. That was all right with Asey. That worked out fine. He'd wanted Cummings to bustle off exactly as he had. He wanted this fellow to act just the way he was acting.

"Did she have that scroll thing in her hand when you saw her last?" he inquired.

Buff turned and looked down in bewilderment. He hadn't even noticed what was clutched in Muriel's hand, and partially hidden by the skirt of her burlap costume.

"No, but she was brandishing it when she first chased after Aunt Maude. I remember noticing it — look, how'd she get here? Who brought her?"

Without answering, Asey stepped over to the gray slate tombstone, and with his forefinger traced the carved outline of the weeping willow tree decoration.

"Why Thamozene Winter should have this instead of a skull an' crossbones at the top of her stone," he remarked, "is goin' to haunt me to the end of my days. Huh. I guess five or six. Five anyway."

"Five what?" Buff couldn't imagine what Asey was referring to. He wasn't looking at Muriel Babcock. His gaze appeared to be focused on the pinewoods bordering the cemetery.

"Layers."

Buff glanced from the pinewoods up to the lowering sky, and then at Asey. If Kay should ever ask his opinion, he intended to tell her quite frankly that the Codfish Sherlock was definitely a screwball character.

"Layers of clothes," Asey went on. "I counted the hem edges of five different skirts she's got on, anyway."

"I didn't notice that," Buff said slowly, "until now. Kay mentioned her looking lumpy. But what for? I mean, why should she be dressed in layers?"

"For the pageant, I s'pose," Asey said. "She starts off bein' an Indian squaw, see, an' then to save time she's gone an' loaded on all her other costume changes underneath. Probably she intended to peel 'em off, layer by layer, as the show went from scene to scene. Leastways, I can't figure out any better reason. Yup, the doc's right about this, in some ways. All the time, new trends an' new angles. *I* never found anyone clutchin' a diploma before."

Buff stared down. Once the scroll was identified as a diploma, you suddenly realized that it couldn't possibly be anything else. Coupled with the easy explanation of the costume layers, it had the effect of annoying him. He'd always thought Columbus was pretty patronizing about standing the classic egg on end!

"Now why," Asey said, "*why* a diploma?"

"Why the hell not?" Buff retorted with irritation. "This is Picturesque Quanomet, isn't it? I wouldn't be surprised at her clutching one of Aunt Tham's breakfast fishcakes — or even the ant-and-molasses picture! Look, where d'you suppose Aunt Maude *is*? I told you Kay thought someone was trying to murder her, and — "

"Uh-huh, you went into all of that," Asey interrupted gently. "You gnawed it to the bone. About Mr. Bird, an' Muriel Babcock. It's got her name penciled on the side. Now I wonder if perhaps it's maybe her own college diploma she's got here?"

"Does it matter?" Anyway, Buff thought, he could assure Kay that while Mayo seemed occasionally capable of ferreting out some minor details, he certainly was not the Man of Action, as advertised. Stand on one foot, stand on the other, peer off into space — that was her Hayseed Sleuth! "You can always unroll the thing, and find out!"

"I suspect," Asey said in reflective tones, "it's a peace treaty."

Screwball! Buff nearly said it aloud. But he managed instead to come out with a plain "Oh?"

"Uh-huh. Indian squaw division. You mind movin' about two feet over to your left, please? Thanks. Make it six inches more."

"Are you just talking for the pleasure of hearing yourself talk?" Buff couldn't hold in any longer.

"Nope." Asey sounded completely unruffled. "I was aimin' to tell you about the peace treaty, but you got in my way.

Seems like the first Quanomet settlers made off with all of the Quanomet Indians' stored-up corn, an' a feud resulted — will you please try to look like you was deeply interested, Mr. Orpington? This feud took up a lot of valuable time on both sides, an' nobody got anywheres. So Parson Somebody's wife got together with a squaw named Mary Cranberry Bog, an' they talked things over, an' put an end to the feudin'. I think this diploma's the peace treaty. Probably the real one was a scrap of parchment or a slice of deerskin, but this diploma'd be visible at a distance in a pageant. It'd look like a treaty to the audience."

"I see." The infuriating part, Buff thought, was that Mayo was probably so damned right. "Look, has it crossed your mind that there may have been a dozen other characters lurking around this cemetery? That I'm just the one you happened to find?"

Asey grinned.

"Uh-huh. Mr. — what in time do folks call you for short? Well, Buff, ever notice that when you try to kill time, you usually only succeed in maimin' it a mite? Step about two feet more over to your left, will you, an' please keep lookin' at me while you do it."

"Are you *watching* something?" Buff asked as he obeyed. "Is that it?"

"Wa-el," Asey drawled, "you might say I'm sort of nursin' along a project that I couldn't see my way clear to rush at. Sometimes in the last fifteen minutes I've had my doubts about its ever hatchin' at all. But I'm now becomin' more hopeful. Buff, without turnin' your head, glance out of the corner of your eyes to the right. See a cemetery lot with a spired stone in the center of it, way over yonder? When I say go, you start runnin' toward that at top speed, will you?"

"Of course, if you want. But why —"

"Between your assorted questions," Asey said, "an' the doc's attempts to bait you, I been sorely tried! When I say go, you *run* — an' keep on runnin' towards the woods after you come to that lot with the spire. See if you can give out the impression of bein' in desperate flight. Don't hesitate, or look back, an' don't trip over some old broken tombstone! Don't pay any attention to what I do — just tell yourself it's back to the concentration camp if you don't get to them pine trees in ten seconds."

"Where do I stop?" Buff inquired.

"Oh, when you find yourself bargin' onto the super-highway, or when you hit the south swamp — I don't care. Don't worry about that part. Just you fling yourself into something that'll impress anybody watchin' from a distance as the real McCoy. Make it look like the old college try — *now!*"

As Buff swung around and darted like a jet-propelled rocket toward the spired stone, Asey chuckled involuntarily to himself and thereby lost a full two seconds setting off in pursuit. He hadn't realized until he saw this fellow in motion that he'd been telling the great Flash Orpington how to run!

He certainly hadn't forgotten much since his college hey-day, either, Asey decided as he pounded along. If this were a real chase, he personally wouldn't have a tinker's chance of laying hand on the fellow. In fact, he was virtually out of ear-shot after the first fifteen yards. And only because Buff rather ostentatiously hurdled the stone fragments and other mis-cellaneous objects lying in his path did Asey himself stave off the calamity of coming a cropper and falling flat on his face.

By the time he reached the edge of the pinewoods, he could hear only the sounds of footsteps racing ahead of him somewhere. Buff was out of sight.

Asey stopped and devoted himself to the process of recovering his breath, the while giving devout thanks that there was no longer any necessity for his maintaining the role of pursuer in this act. The next time he undertook any false flight operations, he'd pick out someone in his own league to chase after.

Anyway, he'd achieved his purpose of clearing the deck for action — at least, he hoped it was for action. To the person who'd been watching for so long from afar, back in the woods directly behind Thamozene Winter's tombstone, this whole proceeding ought to have appeared perfectly natural and understandable. All of it, from Cummings's bustling away to Buff's sudden flight, and his own pursuit.

If the watcher had been yearning to come out into the open, here was the open — ready and waiting for him!

Leaning back against a pine tree, Asey stared at the area ahead from which the watcher should by rights emerge, and mentally reviewed the slow, tortuous course of that wriggling figure he'd spotted. Actually it wasn't a figure — actually he had never seen a figure, as such. Actually it was never more than the slightest movement of bushes and branches and underbrush. He couldn't guess why his eyes had been drawn to it way back there when Cummings had first wise-cracked to Buff about new trends. Even before that, perhaps at the moment the rain had so suddenly ended and he was able really to see around, he'd somehow become aware of that faint motion.

He'd known at once that he never could make a dash for the person without having him beat it first through the woods to the highway, where he probably had his car waiting. Or else the fellow would have melted away in the scrub tangle of the south swamp. Even if Buff's help had been enlisted, nothing ever would have been gained from any wild-goose chase after that commando type. That the person was merely watching, and edging closer in order to watch better, had no meaning anyway.

The point was, what did the fellow want? What was he *after*?

Asey cast a brief glance back in the direction where his Porter was parked. He had to reckon on the chance of Cummings's bustling back onto the scene and the possibility of his frightening this person into running away. But from his own present vantage point he was now in a position to maneuver, and to intercept any wild dash toward the highway. He didn't want to do that except as a last resort. After all this hopeful dallying and planned rushing about, he didn't want to settle for just grabbing the fellow without finding out his purpose.

Buff was now not even a dim sound in the distance, and still there was no sign of anyone ahead. No sign of anyone, anywhere.

Keeping his eyes firmly glued on the woods behind Thamozene Winter's stone, Asey turned over in his mind the issue of Aunt Maude Henning. He couldn't wholeheartedly string along with Buff's assumption that she must be here because her gray sedan was here. From his one previous meeting with that rather overwhelming female, he suspected if she were anywhere in the vicinity she'd surely have appeared long before this — and probably have assumed complete charge of the situation. To his way of thinking, Aunt Maude Henning wasn't one to watch anything quietly from a distance. Aunt Maude would have taken over. Lock, stock and barrel!

And certainly she didn't have the physique or the figure for this commando stuff, either. The thought of her squirming through wet underbrush on her stomach made him laugh aloud.

Asey drew his breath in sharply, and leaned forward.

Someone had suddenly popped into sight, like a jack-in-the-box, on the edge of the woods ahead.

At long last, the watcher had decided to stop oozing along, and to come out into the open!

Asey couldn't see the man's face, but he wore a tan raincoat and a brown felt hat. A city-type hat. He might be five feet ten or eleven, perhaps he weighed a hundred and sixty. And definitely he wasn't a local product, or a summer person, or a tourist. Not with that hat!

And he was staring fixedly toward the Thamozene Winter stone, and Muriel Babcock's body.

"So!" Asey murmured with satisfaction as the man took a hesitant step forward, and then another. "I guessed right!"

After all, no one would lurk around all this time for the sheer fun of it! With his mission accomplished, the murderer ought by now to be over the hills and far away. That he'd stayed was reasonable proof of Asey's original guess, that Buff's unexpected rush in the wrong direction had driven this fellow away before he could get something that Muriel Babcock had.

"An' if it's that doggone diploma," Asey said, "I'm goin' bats an' out of my mind right now! Oh, come on! Get on with it!"

But at that point, as suddenly as he'd appeared, the man popped out of sight again.

"Oh, go get what you want!" Asey muttered in disgust. "Go *on!*"

Thunder began to roll again, and a streak of lightning zig-zagged across the sky. All the place lacked, Asey thought as the greenish-yellow light illuminated the rows of old slate gravestones, was a few witches flying around on their broom-sticks. He never had shared his Cousin Jennie's enthusiasm for old cemeteries even on a pleasant day with the sun shining bright.

And it wasn't possible, he assured himself with some firmness, that Brown Hat could have spotted him.

Or was it? Had he himself, after all, been the one to stick his neck out?

Could be!

And he'd never be able to hear, in all this shattering din, if the fellow started commando-ing this way, sneaking up on him. But such a move would take time. Plenty of time. Brown Hat would have to do some very fancy circling.

In the very next startlingly silent moment between a crash of thunder and a racketing zigzag of lightning, he actually thought he did hear something behind him. A twig under someone's foot?

As he started to turn around, the blanket of rain descended

with as much force as before, and he thought he saw a flash of something moving.

Something pink.

It was the last he thought, or for that matter the last he saw, for some time.

Thunder drowned out the swish of whatever hit him.

He only felt himself begin to crumple.

iv

▼▼

"SNIFF, Mr. Mayo!"

It was a woman's voice, unfamiliar and on the high side, and Asey found that he was resisting its sergeant-major tone with all the passive strength he could muster. He didn't wish to sniff. He didn't wish to do anything except to be left alone in this mental vacuum. He liked this feeling of being suspended in mid-air, apart from the world and unhampered by any problems, or questions and answers. He refused even to think of sniffing, just as he rejected the thought of raising a hand and removing the pine needle boring into his left ear.

"*Sniff!*"

Asey opened his eyes the fraction of a hairsbreadth and was confronted by pink lace. Acres of pink lace. Buff Orpington had quipped about Aunt Maude Henning's pink lace dress. With — with leg-of-mutton sleeves. That was it!

"Sniff at this! *Sniff!* Sniff, Mr. Mayo!"

The comfortable mental vacuum suddenly gave way to a wall of mirrors that distorted everything and blew perspective to the skies. The crimson fingernails on the cut-glass smelling salts bottle being shoved under his nose loomed up larger than Thamozene Winter's tombstone. And they were the same shape. Blood-red tombstones. The hand they belonged to was like the inside of a cat's paw, plump and padded. It didn't go with the pink lace background. It wasn't a pink lace hand.

Why was the pink lace dry? Asey asked himself that while the swirls of its intricate pattern wavered before him like a mad television image. Why should Mrs. Henning be dry? He wasn't. He was drenched. He felt soggy.

"Sniff. *Please.*" This time it was a most conciliatory coo.

"Listen here, Maude!" Dr. Cummings's voice came from somewhere behind Asey's head, and it sounded dangerously tried. "There's absolutely no sense ordering him to sniff! If he comes to and wants to sniff, he'll sniff, and if he doesn't, he won't! Matter of fact, he detests smelling salts like poison — they make him sneeze his head off. You might just as well give up!"

"I can*not* stand callously by, doing nothing, while another human being is stretched out unconsc — "

"Nobody's being callous!" Cummings broke in. "Absolutely nothing's the matter with him except he's been biffed over the head and knocked out. He's coming to nicely without any help from us. The man's indestructible. Probably won't even have a headache."

Asey didn't feel quite equal to opening his mouth and calling the doctor a liar. He had the headache to end all headaches, and a pain in the neck to end all pains in the neck. He throbbed.

"If you hadn't made that vicious attempt to move him," Cummings went on, "and crooked his neck over that damn bough — thank God I saw you before you mauled him around to any great extent! Weren't you ever exposed to *any* of the basic principles of administering first aid?"

"I taught it," Maude Henning informed him, and there was a slight chill in her voice. "I was Co-ordinating Chairman of Civilian Defense from — "

"I should have guessed as much," Cummings interrupted acidly, "from the barbarous way you were wringing his neck! Oh, I certainly ought to have recognized that technique, it had *all* the earmarks of Civilian Defense First Aid! On my word of honor, Maude," he added with sincerity, "when I first caught sight of you apparently strangling him, I suspected you'd bashed him yourself and were trying to deliver the *coup de grâce!* Now face the fact you can't organize the human frame as if it were a pageant, and get up, and stop waving that silly bottle under his nose — what the hell are you doing here, anyway?"

While skirts rustled and accompanying sounds indicated that Mrs. Henning was somewhat laboriously getting to her feet, Asey unobtrusively altered the position of his head an inch. Miraculously, all his pains and aches stopped at once. He only throbbed over one eye.

"Hm." Cummings cleared his throat. "Hm. I think he'll be all right *very* soon! Maude, how in God's name did you manage to keep dry during that deluge? Where were you, anyway?"

"Isn't it simply wonderful? It *worked!*"

"What worked?"

"The waterproofing," she said. "I was really torn — as I told your wife — between this dear old pink lace, and my Alice blue taffeta with the panniers. Because of course I knew all the time it would rain today, or tomorrow, or Saturday."

"Indeed?" Cummings said. "Indeed! Weather experts have only spent the last seven weeks beating their brains out over when it would rain again, but you *knew*?"

"Of course I knew!" Her laugh that tinkled out reminded Asey of Jennie's silver tea bell. "It always rains during a pageant, always! Usually it starts during dress rehearsal. So Bobby and I got some of that stuff and waterproofed this, and it works! Isn't it too wonderful — oh, look, he *is* all right!"

She pointed down at Asey, sitting cross-legged with his back against a pine tree.

"Hm." Cummings looked at him quizzically. "Old Ironhead. Who did it, d'you know?"

"Wouldn't smelling salts *help*?" The cut-glass bottle was hurriedly thrust at him. "Don't you think that just a sniff — "

"No, thanks," Asey said. "Did you happen to catch sight of who hit me?"

"Isn't it the most extraordinary thing that someone *should* have, really! And how fortunate you weren't seriously hurt — no, I didn't see anyone. I just stumbled over you, as you might say." The tinkling laugh rang out again. "I nearly stepped on you! You probably wonder what I was doing here, I'm sure, with your detective mind!"

"May I point out, Maude," Cummings said, "that with nothing remotely resembling a detective mind, I've asked you fifty thousand times why you're here? I thought you detested cemeteries. My wife told me so."

"It was the one place I could think of to go," she lowered her voice confidentially, "where absolutely *no* one could possibly find me, and ask me questions! It's been a most trying morning, and I needed a few minutes all to myself. I simply *had* to be alone!"

"Just the Garbo in you coming out, hey?" Cummings inquired. "Now listen, Maude, *I* know that voice! That's the voice you put on when you explain to me how you couldn't possibly lose one single ounce in the last two weeks because if you'd refused desserts, you'd only have hurt the feelings of whoever made 'em especially for you, and you can't *bear* seeing people burst into tears, and so on and so forth! You — "

"But I do hate hurting people's feelings! I *do!*" she protested. "And I've lost six whole ounces since dress rehearsals started! I told you I would!"

"When you use that voice," Cummings said, "you can make things sound so damned plausible! You probably could explain atomic energy, and I'd just nod and say yes, and believe every syllable. It's a wonderfully effective and lulling device — but now break down and tell us, what *were* you doing here? What *are* you doing here?"

"Why, I told you, Doctor!" Her blue eyes were wide open and as guileless as a child's. "I came here for peace and quiet!"

Cummings sighed. Then he looked quizzically over at Asey.

"Okay, Sherlock," he said. "I tried, but she gives me minstrel show lines. She says she came here for peace and quiet, and I *think* Mister Bones is supposed to snap back that lots of people who came to cemeteries with peace and quiet in mind were, in effect, rudely disillusioned. It's your ball!"

"But I did come for peace and quiet! You see the little pump house, over by that clump of bushes? I went in there and sat down — "

"On an upholstered chair," Cummings interrupted, "doubtless provided by the cemetery management?"

"I sat down on an overturned bucket, and just meditated. I simply had to clear my mind." She smiled brightly at Asey. "I'm sure that Mr. Mayo *often* has to sit quietly and clear *his* mind, too — don't you?"

"Sometimes," Asey told her blandly, "it seems to me I don't do anything else but. How'd you happen this way, over to this part of the woods?"

Mrs. Henning hesitated, and for a brief moment Asey thought she might be going to panic. But then her poise returned, and the tinkling laugh rang out.

"It sounds so terribly foolish, but I — well, I guess I just went in the wrong direction, that's all! Cemeteries are all so terribly alike, if you know what I mean. All those *stones!*"

"Uh-huh," Asey said. "But your sedan's right there by the pump house, an' you can't very well mean that you went in the wrong direction toward *it,* I'm sure. Did you have any special purpose in makin' your way to this particular spot here?"

Instead of looking cornered, Mrs. Henning seemed almost relieved by his question.

"I'm so glad you asked me that, Mr. Mayo! You do put things so extremely well! You're so clarifying! I mean, sometimes little obstacles crop up in one's work, don't they? Little problems intervene. If one magnifies them, they tend to become significant, when as a matter of fact, if one ignores them, one realizes they're simply bits of fluff that are gone with the wind!" She snapped her fingers expertly. "Just like that!"

"Isn't it the truth?" Asey said. "If one doesn't make a violent attempt to nail 'em down when one has one's finger plumb on 'em, they might tend maybe perhaps to escape one forever."

Cummings chuckled. "If there's anything I enjoy more than double-talk," he said, "it's double-talk. I think he's won, Maude!"

"I can't imagine what you mean!" Mrs. Henning sounded perfectly sincere. "I simply said that one shouldn't magnify the little obstacles that interv — "

"Uh-huh," Asey broke in. "We know. What I meant was, s'pose we put our finger on this bit of fluff before it goes with the wind. Actually, you saw someone, an' you come over here to investigate. Right?"

"That's — well, it doesn't really matter, does it?" Mrs. Henning said hastily. "When you put that question so concisely, I realized I shouldn't have magnified that situation. It didn't *signify*. Problems arise, don't they, and one should gauge and assess them, and face — "

"S'pose," Asey said, "that we face this one, please. Your niece came to my house early this mornin' an' told my Cousin Jennie she thought someone was tryin' to murder you. She told a good enough story to make Jennie set off on the run to help look after you, an' Jennie left me a note strong enough so's when I read it, I came whippin' over to the ball field myself to see what was goin' on. Now your niece had some notion — "

"Dear, dear Kay!" Mrs. Henning said with warmth. "The dearest girl in the world! Her mother was my most intimate friend, you know, and I always marveled at her patience with my brother — you know Davis? An unusual man in many ways, gifted generally, and — "

"And generally God's gift to womankind," Cummings said. "D'you know, Asey, I've even found my wife gazing after him dreamily, although he's frankly always put me in mind of an amiable St. Bernard — dog, that is. Davis is unquestionably gifted. He's versatile. Now, Maude, get back to what's been bothering Kay."

"The dear girl! Of course, Bobby's such a vigorous child — if only he had his father to help wear him out! Dear Kay's done her best, and goodness knows Davis is wonderful with him, and I'm sure I've bought him every vigorous toy in the Schwarz catalogue! I've bribed the swimming instructor at the club to make him swim and swim, and I have the Harriman boy play games with him. But Bobby *is* vigorous!"

"Are you trying to say Kay's so worn-out coping with that child," Cummings said, "that she's developed some neurotic notion about your being persecuted?"

"Oh, no! I think she's very tired, and with the pageant taking so much of my time, she's had to run the house, and do the shopping. And it has been so dreadfully hot all summer! When one is fatigued, one's perspective so often *fal*ters — "

"But what she told Jennie was all true, wasn't it?" Asey interrupted. "I mean all this business of the grandstand bein' sawed, an' your tires bein' tampered with, an' some wirin' blowin' up, an' someone lurkin' on the balcony outside your window last night?"

"My dear Mr. Mayo, I never yet put on a pageant in which some little problem or other did not arise!" She waved her hand in an airy gesture of finality, as if she were dismissing the topic.

"Maude," Cummings said wearily, "I do wish you'd stop this bush-beating! Who's responsible? Who's behind all this?"

She frowned. "It's Clifton Bird's opinion that the rowdy element — "

"I don't care two hoots what that twittering little schoolmaster thinks! Who do *you* think is responsible?"

"Really, Doctor, if I permitted myself ever to become upset by the little problems that always crop up during the span of a pageant — "

"Hold on a second, Mrs. Henning!" Asey said. "You're makin' one whale of an effort to belittle things. But the fact remains that you got upset enough over this particular problem so it made you leave off your meditatin' " — he watched her face closely — "in the peace an' quiet of the pump house, an' caused you to march clear across the cemetery over here. Why? What for? So's you could have a quiet, peaceful chat with a bunch of rowdies? In a pourin', peltin' rain?" Something prompted him to add, "An' with that dress on?"

To his surprise, her expression softened. Almost absently, she took a little fold of the full lace skirt between her thumb and forefinger, and stroked it.

"Well," she said hesitantly. "Well — "

Asey shot a warning look at the doctor. If some sentimental memory attached to that pink dress could succeed in eliciting any sort of straight, factual story from Aunt Maude Henning, he didn't want Cummings to break the spell.

"Well," she drew a long breath, "I never ever really agreed with Clifton about the rowdy element. I've run too many pageants. I know rowdy elements better than he does. But I did let myself think for a brief moment that — well, I permitted myself to magnify the situation. I wondered if possibly we might not be being faced with what you might refer to as the *subversive* element."

She stopped suddenly, and from the way in which she glued her lips firmly together, Asey felt sure she wasn't going to add any more, and that she was already regretting having said as much.

"Okay," he said briskly as he got to his feet. "*I* know why you came over here, of course! You saw a man in a tan raincoat an' a brown felt hat, an' you wanted to find out who he was."

She stared at him blankly, and so did Cummings.

"Oh, no!" she said. "It wasn't any man in a tan raincoat and a brown hat! It was the man with the beard."

Asey tried not to let his eyebrows move, but it was a losing fight. They went up anyway.

"Beard?" Cummings demanded in a voice vibrant with disbelief. "With *what* beard?"

"Just the one with the beard."

"D'you mean he had a long, white, flowing, Old-Man-of-the-Sea beard, like something washed up on the beach after a storm? Or a short, Vandyke, artist-type beard? Or — "

"S'pose," Asey intervened before the doctor had any

chance to sink his teeth into the beard issue, "we let her tell us all about him. What kind of a beard, Mrs. Henning? Did you get a chance to see?"

"A shaggy beard," she told him simply.

"Ah!" Cummings said. "Ah! A subversive-type beard, hey?"

But his irony was totally lost on her. She merely nodded.

"Did he have a limp?" Cummings inquired interestedly. "And a black patch over one eye? In God's name, Maude, if you're compelled to invent a man with a *shaggy* beard, give him all the trappings!"

"He didn't limp, and he didn't have any patches. He just looked like the pictures of those old-fashioned anarchists who used to go around blowing up kings — you know, back when there *were* kings. That was why I noticed him at first. He was *so* shaggy, you see. Too shaggy, I felt, for one of our pageant characters. Our beards are really splendid — so beautifully trimmed! I really think," she added with enthusiasm, "that I never saw better beards than those Spinosa sent. He did all our beards and wigs, you know."

"An' when did you first notice him?" Asey asked.

"Spinosa? Oh, I always have him do my pageants if I possibly can cajole him into — "

"I mean Shaggy-face," Asey said. "When did you spot him first?"

The question seemed to confuse her.

"I really don't remember," she said uncertainly. "I think it may have been yesterday, or possibly the day before. These few days of final preparations and rehearsals are really the vital moments of a pageant. So much goes on, it's very difficult to recall the exact time of one isolated little — er — er — "

"One isolated little shaggy beard," Cummings blandly suggested as she paused. "Without any accompanying limp, or patch. Frankly, I think I can understand your general hesitancy and obvious state of chokiness. Because *I'm* having trouble in swallowing this. It chokes me, too! D'you find small tufts of that subversively shaggy beard adhering to your tonsils, Asey?"

"Wa-el," Asey drawled as he leaned over and picked up his yachting cap from the pine needles, "wa-el, let's be fair, Doc. If I could see a man in a tan raincoat an' a brown hat, why Mrs. Henning could see a man with a beard. *I* don't know who Brown Hat was, an' I don't s'pose she knows who Shaggy-face was, either. But golly, I wish she had some inklin'! I'd kind of like to know who it was that crept up an' bopped me. An' why."

He had pretty well managed to convince himself that he hadn't been hit by Brown Hat. There simply hadn't been time enough for Brown Hat to have sneaked up on him. Without any doubt, a third party had been hovering around.

But on the other hand, he shared the doctor's skeptical attitude about men with shaggy beards. Roughly speaking, a man with a shaggy beard was the adult equivalent of a child's make-believe dragon whose hungry tongue demolished cookies and jam while its lashing tail conveniently smashed windows right and left. In a nutshell, it was one of those inspirational explanations which always seemed like such a good idea at the time.

"An' why," he repeated thoughtfully, wondering to himself if there were any earthly use in his pretending to accept

Shaggy-face as gospel truth, just in an attempt to find out what she would choose to do then. "You got any sterlin' thoughts on that, Mrs. Henning?"

"What *I* think," she spoke in her most confidential tones, "is that this person hit you because he suspected you were after *him!* I mean, I'm touched at dear Kay's worrying so on my account, and I knew she meant *so* well — but by enlisting your aid, she really magnified the situation, didn't she? Motivated by the best intentions in the world, she acted unwisely, just as I acted unwisely in rushing over here when I caught a glimpse of that man with the beard. I should have ignored the whole thing as I have — well, as I've told you, experience has taught me that the best policy is to ignore these little problems that crop up."

Asey put on his yachting cap, and then hastily removed it.

"Either the rain shrunk it three sizes," he said in response to Cummings's question, "or else my head's lumped up three sizes. Now maybe you're right, Mrs. Henning. Could be. Could well be that someone suspected I was after him. Only it sort of seems like he'd been wiser never to have bothered me at all, if you think it out. I never knew of his existence, an' I never would of known if he hadn't forcibly called my attention to it, so to speak. Wa-el, I guess we'll have to sum up this episode by callin' it just a little pageant problem, like you said. Most likely it's all a matter of petty jealousy."

He avoided the doctor's incredulous stare, and disregarded his muttered commentary about a lot of damned silly nonsense.

"Most likely somebody got awful sore at bein' left out of the show," he went on, "an' decided for spite to louse things up as much as he could, or as much as he dared. Why, I remember a man over home once who chopped down the town flagpole because he wasn't the one chosen to hoist the flag first time it went up."

"*I* never heard — " Cummings began.

"Most likely," Asey firmly silenced him, "most likely this person here got hold of a beard somewhere so's he could mix in the pageant doin's without bein' recognized, an' maybe pretend to be part of it anyway."

"That's just what I thought!" Maude Henning said. "I thought exactly along those very lines at first! Then, of course, there was the strong possibility that someone actually *in* the pageant is exercising a most perverted sense of humor, and has altered one of Spinosa's beards. And I do hope not, because his repair charges are simply too exorbitant!"

Asey tried on the yachting cap again, and perched it at an angle.

"Was he wearin' the beard on your balcony last night?" he asked casually, still adjusting the cap.

To his unbounded pleasure, Mrs. Henning nodded absently while she watched his efforts to make the cap stay on his head.

"Oh, yes, you could see it so *very* plainly in profile. There was just enough light so that he was silhouetted against that broad white pillar — oh! Oh, dear!" She broke off in exasperation and bit her lip. "What have I gone and said!"

"Now," Cummings said to Asey, "I see what you were up to. A sneaker. Maude, why in God's name didn't you break down and tell us this right off the bat?"

"Oh, I never meant to let that out! Never! I wouldn't for

worlds let dear Kay know that *I* was at all worried. But I was simply numb with fear last night that someone was after Bobby — trying to kidnap him. And I never, never wanted her to guess the extent of my anxiety!"

"Huh." Asey thought back to Jennie's note, and her succinct report of Kay Pouter's story. "An' just what," he inquired, "did you intend to do about it if this fellow'd tried to pull a kidnap job?"

"Oh, I had my little gun, of course. Right in my hand." She might have been talking, Asey thought, about a garden trowel or a cake-mixing spoon. "All the time he was there. Naturally I pretended to be asleep. I snored. But I was quite prepared for anything — and I thought it so much wiser to wait and see what he was up to than just to rush *in*to — did you say something, Mr. Mayo?"

"No, Mrs. Henning, I didn't say a word. I choked," he told her with perfect truth. "Go on."

"Well, ever since an exceedingly disagreeable experience in a Vermont pageant fifteen years ago — this poor, demented creature threatened to murder me for misrepresenting one of his ancestors, as he thought — well, after that, I've always carried my little gun everywhere I put on a pageant. It's just a little derringer," she added. "A forty-four."

"Er — loaded?" Cummings sounded as if he'd just sat on a tack.

"Oh, yes! My husband always thought women should be able to protect themselves. He taught me how to shoot. And of course there's the jiujitsu I learned for Civilian Defense. I taught that to several hundred groups in the Women's Division."

The doctor winced.

"Maude, I shall studiously avoid tangling with you, ever!" he said with deep sincerity. "If your little forty-four misfires, or your jiujitsu fails, there's always the ugly possibility of your resorting to first aid. See here, when *did* you originally notice this fellow?"

"I'm so ashamed to think I truly can't remember! We've been having bits and pieces of costumes for nearly a week, and it's hard to recall when one single beard appeared. Even this shaggy one. But I've sensed that something was going wrong with the pageant ever since I — we, that is — decided to accent our underlying purpose. If you've seen our posters, Mr. Mayo, you know that our basic purpose in this pa — "

"Uh-huh," Asey said hastily. "I know. The patriotic issue. What we stand for, the history of America, our glorious heritage, an' so forth. So you honestly think that Shaggy-face is a genuine subversive element, huh? An' just how would you work that in with Bobby's bein' kidnaped? As a sort of general sabotage against you, I s'pose, an' thus sabotage against the show, an' thus against what we stand for, an' thus an' so on. Wa-el, could be. But it's a mite complicated, ain't it — say, are there many beards in this show?"

She nodded. "We're really quite bearded. More so than I'd like, personally, but Muriel Babcock has absolutely insisted that we be historically accurate."

"She's your general manager, isn't she?" Asey asked casually.

"Muriel's official title is Chief Historical Advisor."

Each word, Asey thought, might have been chipped off a block of ice.

"You never had any suspicion that someone might be aimin' to kill her," he said, "instead of you, as your niece figured?"

"I had a suspicion this morning," Maude Henning returned, "that if I didn't rapidly achieve peace and quiet, and clear my mind, and restore my perspective, I might succumb to the impulse to kill her myself! That's why I left the rehearsal and came here!"

"Why, Maude!" Cummings rose to the occasion as Asey guessed he would. "I'd no idea Muriel had tried you to that extent! God knows she's the most persistent woman I ever met — and that's no puny statement! And certainly her mind is one-track. But you shouldn't let Muriel get into your hair. She's utterly harmless."

Maude Henning drew a long breath.

"I suppose I might just as well say it! Since Kay has enlisted Mr. Mayo's aid, and since he knows so much, I might as well tell him everything. When I sensed that things were going wrong with the pageant, I immediately put my ear to the ground — "

"Don't tell me you heard Muriel Babcock undermining! Doggedly boring from within — By George, come to think of it, Muriel *is* the doggedest borer from within — " The doctor looked at Asey, and stopped short.

"I discovered it was Muriel who was responsible. For everything."

Asey whistled softly.

"For everything, Mrs. Henning? Like the tire business, an' the grandstand sawin', an' all?"

She shrugged. "It would take someone like you to prove

the authorship of yesterday's overt acts. But I discovered it was Muriel who lied to Thamozene Sturdy, and provoked her into leaving the pageant and stirring up local resentment. I found Muriel was lying to Clifton Bird, angering him with critical comments which she claimed I'd made about him and his work. She's deliberately been causing minor confusions — losing lists, changing sequences, altering episodes, giving out conflicting instructions. She's — Mr. Mayo, Muriel Babcock is the most thoroughly vicious and malevolent woman who has ever crossed my path! And I think — I truly think that — "

"That she's Shaggy-face," Asey said as she paused. "That it?"

"I *do* think so!"

"Maude, d'you realize what you're saying?" Cummings demanded. "That *Muriel's* been clapping on a false beard and — oh, no! Never!"

"I was so sure last night that it was Muriel Babcock on the balcony, I nearly — look! Look over there! Are those state policemen?"

"Seems's if," Asey said. "Doc, I plumb forgot to ask if you'd called Hanson."

"Bobby's masterly with gadgets," Cummings said. "He made the phone work. Hanson said he'd send a couple to hold the fort until he could mobilize, and for you to carry on till he did. The — "

"But what would state police be doing here?" Maude Henning persisted.

"Muriel Babcock's been murdered in front of a gravestone named Tham — "

Cummings broke off as she toppled gently down on the pine needles.

"Your ball," Asey said with a chuckle. "Your department, Doc. Don't look so helpless. She's only just fainted."

"But — wait! Don't go!"

"Take her smellin' salts," Asey said, "an' tell *her* to sniff-sniff-sniff! I'll be back — "

"Wait — what d'you think of this recital of hers? What d'you make of it? What's your guess — that she brought Muriel here in her car, and biffed her, and then hid in the pump house when Orpington steamed along — by the way, where *is* he?"

"I don't know," Asey said. "I don't know if she's told us the truth, or if she hasn't. I don't know why I got biffed — I got to see Hanson's boys, Doc, they're goin' the wrong way. Ahoy!" He cupped his hands to his mouth. "Ahoy — over there! To your right!"

"They see her now," Cummings said. "What's the matter, Sherlock? The oddest expression just came over your face!"

Asey looked down at the figure of Maude Henning, grinned, and beckoned the doctor to follow him as he turned away.

"What's up?" Cummings demanded. "What — "

"Shush — not so loud! Remember when Jennie caught that German spy on the beach, complete with his rubber boat, durin' the war?"

"*Do* I! And then kept him tied up in the woodshed while she finished baking, for God's sakes, a batch of sugar ginger-bread!"

"Uh-huh," Asey said. "There's a sort of a grand flourish,

Doc, that women sometimes tend to like to make. Jennie couldn't see any reason for burnin' up her gingerbread on account of an ole spy. An' Aunt Maude Henning couldn't see any reason for crushin' her leg-of-mutton sleeves on account of she felt Mrs. Post'd expect her to faint just then. So she toppled with grace an' with real forethought — consider the deft way she missed that pronged branch off her right shoulder! She's fakin', Arrowsmith. I'm sure of it. Give her a good faceful of her smellin' salts — "

Five minutes later, after concluding a brief summary of the situation for the benefit of the two state troopers, Asey asked what they'd done with the cane.

Sixty seconds later, it was tentatively established that there was no cane in the near vicinity of Thamozene Winter's stone.

And sixty seconds' additional scouring on the part of the three of them conclusively established the fact that there wasn't any cane within a radius of a hundred and fifty feet.

"Okay, boys," Asey said. "We're not goin' to tackle the woods. Now let's take a look at her diploma — huh. Which of you unrolled it?"

The shorter of the pair said somewhat truculently that nobody had unrolled nothing.

"Okay," Asey said. "Someone's swiped that cane, an' someone's unrolled the diploma. Took something that was rolled up inside of it, I suspect, an' then rerolled it wrong side to from what it was at first. The penciled name's on the inside edge now. Fine. Fine an' dandy. Now we got that part all straight!"

"Say, Hanson won't like it if anything's got touched or swiped!"

"On the contrariwise," Asey said, "I think Hanson's goin' to be real pleased."

"You hadn't," the short man said, "ought to have left her alone!"

"I didn't," Asey told him. "I been watchin' this spot like a hawk, except for a little interlude when I was knocked out. I'm cross-eyed from starin' over here an' tryin' to watch a fat lady in pink lace at the same time. Anyhow, Hanson's goin' to be as happy as a clam at high tide with this cane an' diploma business. Because now we know just what happened, an' the reason for things. An' why I got beaned."

"Is that so?" The short man stared at him with suspicion. "Is that so?"

"Yup, it's so. Orpington scared someone away, see?"

"Who's he? Where is he?"

"At the moment, I wouldn't know. But Orpington scared someone off before they got whatever they was after — whatever they killed her for. So they hung around till the coast seemed clear, an' then they seen me. So they knocked me out of the way, an' then whipped over here, an' got whatever it was — papers, I surmise — that was rolled up in the diploma. Why they took the cane," he added reflectively, "I don't quite know."

"Oh, you don't, huh?" the short trooper inquired with rising inflection.

"Nope, I don't. Personally, I'd have left it, an' I'd of watched my diploma rerollin' real careful. But I s'pose they was in a terrible rush, an' that rain must of been disconcertin'. An' of course that long, long wait must of been pretty frustratin' an' soul-wearin', too. Trouble with the average murderer is, they just won't ever figure that some Buff Orpington or other'll probably loom on their horizon at an awkward time. Plannin' is one thing, but improvisin' is another."

"I bet," the trooper said, "that you got a hundred in your Junior G-man radio test Saturday! Listen, bud, if you know so much about all of this, you can just stick around with us until Hanson or this Mayo guy gets here, see?"

"I guess I forgot to tell you my name," Asey said. "I'm Mayo. An' right now I'm goin' over to assist Doc Cummings with the fat lady he's restored to health an' vigor. You boys'll please stay here, on this spot."

"Yes, sir."

"An' if you see anybody roamin' around in a tan raincoat an' a brown felt hat, grab 'em. If you see anyone with a beard, grab them too."

"Yes, sir!"

Asey caught up with the doctor and Mrs. Henning as the latter was removing a pink cloth knitting bag from the front seat of her gray sedan.

"Maude feels a lot better," Cummings said blandly. "Quite recovered. In the pink, in fact. But she thinks I'd better drive her home in my car, and in view of her recent deep agitation over poor Muriel, I feel that's probably the wisest course. We'll also pause by your car and pick up Bobby, and take him along — say, whatever *did* happen to the Orpington lad?"

Asey shrugged. "I wouldn't know, but I don't worry about him."

"It's occurred to you that *he* might have knocked you out?"

"An awful lot," Asey said, "occurs to me."

He made a mental note to remember to ask Jennie what made those leg-of-mutton sleeves puff out, and stay puffed out. Every time he looked at them, he was consumed with curiosity. The dress was clearly an old-timer and not a new facsimile. But if Aunt Maude Henning had modernized the job to the extent of laying in a pink zipper on one side of her waist, and pink zippers on both wrists and shoulders, perhaps she'd also had modern wiring laid in to solve that mutton-leg look.

"Don't forget your hat, Maude," Cummings said. "I don't understand, Asey, how you can ignore Orpington — "

While the doctor ran on about Buff, Asey continued to ponder the leg-of-mutton angle. With sleeves that size, why should Mrs. Henning or anyone else require such a capacious knitting bag? She could easily tuck half the world away in either leg.

"Doc," he broke in on Cummings's discourse, "did you make arrangements with Hanson about an ambulance an' such? Good. I'll be around when you get back. An' I'll have a cop or somebody drive your car home for you sooner or later, Mrs. Henning. Be seein' you."

He was three quarters of the way back to the Thamozene Winter stone when he abruptly about-faced and started running toward the place where Cummings's old sedan was parked. He'd forgotten to tell the doctor to ask around about Jennie, or even to find her, if he possibly could, and bring her back with him. Properly primed, Jennie could unearth more

about Aunt Maude Henning and Muriel Babcock in ten minutes than he or Hanson could in a thousand years. Probably
she'd already made a start. She knew Buff Orpington's landlady, whose fragile appearance had so misled him. Not
Whistler's Mother, Asey thought, but Whistler's Mother
with Benzedrine, was more in keeping with what he'd ever
heard about the loquacious Mrs. Sturdy. Anyway, Jennie
could drill down to the pageant bedrock in no time at all.

As he heard the familiar coughings of Cummings's motor
turning over, he increased his speed.

But before he could reach the lane, the old sedan went
sailing along it and out of sight, in spite of his frantic wavings
and hailings.

Mrs. Henning even went so far as to wave back.

"Doggone it!" he said with irritation. "Don't they know
when someone's tryin' to chase after — oh, if the doc would
ever learn to glance into his rear-view mirror once in a while!
Why in time didn't *she* take some notice? She was on this
side — hey, *was* she wavin'?"

Or had she dropped something?

After all, that hadn't been a farewell gesture with the
finger tips up. Her hand and fingers had been pointing
straight down, toward the ground.

"She did! By golly, she dropped something! She was
throwing something away!"

He found himself marching in a beeline toward the spot,
like a golfer marching toward his ball after a badly sliced
drive.

Of course he was crazy. There was no earthly sense in
stringing out his flighty inspiration about her sleeves being

such a handy catchall. Sure, they could provide a handy storage space. But that wasn't any reason for his suddenly wondering if her left sleeve hadn't a curious little oval bulge toward the elbow that was quite lacking in the right. Or for his fanciful assumption that she'd necessarily have availed herself of those pink lace mutton-legs as a hiding place for some vital small object.

Or that if she had, she'd choose to rid herself of it at this point.

Still and all, she'd been in a whale of a hurry to be gone, now that he thought it over. She'd almost forgotten to take her big feathered hat until Cummings reminded her, and the toe of her pink satin slipper had tapped away impatiently while he went on and on about beards.

Had she perhaps guessed that a hasty solo exit on her part would instantly have aroused his suspicions? And was that why she'd prevailed on the doctor to take her home, in order to lend an aura of dignity and general whitewash to her withdrawal?

He reached the lane, and sighted his line — just to the right of the old receiving vault.

Crazy as the project probably was, he intended to grub around for some small oval object that Aunt Maude Henning might have tossed away.

Great drops of rain were splashing down on the nearby tombstones when he finally stood up and surveyed with honest perplexity the object in the palm of his hand.

"All the time, new trends!" he muttered. "Now why in time should she drop a pink glass egg into the creepin' myrtle? Why would anyone lay a pink glass egg — "

At the sound of a car approaching along the lane, he stepped hastily out of the rut where he was standing.

But after one swift glance at the driver, he unhesitatingly jumped back into the middle of the lane and remained there.

v

THE coupé wasn't going fast. But the driver braked so violently and twisted the wheel so energetically that the car bucked, and jumped the ruts at an angle, and then stalled.

Never in his entire life, Asey thought as the man viewed him with reproachful eyes, never had he seen such a shaggy beard!

"I very nearly ran you down!" the man said plaintively. "And it was all your own fault!"

You couldn't compare that beard with anything in the animal or vegetable kingdom, Asey decided. For unadulterated wild abundance, it was in a class by itself.

"I'm sorry I caused you this trouble." He planted both forearms on the car doorsill, and regretted the lack of a running board on which to plant his foot possessively. "I'm real sorry. Fact was, I stepped on a snake in the myrtle yonder, an' it kind of disconcerted me, Mr. — say, I'm sure I know who you are, but I don't recognize you with all that flourishin' mane."

"Bird," the man said. "Clifton Bird. Of Quanomet. But — ah — I'm afraid I don't quite — "

"Sure! Sure-sure! Bird, that's it! Sure. Of course. You was

pointed out to me only this mornin' down on the ball field."
Asey had never laid eyes on Mr. Bird before, but his hearty
tone carried so much conviction that for a moment he almost
persuaded himself that they'd at least gone through the sixth
grade together. "You're Mrs. Henning's chief cook an' bottle-
washer in the pageant. Sure. Doc Cummings told me about
you. Only you wasn't hidin' behind such a crop of foliage.
That's sure some beard you're sportin', Mr. Bird!"

Mr. Bird nervously cleared his throat, and such portions
of his cheeks and forehead as were visible turned a dull pink.

"I'm on my way home," he said with some embarrassment,
"to remove this — this *thing*. The Chairman of the Make-
up Committee, Miss Poole, insisted on trying out on me some
new idea — a new substance, that is — which she thought
might prove effective in the application of our pageant
beards. More adherent, as one might say. Naturally I protested being used for such experimental purposes, but to no
avail. I was the guinea pig. Miss Poole is a — a peculiarly
persuasive individual." Mr. Bird suddenly blushed to the
roots of his sandy hair. "But perhaps you are acquainted
with Miss Poole?"

"I'm afraid," Asey said, "I ain't had the pleasure."

"Miss Poole is the Spirit of Quanomet," Mr. Bird said.
"And while I seriously question whether the — er — founding fathers would have considered her in precisely that light,
it is to be admitted, as Mrs. Henning pointed out, that any
town ought to rejoice at being personified in such a — er —
such a comely fashion."

"Powers model stuff?" Asey inquired.

"Quite! Oh, quite! At all events, Miss Poole has now established the fact that her inspiration for attaching beards was almost too overpoweringly successful. That is to say, none of the ordinary means at hand seemed capable of removing this thing from my face."

"Stuck with it, huh?"

Mr. Bird nodded. "So I am hastening home to see if acetone, or any variety of paint remover, or some strong combination of them, or possibly even lye, may not — er — release me from this bondage. This beardage. I feel *silly!*" he added in a poignant burst of confidence. "Inordinately silly, Mr. — it *is* Mr. Mayo, isn't it? Mr. Asey Mayo?"

"Uh-huh. I can't help wonderin'," Asey said, "what a beard that looks like that could ever be doin' in something called 'Quanomet Through the Ages'! I can't seem to fit this into our glorious past. Did somebody ring in a historical act about the town's first circus, an' their Wild Man of Borneo?"

"Indeed you might well ask that!" This time Mr. Bird nodded with such vigor that the beard suddenly looked like a bearskin laprobe waving in a brisk wind. "I feel it's an error. A definite error. I feel it is not in the slightest degree Arabian!"

"How's that again?" Asey asked. "The slightest degree which?"

"Arabian. Possibly I should have said Iranian."

"What in time is either one of 'em doin' in Quanomet's glorious past?"

"It's the future, not the past," Mr. Bird explained. "It's for the final episode. The last scene. 'Quanomet's Glorious Future.' "

"Expectin' an Arabian-Iranian invasion, huh?"

Mr. Bird looked at him in dismay.

"Oh, no!" he said seriously. " 'Quanomet's Glorious Future' is essentially our country's glorious future, of course. 'With All Nations United,' as the program will say — dear me, I do wish I could trust Mrs. Pouter's casual optimism about the delivery of those programs! 'United in Universal Peace and Brotherhood.' "

"I see," Asey said. "Uh-huh. I get it. Quanomet, the happy meltin' pot."

At least this shaggy beard appeared to be a legitimate decoration, he thought to himself. There was a reason for its existence, and for its being worn. That Clifton Bird's Palm Beach suit was wringing wet didn't matter a whit. Nobody on the ball field could ever have escaped bone dry from the morning's downpours. And certainly there wasn't any visible evidence of his having commandoed through underbrush. He wasn't smudged, or briar-torn, or scratched by blackberry thorns.

Which was a great pity, Asey reflected. Because never on earth could there be another beard that fitted in so well with Mrs. Henning's simple description. If a shaggy beard existed, this was it. And when he'd stepped in front of the car, he'd thought for sure that he had it, too.

In fact for roughly three seconds back there, he'd thought he had everything for sure.

It hadn't been crystal-ball stuff. It simply had flashed through his mind that the boldest step any bright murderer could take at this point was to stick on his phony disguise and drop by to see how the situation was shaping up. If he found his beard had been previously spotted and was under suspicion, he could concoct some alibi from the pageant. Unquestionably he'd already have furnished himself with bullet-proof alibis for time and place.

But little Mr. Bird had only to open his mouth in gently plaintive complaint to dispel any suggestion of the bold, bright murderer. He hadn't even ripped out a few juicy cuss words at someone's marching in front of his car.

"Too bad," Asey said aloud. "I sure — uh — say, Mr. Bird, why was Miss Babcock runnin' around the ball field with a diploma in her hand?"

"Ah, yes! The diploma. That, Mr. Mayo, is to represent the legendary Quanomet Indian Treaty. You see, history actually offers some factual basis for the local legend that an Indian squaw — "

"Uh-huh. Eliza Bayberry Bush and the Parson's good-wife. I know. An' why did Miss Babcock have on so many layers of clothes, so's she could make quick changes for the show? Good. I guessed as much. What with your bein' stuck right smack there in the theater of operations, so to speak, I s'pose you pretty much see an' know about everything that goes on."

That was the simple way of finding out, just for the record, where and how Mr. Bird had occupied himself all morning. He had only to nod, and that would provide him with an alibi, whether he knew it or not.

But Mr. Bird shook his head.

"Since seven-thirty this morning," he said wearily, "I have made sixteen — no, I think it may be seventeen — trips to the village, including side trips to Mrs. Henning's home, the express office, the Town Hall, the printer, and the summer playhouse. If there were only one place in which I could be stuck right smack, as you phrase it, I assure you it would be a pleasure. I'm almost afraid to contemplate what lies before me these next few days. Er — could I give you a lift anywhere, perhaps?"

And that, Asey thought, was the simple way of suggesting that he couldn't back the car onto the lane with him leaning on the door.

"Thanks," he said with a grin, "but my car's parked down over the rise. You probably noticed it comin' in."

Mr. Bird looked blank.

"I don't hardly think you could've missed it," Asey continued as he stepped away from the door. "A chrome job, on the flashy side. A Porter — "

"I once had your car pointed out to me, Mr. Mayo, and I know what it looks like. But I did *not* see it parked back on the lane!"

"Wa-el, if you didn't see it, then I guess it plumb ain't there." Asey spoke in his most drawling voice, but he surveyed Mr. Bird through narrowed eyes. Why was this little fellow so desperately bothered all of a sudden? Of course he'd seen the Porter! "I guess gremlins whisked it away."

"Do you suppose it could have been stolen?" Bird asked anxiously.

Asey shrugged. "Probably just momentarily borrowed again. Huh. We been advertisin' that model as a car for persons who like to go places in a hurry, an' it seems like people are takin' that slogan literal this mornin'."

"But shouldn't you notify the police at once if it's been — er — stolen?"

"Swipin' that car," Asey said, "is like bearin' away the bank's safe on your shoulders. Now I wonder if Buff — oh, well. If you didn't see it, then somebody backed it out on the beach road just before you came, an' after the doc'd collected Bobby — "

"I do wish," Mr. Bird interrupted in a sudden burst of firmness, "that you'd get inside my car! You're getting wet!"

"I got wet. I can't get any wetter," Asey told him. "One more thing before I forget it, an' then you can run along an' peel off your mane. Are there any more beards like yours in the show?"

"No, mine is unique, and obviously a mistake on the part of Spinosa, who supplied our beards and wigs — Mr. Mayo, I *do* wish you'd get inside the car! I — I have something I wish to tell you, and it's so difficult with you out there getting wetter and wetter! I feel increasingly sure that your interest in the pageant must have some — er — basis, and if that fabulous car of yours has been stolen, I wonder if — that is — well, there is something I feel you really ought to know!"

"S'pose you pull up ahead," Asey suggested, "an' get yourself out of anybody's way."

Next to Cummings, the little man was the most inept driver he'd ever seen. It took minutes and a dozen stallings before he succeeded in easing the car across the ruts to the side of the lane.

Restraining his native impulse to take the wheel himself and spare the car any further beating, Asey waited and wondered what Mr. Bird wanted to get off his chest. And why he personally cared, and what had inspired his sudden solicitous and almost paternal interest in the man. After all, he wasn't an impetuously youthful or appealing character, like Buff Orpington — how old *was* he, anyway? That schoolmarm way of talking could so often fool you into thinking that people were a lot older than they actually were.

He sighed with relief when the coupé finally stalled in the creeping myrtle.

"Okay. That's — uh — good enough, Mr. Bird. Hold it there."

As he opened the car door, he became aware of the pink glass egg, still tightly clutched in his left hand. That could wait a bit, he thought, and quietly slipped it into the pocket of his jacket. That crazy pink egg, and whatever had been removed from Muriel Babcock's diploma, were two things he'd just as soon put on ice. The longer he could stave off trying to figure them out, the better.

"Well, Mr. Bird," he said, "what's the trouble?"

"Mrs. Henning always says that in the — er — the heat of a pageant, little problems always arise. She — "

"Uh-huh. I know she always says that. So what's your little problem?"

"This — that is to say, I — er — the situation — "

Hesitantly, almost falteringly, Clifton Bird embarked on the story which Asey had already heard from Buff. He told about the dagger incident, and how his own tires had been tampered with on the previous day, and he covered both topics at considerable length. This little man, Asey decided with a growing sense of ennui, was not one to leave even the tiniest pebble unturned.

"So," he concluded, "witn utmost reluctance, I have come

to the unhappy and regretful realization that someone really is attempting to sabotage our pageant, and — er — possibly myself, also."

Aside from the wealth of irrelevant detail, his account coincided with Buff's. Yet Asey had a curious feeling that Bird was omitting something.

That wasn't unusual. People often did a little editing after they'd added two and two — and Bird had clearly totted up Asey's own presence, and all his questions, and his car's disappearance, and decided that the sum total indicated trouble of some sort.

But this wasn't the time to try and extract the omission, or to inquire into Bird's theories of what might have motivated the sabotage, or even to inquire into his own purpose in relating all this.

"You got this dagger with you?" he asked briskly. "I'd like to see it."

"I'm afraid I left it among the pageant firearms in the men's dressing tent. Probably I shouldn't have, but it — it upset me. I fear I didn't think things through. I was very frightened. And so very tired. It's been a very fatiguing morning. In fact, the last three weeks have been fatiguing to an extreme. Acting as Mrs. Henning's assistant is like — er — like — "

"Like livin' in an activated Bendix washer, I kind of suspect," Asey said. "You got any idea who's responsible for this dagger business?"

Bird looked out across the rows of tombstones, and frowned.

"I'd never really have brought this to your attention, Mr.

Mayo," he said at last, "if you had not evinced such a definite interest in my beard. Because I suspect that this was the work of a man with a beard."

"Who? You know everybody in the pageant."

"I honestly don't know who this person is," Bird said swiftly. "I wasn't able to recognize him as anyone in the cast."

"An' what kind of a beard did he have, exactly?" Asey returned.

"Well — er — actually, it wasn't unlike mine. That is to say, it was — er — well, like this thing!"

"Mr. Bird, you know perfectly well I can't be any help in this sabotage issue if you don't tell me the truth — hey!" Asey had a sudden brain wave. "Hey, did you let Miss Spirit of Quanomet rivet that beard on you so's *you*'d be disguised, so's this fellow wouldn't take another stab at you?"

Bird said no so many times and in so many different ways that there wasn't much doubt in Asey's mind that such had been the case.

"Come on," he said when Bird ceased protesting. "Come clean!"

"Well, I was actually persuaded into this experiment against my will and better judgment. Once the beard was on, however, I must confess to having felt a deep sense of ease and — and of safety. I don't resemble myself. I am sufficiently altered in appearance so that a stranger might — er — stay his hand."

"Did you know someone'd been after Mrs. Henning?"

Bird nodded. "I fear I took too lightly Mrs. Pouter's expressed fears for her aunt's safety. Quite frankly, Mrs. Henning is so stalwartly determined, I felt that no one would dare to injure her. She is so magnificently oblivious to little problems — "

"Uh-huh. I know. Now what about Muriel Babcock? Has *she* said anything to you about bein' hounded?"

"Yes."

Asey looked at him questioningly.

"Yes," Bird repeated, "she has. Indeed, yes."

"Like what?"

"She told me yesterday morning that someone had tampered with the engine of her car, and she informed me this morning that someone had entered her room last night, but that her screams had driven the intruder away. An hour or so ago, down on the ball field, she announced in panic that someone had tried to stab her."

Asey leaned back against the car seat and critically considered what he could see of Mr. Bird's face.

"Sometimes," he said after a moment, "I get thrown so hard by my fellow men that I kind of feel bruised an' smartin'. Here you sit an' recite all that as emotional as if you was readin' the choices on a sixty-five-cent lunch. Look here, Mr. Bird, why in thunder didn't you *do* something about Muriel Babcock? Whyn't you tell the cops what she told you? Or even the local police, for Pete's sakes? Whyn't you tell someone?"

"Because," Bird looked him squarely in the eye, "because I didn't believe one word she said. I don't believe it. I do not believe anything Miss Babcock says. And to be very honest with you, Mr. Mayo, if I thought what she told me were true, I doubt if I should raise my hand to assist her — or even to attempt to aid her in any way. Anyone entertaining any base motives in connection with Muriel Babcock has my full and unqualified approval. There! I cannot tell you," he added, "what a relief it is for me to have said that out loud. I hate her."

"They tell me she's an awful persistent person," Asey quoted Cummings, "an' awful tryin'. But isn't she sort of a harmless creature to feel so violent about?"

"Probably there are those individuals," Bird returned, "who consider a cobra harmless. Or a black widow spider. I recall that one of my former teaching colleagues maintained in his household a venomous krait as a pet. One man's meat, Mr. Mayo, can quite often be another man's poison, can it not?"

"Wow!" Asey said softly. "You don't like her even a little bit, do you? What in time did she ever do to you, anyway?"

"She was most kind to me when I first came to Quanomet to live, and I must in all fairness say that I appreciate what she did for me at that time. I was — and am — interested in genealogy, which is one of her hobbies, and I saw quite a lot of her." He paused. "I was most desirous of entering fully into the life of the town, and particularly concerned with the Quanomet Fire Society — er — I suppose that you are a member of that very distinguished and historic organization?"

Asey laughed. "Sure, all good Cape Codders hereabouts join that as a matter of course, I guess. Oh — so you got Cape family, huh?"

"Yes, indeed, and I'm extremely proud of it," Bird said. "Perhaps you might enjoy seeing — er — if you'd be good enough to turn and reach me that briefcase from the shelf behind your head, I'd gladly show you my — what's the matter? Did you say something?"

"Only ouch," Asey told him. "I twisted my neck. Got a little crick in it."

He hadn't. His exclamation had popped out of him when he'd turned and noticed that next to the briefcase there was a roll of thin paper which could have fitted inside of Muriel Babcock's diploma like a hand inside of a glove.

"I'm sorry," Bird said. "I hope it subsides. If you'll forgive my saying so, perhaps it might be wise for you to think about putting on some dry clothes. You don't want a stiff neck. That roll of papers," he added as he took the briefcase from Asey, "might also entertain you. I know how all Cape Codders take a passionate interest in their family trees, and I'm sure that you'll find my maternal grandmother's lines most unusual. Her name was Sophia Hopkins, and her mother was a Nickerson of the Jonathan Nickerson line which originally settled in what is now known as South Pochet. Now Sophia, as you will see here on this paper, married first an Ebenezer Higgins of Weesit, whose father — on this chart, over here — was own cousin to — "

After five solid minutes of that sort of thing, Asey began to wonder if brute force would be necessary to drag Mr. Bird away from the sheaves of papers and the genealogical charts which he'd unrolled and spread out. Gentle hints of his own personal lack of interest fell on deaf ears, and pointed interruptions had no effect at all. Even spilling the papers on the car floor didn't disturb the man. Mr. Bird knew it by heart.

"Now *her* mother, here — "

"Mr. Bird!" Asey raised his voice. "Yoo-hoo, Mr. Bird! Look, my cousin Jennie Mayo is your girl for this stuff. She eats it up. But I got such doses of family trees when I was a boy, I've kind of avoided 'em like the plague ever since. My grandfather made me learn side branches of Mayos for ten generations back, an' I got larruped if I stumbled. How'd we get into this?" He rolled up the chart on his lap. "Talkin' about Muriel Babcock — oh. I s'pose she most likely helped you assemble all this family tree business, huh?"

"On the contrary." Bird started rolling up the other charts. "On the contrary!"

Something in his manner made Asey suddenly realize that he'd hurt the little man to the core. He couldn't tell what was going on behind that shaggy beard, but Bird's eyes looked like those of a stepped-on puppy.

"I'm afraid I don't get it," he said. "Did she hinder you? How could she?"

"Miss Babcock hindered to a point of almost making it impossible for me to gather the data at all." Bird's voice was bitter. "She refused me access to the records of the Quanomet Historical Museum."

"Oh? Why?"

"I rather think," Bird said slowly, "that when she grasped how very much it meant to me to be able to produce the proper genealogical papers qualifying me for membership in the Fire Society, she merely decided to thwart me if she could. It was foolish of me to tell her about it, of course, or to let her suspect how I felt. One should never confide one's hopes and one's — but I don't wish to bore you, Mr. Mayo."

Asey protested primarily from a sense of duty. He'd never taken any deep interest in the Fire Society, himself. Originally a co-operative fire-fighting unit with a hand pump and a few feet of hose, it had become in the passage of years merely a social club which native Cape Codders joined because their grandfathers and great-grandfathers had belonged. The organization gave an annual clambake at which everyone wore red shirts and antique fire helmets, he remembered. Occasionally it succumbed to a wave of civic-mindedness, but offhand he couldn't recall any constructive results.

"The Fire Society," Bird said, "means so very little to those of you who belong as a matter of course. But to an outsider living here, it's something to be desired, and attained. Er — I wonder if you can possibly understand what I'm trying to say."

"Sure," Asey said. "Somebody moves to a new place, an' they break their necks to join the Country Club. It's not so much an end as a sort of steppin'stone. Once you're in, you go on from there."

"Yes," Bird said. "But to me, membership in the society was a part of coming home. Once in, I thought perhaps I might run for the School Board, and then perhaps I might think about the State Legislature. Not that I couldn't attempt either one without ever having heard of the Fire Society. But being a member would give me a certain status. A certain position. People would know that my family came from here. I would *belong*."

Asey nodded, and reflected briefly on the things that people hankered for. One man's meat wasn't necessarily another man's poison. More often it was just someone else's cold mashed turnip. Porter, who'd founded Porter Motors, felt to the end of his days that he was a failure because he'd never been asked to buy a pew in the Weesit church. He'd never understood why, in spite of his donations of stained-glass windows and an organ, he had to sit in a back row while the people who cut his grass sat up front. It never had occurred to him that sitting in the front row proved nothing about anyone's worth or stature.

Neither did membership in the Fire Society. But Asey refrained from saying so.

"An' Muriel Babcock gummed you up? Deliberately? What on earth for? Er — what'd you ever do to *her*, Mr. Bird?"

"I assure you that my interest in her was purely — er — purely — "

"Platonic?" Asey suggested helpfully.

"Quite. Also historical, and genealogical. At all events, since I was prevented from consulting the data at hand, I've only recently succeeded in getting my material together from odd and remote sources. It's taken me two years — think of it! Two years to assemble what I probably could have acquired in two months or less!"

"Huh. An' this was just spite on her part?"

"I have never been able to think of any other reason," Bird said simply.

"But how could she ever keep you *out* of the museum?"

"It's hers. The material in it is hers. If she wishes to refuse permission to anyone to view old records, she is within her rights. She quite literally owns that building, you know, and every last thing in it. Because the townsfolk have been led to expect that it ultimately will become the property of the town, they have donated many priceless things to it. But Miss Babcock is not, as I said, entirely truthful. She has never actually promised to bequeath that collection to Quanomet. If she wishes to dispose of it or any part of it for her own gain, she may do so at any time."

"So?" Asey said. "I never knew that."

"But it's true. And it's my impression that she has more than once disposed of — " He broke off. "About my charts, Mr. Mayo. Sometime I should like to discuss them with your cousin, and particularly in regard to my grandmother's second husband, who — "

"Jennie'd love it," Asey said hurriedly before Bird got wound up again on family trees. "Uh — isn't it strange, all things bein' considered, that Mrs. Henning let Muriel Babcock have any say in this show at all, let alone such an important job."

That was not good fishing, he thought critically. But his bait worked anyway.

"Considering that Miss Babcock's money has backed and financed the pageant," Bird said, "Maude Henning had very little choice in the matter. In fact, Miss Babcock fully intended to be chairman herself."

Asey raised his eyebrows. "Oh?"

"Only Maude's tenacity and heroic will prevented such a tragedy," Bird said. "Plus, of course, a certain amount of background machination. Her wide experience in club work has taught Maude to be an extraordinarily gifted manipulator. Even now, I doubt if Miss Babcock quite understands why she was not elected chairman. According to her point of view, she had definitely purchased the position."

"An' I s'pose she's pretty much been takin' it out of **Mrs.** Henning's hide ever since, huh?"

"Indeed she most certainly has! She has not missed one opportunity to — er — to louse up the pageant, if I may be crass about it. Not one!"

"An' Mrs. Henning's coped with her?"

"Every step of the way. Maude is a genius," Bird said with honest admiration. "Mr. Mayo, can you explain this sort of thing? I mean, when anyone possesses as much money as Miss Babcock, how can she be so small, so petty, so utterly selfish? So thoughtless? So inconsiderate? So — so ruthlessly demanding?"

"Wa-el," Asey said, "when you come right down to brass tacks, the rich usually have most of the bad habits of the poor, don't they? Now let's — "

"Take her Quanomet Museum, for example," Bird went on. "That could be such a splendid little museum! But because it's Miss Babcock's, everything must be secondary to her own specific interests. It is, in consequence, a hodge-podge. A jumble. A *mess!* It is — "

"S'pose," Asey began, feeling that the conversational wedge might divert Mr. Bird in case the museum proved to be another of his favorite topics, like family trees, "s'pose we — "

"It is badly arranged," Bird continued, "and badly balanced. Its exhibits have been chosen solely for Miss Babcock's own pleasure. No one viewing it can have any conception of its true wealth of local treasures. Whatever she finds dull is thrust into the cellar — that's where she keeps those superb genealogical items willed her by old Mrs. Kenrick! And all — "

"S'pose," Asey patiently tried again, "that we drive along so's I can — "

"*All* of the Sturdy family papers! Think of it! And the Lombard family's wonderful collection of Sandwich glass is *never* displayed. It's thrust away carelessly in closets, or stuffed up under the attic eaves. The only item which Miss Babcock sees fit to put on display is that egg! And — "

"Hold on!" Asey grabbed Bird's arm and shook it. "Wait up here, chum! *The* egg? What egg?"

"That pink egg!" Bird said with scorn. "Of all those magnificent pieces, only that pink egg — "

"Mr. Bird," Asey said, "you've now touched on a topic as excitin' an' near to my heart as your family tree is to you. Let's crack this pink egg wide open. First off, why a pink glass egg in the first place? Why'd anybody make a pink egg? What's the reason for it?"

Bird shook his head.

"You mean you don't know?" Asey demanded.

"Frankly, no. I myself do not believe that it is even Sandwich. But Miss Babcock chooses to display it prominently in a large glass case. Together with her definitive monograph on the subject."

"All the time, new angles!" Asey said. "Muriel Babcock's actually written something about this pink egg?"

"She has proved, at least to her own personal satisfaction, that it is Sandwich," Bird said. "Since she is blindly accepted as an authority on everything pertaining to Quanomet, her opinion on the Quanomet pink egg has not been challenged or questioned. Her monograph — now let me see if I can recall that title. 'The Influence of Indian Trades Goods Traditions on the Forms of Product of Sandwich and Other Glaziers of the Period.'"

Asey stared at him. "How's that again? That is, if you feel up to repeatin' it!"

Bird obligingly repeated the title. "There is also a footnote, as I remember, on the evolution of certain loose-top snuff-boxes."

"When you render it into common speech," Asey said, "what's it boil down to?"

"Mercifully," Bird said, "I have never read that monograph. But I have gathered that Miss Babcock decided that perhaps certain baubles used by the early settlers for the purpose of trading with the Indians had some effect on trades goods manufactured at a later date."

"Huh. That requires a little mullin' over," Asey said. "Because Parson Whozis's wife traded lumps of glass with Mary Quahaug, why then Muriel Babcock figured that other people therefore went an' made a pink glass egg two hundred years later? Don't tell me! I hate to think that maybe I could be right!"

"Essentially, yes. That was her train of thought," Bird said. "Er — what's your own opinion concerning the egg, Mr. Mayo?"

"Wa-el, I never heard tell of there ever bein' *any* pink Sandwich glass," Asey said, "an' if there was, if some joker of a workman went an' created a pink egg, it's my own guess he either wanted to scare his wife when she went out to gather up the mornin' hen fruit, or else she told him she needed a new darnin' ball, an' so he made her a special model for a Christmas present. Is this it?"

At the sight of the pink glass egg in Asey's hand, Mr. Bird practically turned to stone.

"Yes! Yes, that's it! But — how did you get it?" he asked in a bewildered voice. "She *never* permits that to leave the museum! Where did you get it? Why, this is a most unusual occurrence! This is most amazing! We wanted that so badly for the pageant, and she absolutely refused to let us have it! Absolutely!"

"I'm rapidly reachin' a point," Asey said, "where I'll swallow almost anything I'm told about 'Quanomet Through the Ages.' But exactly how an' where does this pink egg fit into the picture? As a bauble for the Indians in the Peace Treaty division, perhaps? Or is it goin' to represent the Atom Bomb of the Glorious Future, in Technicolor?"

"We wanted it solely for publicity pictures," Bird explained. "Maude Henning very rightly felt that a pink glass egg would be certain to attract the attention of the press — and of course anything which directs public attention to our pageant is advantageous. If we were pinned down as to its actual role in the show, we decided we could utilize it in the Peace Treaty scene as a gift bauble — er — thrown in as a symbol of good will. But Miss Babcock absolutely refused to permit — "

"Would you change places with me?" Asey interrupted briskly. "Just wriggle over here. Thanks."

"Why, most certainly," Bird said, but he didn't sound in the least certain. "Er — just a moment, my beard has caught on the gear-shift knob. But what — er — oh, I see. You wish to drive. But what — where are we going?"

"I know you won't mind my grabbin' the wheel," Asey said with firmness as he eased the car onto the lane, "but I'm in sort of a hurry. I want to go to the Quanomet Historical Museum, an' I think maybe I know more short cuts than you do."

"But it will be closed, Mr. Mayo! The museum is open only when Miss Babcock is there, and she will be at the rehearsal all day!"

"Let's not brood about that angle," Asey told him.

"But if you can't get in, then what is the use of — "

As the car slid onto the new highway, Bird broke off, gripped frantically at the door strap, and closed his eyes tight.

He didn't open them again until the car came to a stop, when he turned to find Asey devoting himself to a thoughtful survey of the Quanomet Museum, which had started life as the town's two-roomed grammar school back in the eighteen-eighties.

"What a truly fine driver you are!" Bird said in a choked voice as he wiped his forehead with his handkerchief. "I'd been told that you drove like a — that is, that you let no grass grow, so to speak, under your feet, and I — er — how true!"

"Uh-huh," Asey said absently, and wondered if Muriel Babcock bought her wagon-blue paint in wholesale carload lots. The old frame building was white, but its two front doors and the trimmings were blue. The well sweep in the front yard was blue. There was a nailsick dory painted blue and planted with petunias. The school-bell cupola on the roof was blue. So was the ridgepole. "Kind of likes blue, don't she?"

"Aren't you observant! It's her favorite color. Not," Bird added critically, "precisely fitting for a museum, in my estimation!"

"Wa-el, she could turn it into Ye Olde Well-Sweep and Pink Petunia Gifte Shoppe any time she got tired of the museum part," Asey said. "She'd only have to change the letterin' on the blue an' white sign!"

"Quite. You'll notice, Mr. Mayo, that both doors are shut, and I'm very sure you'll find them most securely locked. Miss Babcock is very proud of her special burglar-proof locks —"

But Asey was out of the car, and walking slowly around the petunia-filled blue dory.

"Of course" — Bird hastened after him — "the flowers did look much better before today's rain beat them flat —"

"I knew it!" Asey reached out suddenly into the dory, and then he dangled a tagged key before Mr. Bird's startled eyes. "I felt it in my bones!"

"Now how could you ever guess —"

"Any woman who paints old dories blue an' plants 'em with petunias," Asey said, "usually hides her keys in the petunias. My cousin Jennie Mayo uses the second geranium on the left in the kitchen window box, but it's all the same thing. Let's go in an' take a look."

One swift glance around inside confirmed Bird's earlier comment about the place being a jumble and a hodgepodge. If nobody bothered telling you it was supposed to be a museum, Asey thought, you could easily take it for a combination secondhand store and junk shop, or somebody's cluttered attic that hadn't been cleaned out since the Year One.

"See, Mr. Mayo — here's the display case where the pink egg belongs. The monograph is still here."

"Uh-huh."

The removal of the egg had presented no problem, he reflected. All anyone had to do was to unhook the hinged rear wooden door. And Aunt Maude Henning was a girl who'd automatically take it for granted that the front door key would be in among the petunias. That was the way her mind would work.

"Is there anything I might possibly be able to explain for you?" Bird asked eagerly. "About any of the other exhibits, that is? While I'm naturally most familiar with items pertaining to genealogy, I'd be glad — "

"No, thanks!" Asey said quickly. "Nope, I found out what I wanted to know."

He could always rush off and grab Aunt Maude, and bring her here, and confront her with the empty case, and get good and melodramatic about it — and draw a blank look. Or he could ask her outright why she'd tossed the pink egg away in the cemetery — and draw a bland denial.

"Aren't you going to put the egg back where it belongs?" Bird asked.

Asey shook his head. "I guess maybe I'll just keep it up my sleeve."

"But Miss Babcock won't like it!"

"Muriel Babcock," Asey returned, "isn't hardly in any position to object. You see, it's this way — "

Very briefly, he told Bird what had happened.

Just as the sight of the pink egg had done, the news had a momentary effect of turning the little man into a marble statue.

Then he crumpled limply into a Hitchcock chair, ignoring the fact that it was already occupied by two china-headed dolls dressed in flounced crinoline and lace-trimmed pantalettes.

"And what I have said!" His voice was full of anguish, and his eyes had that kicked-puppy look again. "What I have *told* you! What I have said about her! Oh!"

"It's so hard for me to think," Asey said, "that you didn't perhaps catch just a wee glimpse of the police car at the cemetery, Mr. Bird, an' maybe guess at the start that something was wrong!"

"But I assure you I didn't! I never once suspected — "

"Okay. Now you know what's gone on, d'you feel like breakin' down an' tellin' me the truth about this man with the beard you say you seen? Because I've got kind of tired extractin' information like I was a polite an' painless dentist. Seems to me I been pullin' gentle at rear molars for altogether too long this mornin'!"

"But there really *is* another man with a beard! I felt sure when I told you that you didn't believe me, but there really is! And truly, I don't know who he is! I don't know his identity — "

"But you know where he lives!" Sometimes if you shot that sort of question quick enough, it worked.

"No, only that — " Bird stopped, and Asey knew it wasn't working this time. "No."

"I keep thinkin'," Asey said, "that it might prove an awful profitable experience for you to go back to the cemetery an' view this situation in a realistic fashion, Mr. Bird. S'pose we do just that. S'pose we go there right now, you an' me. Come along!"

He gestured for Bird to precede him, and then slammed the blue door shut and started down the walk to the car.

"Really, I — er — that is, I don't — "

"Because if you saw Muriel Babcock," Asey went on, "maybe p'raps you might have a clearer conception — huh, looks like the sun was tryin' to come out again, don't it? If you see her, I think p'raps you might almost figure that but for the grace of God, Mr. Bird, there you — "

"Yoo-hoo! Asey! Yoo-hoo!"

The hail issued from a passing sedan, which skidded to a stop on the wet street, and then backed up in a series of enthusiastic jerks.

Jennie Mayo, dressed in a long, full-skirted calico print dress, emerged from behind the wheel and bustled over toward them, her starched blue sunbonnet bobbing as she hurried along.

"I must say, Asey Mayo, this's just about the last place on earth I ever expected to find you — how do you do, Mr. Bird! You've probably forgotten me, but I met you at that church supper the night you gave such a nice talk to the Ladies' Aid about genealogy, and I been meaning ever since to write and ask you if your great-grandmother — "

"No!" Asey broke in with firmness. "No! No, Jennie, life is too short an' time is too fleetin', an' if I hear that word 'genealogy' just once more today, I'm goin' to start screamin' like a couple of panthers! Where've you been, anyway? The doc an' I decided not to go fishin' after all, so when we come home an' found your note, we hustled over to the ball field — but we couldn't locate you, an' nobody knew anything about you or where you'd gone to."

"Well," Jennie told him complacently, "I found out everything! Who was bothering Mrs. Henning, that is. It wasn't a bit hard once I got started."

"Oh?" Asey said. "Man with a shaggy beard, I presume likely?"

He hadn't intended that as a serious remark, and Jennie's response set him back on his heels.

"Drat it! Can't anybody ever find out anything that *you* haven't gone and found out first?" She sounded thoroughly annoyed. "Anyway, for the last hour, I been driving all over Kingdom Come trying to find *you* — Asey, do you know there's another Porter just like yours around town? I followed it twice."

"Who's driving it?" Asey demanded.

"Some stranger in a brown hat. I was positive it was your car — of course I couldn't tell from the license plates because they were all muddied up from the rain. But — see here, Asey Mayo," her tone changed abruptly, "what's gone on? Has something happened to Maude Henning?"

"There seems to of been a slight shift," Asey said, "in the matter of who was bein' plotted against. Nothing's happened to Mrs. Henning. But Muriel Babcock — golly, I need a wire recordin' of this! Listen hard, now, an' don't interrupt me!"

Jennie clucked her tongue sympathetically when he finished.

"Tch, tch, the poor thing!" she said. "Course, I must say I don't know anybody who managed to rile more folks than she has — it comes from her always having to let people know how awful much *she* knew, or else correcting 'em all the time. Thamozene Sturdy told me way back last spring she'd stood about all *she* could of Muriel's being so superior! But on the other hand, she certainly never deserved anything like this — oh, what a pity I didn't know! I wouldn't've wasted my time tracking down that man with the beard. And I was *so* proud of myself for having got him!"

Asey glanced toward her car. "Uh — where you got him?"

"I wish you wouldn't always keep harping on that ole German spy!" Jennie said. "Can't you ever forget that? What else could I do with him but stick him in the car trunk? He was twice my size, and I wouldn't've stood a chance if he'd worked loose from my clothesline I tied him up with, and you know it perfectly well!"

Bird suddenly sounded as if he were choking.

"Don't let her upset you," Asey said. "You'd never guess if you saw her in a rocker, tattin' away with the cat purrin' on her lap, that she sometimes has her vicious moments! Look here, Jennie, where've you got this fellow? Who in time is he?"

"I only meant I know where he is. He's a foreigner, and his name is Tanek or Tonik, or something like that. At least, that's what the clerk with the pince-nez called him. And what I thought" — she ignored Asey's effort to get a word in edgewise — "was that you'd probably ought to call in the F.B.I., because if ever I saw a man that looked like a sub — oh, what is the word the newspapers call everybody nowadays instead of just communists and such?"

"Subversive element?"

"That's it! But of course *he* was after Maude Henning, and not Muriel, so — "

"Whoa up!" Asey said. "How'd you locate him?"

"Why, it was easy enough — I just asked Bobby Pouter if he knew who'd been bothering his aunt," Jennie explained nonchalantly. "You know how noticing youngsters always are! Well, he told me he'd seen a man with a beard hanging around their house, and around rehearsals, and so on, but he hadn't said anything because he didn't want to get his mother worried. He's a real nice bright boy, that Bobby, and he'd been keepin' watch over his aunt all by himself. He wants that portable Geiger counter thing real bad, and *I* think he deserves to have it for his birthday. Asey, couldn't you get him one wholesale from — "

"After the way I've been havin' to root out little morsels of information," Asey said, "all these assorted tidings of yours are like bein' smashed in the face with a lot of lemon meringue pies. Look, Jennie, somewhere between the man with the beard an' this portable Geiger counter, I got lost!"

"Sometimes it seems to me," she returned with asperity, "that for a man they call the Codfish Sherlock and think of as so awful brainy, you're the stupidest thing! Don't you see, that poor child's been scared stiff, but he hasn't wanted to upset his mother because he wants that Geiger counter so much, and so he's been trying to watch the man with the beard and protect his aunt all by himself! And *I* certainly think that you might get him one, with his poor father killed in the war, and — "

"Okay," Asey broke in. "Geiger counter is written on my heart for future reference. Only before we drown in heavy water, tell me how in time you ever found out *which* man with a beard? Whyn't you pick out Mr. Bird here, or somebody in the pageant?"

"I never once thought of Mr. Bird!" Jennie said flatly. "*Or* anybody in the show! All those beards are false! Just look at this dreadful shaggy thing of Mr. Bird's — anybody'd know him underneath it right away! I wasn't fooled for two seconds! I knew him right off!"

Asey stifled a smile as he recalled the little man's serenely confident assumption that his beard constituted a highly effective disguise.

"After all," Jennie went on, "there's *some* things a beard can't cover up! Like — well, like eyes," she added rather hurriedly, and Asey suspected she'd been going to say "size," but thought better of it. "Eyes, and so on. Anyway, Bobby said it was a man with a *real* beard. Then he spotted him over by the grandstand — this was at the ball park — and pointed him out. So I just followed him when he left in his car, and I found out — Asey, when did they take her away from the cemetery? Muriel Babcock, I mean?"

"Not as of — oh, how long we been gone from there, Mr. Bird? Say fifteen minutes?"

"Less than that, Mr. Mayo, I'm sure. Our — er — trip here was quite brief, and we did no more than take a hasty look around inside the museum. Let me see, it was still raining when we arrived here, so perhaps if we knew when the rain stopped, we might quite accurately determine — "

Over Asey's increasingly impatient protests, Mr. Bird and Jennie proceeded to establish exactly when the rain had ceased.

"Okay, okay! Call it twelve an' a half minutes!" he finally said. "Only don't let's work it over any more — who cares, anyway? Muriel Babcock was there in the cemetery when we left twelve an' a half minutes ago, an' I suspect she's still there now, an' will be for — "

"But she isn't!" Jennie interrupted. "Because about ten minutes ago, I took the short cut through that place, and it was empty!"

"Oh, come now!" Asey said. "You just didn't notice the police car, or the cops. You were too dead bent tryin' to locate me — "

Jennie said that the cemetery was empty, and she guessed she knew an empty cemetery when she saw one.

"And furthermore, even supposing I maybe missed the police car, I know there weren't any police! I tell you, that cemetery's empty! There wasn't a soul there but Thamozene Sturdy — what did you say?"

"I won't repeat it out loud," Asey told her. "Call it an exclamation of amazement. An' go on!"

"So I stopped just long enough to say how-do-you-do to her, and I guess if anybody in this wide world'd known if there were cops and a body around, and particularly Muriel Babcock's body, Thamozene Sturdy would! So there!"

Bird, Asey reflected, had also claimed that he hadn't seen

the police car. Maybe those two cops had left it outside the cemetery. Or else they'd just so happened to park it inside that people driving through from the shore road didn't notice its presence.

But Jennie's logic was faultless. If the cops *had* been around and on deck, Whistler's Mother would certainly have been the first to spot them, and find out what for.

"What was she doin' there?"

"Thamozene? Oh, she always decorates an ancestor today. I mean, it's the anniversary of Cap'n Obed Sturdy — the one that fought on the *Constitution*. He was lost at sea in some battle or other, but she always puts flowers at his stone today. She started to tell me the story, but I cut her short. If you don't watch your step with her, you know, you can fritter away four or five hours in listening. I never give her a chance to get started. Oh, look — there goes the car that's like yours, Asey! With the man in the brown hat — "

"I'm takin' Bird's car," Asey said. It was headed in the right direction. "Jennie, take yours an' go to the cemetery, an' see what's goin' on — an' don't let him drive!"

He was in the coupé and on his way up the street after the chrome-plated Porter before his admonition about Bird's driving was fairly out of his mouth.

After all, the fact that it was being driven by a man in a brown hat made it none the less his own car. He'd meant to tell Jennie so, but never got the chance. And it proved for sure who'd swiped it from the cemetery.

He cut around the corner, and then braked to keep from bumping into the Porter as it slowed and turned up a driveway on the left. A graveled driveway leading to a large, mustard-colored shingled house. With a welter of gables and porches. And a porte-cochere.

And a driveway sign that said "Babcock."

"On second thought — "

Instead of following the Porter, Asey continued very slowly on down the street.

In the rear-view mirror, he watched the man in the tan raincoat and the brown hat get out of his car, and mount the steps to the front door.

Tucked under his arm was a cane.

"An' I like to think," Asey said as the door was opened and Brown Hat entered the house, "it's *the* cane!"

vi

▼▼▼▼▼▼▼▼▼▼▼▼▼▼▼▼▼▼▼▼▼▼▼▼▼▼▼▼▼▼▼▼▼▼▼▼▼▼▼

IT had to be the missing cane, that was all. While he was now reasonably resigned to the possibility of six million shaggy beards cropping up, there simply couldn't be more than one Brown Hat, or one crook-necked cane!

He turned to the left at the corner just beyond, and stopped the car.

The rear ell of the Babcock house was visible through the scraggly remnants of an old quince orchard, and the continuation of a low, mustard-colored picket fence indicated that the entire block on his left was Babcock property.

Asey hurriedly thrust up on the shelf some of Bird's charts which had fallen down when he drove off from the museum in such a burst of speed, and remembered to grab the car keys as he got out.

On the whole, he thought as he stepped over the picket fence and started striding through the orchard, on the whole he was glad he hadn't given in to his first impulse and gone rushing headlong after Brown Hat. Something told him that Brown Hat wouldn't most likely have obligingly co-operated with smiling answers to questions like "Why did you swipe my car, huh?" Or "What was your general purpose in lurking around the cemetery, anyway?" Or "By the way, is that the cane Muriel Babcock was killed with?" Or "Will you be so kind as to hand over whatever you stole from inside that rolled-up diploma?"

Of course he was taking a chance in assuming that Brown Hat wasn't just dropping by to leave a calling card at the Babcock house, and that the fellow might not be off and away within the next ten seconds. But there hadn't been anything tentative or hesitant in the way he'd marched inside the house. He'd given out the impression, Asey decided as he skirted a vegetable garden and started up a path toward the back door, of a man who'd meant to stay a spell.

The sound of voices, yelling voices, brought him to a standstill by the side of the drying yard that was enclosed by a mustard-colored latticework.

Not just yelling voices, either. But quarreling voices. In the room with the open window, the one at the junction of the main house and the ell, a woman and a man were going at it hammer and tongs.

That, Asey bet, was Brown Hat!

Brown Hat, and some woman in the Babcock household.

It took a good full minute before he could adjust his ears to a point of actually understanding what they were yelling at each other about. For the woman's voice was shrill, and breathless, and had a curious quality of never seeming to deviate from a single high-pitched note. It never went up or down, but just on and on. The man's voice was rasping, and he stammered just enough so that whole phrases were unintelligible to Asey until he caught onto the fellow's habit of running words together very quickly after that slight hesitant pause.

But you didn't need any interpreter to know that these two hated each other, he thought. You could tell that right off the bat, simply from their tones.

"You can't stay here!" the woman was nearly shrieking. "She said you couldn't stay here again! Never! You get out of this house! You get straight out of here! You get out *now!*"

"It's my — my house too and I shall stay here if I want to!"

Asey raised his eyebrows. If the Babcock house was his too, then this fellow might very possibly turn out to be Muriel's brother, George Pettingill!

He smiled when the woman confirmed his guess with her next shrill words.

"You get out of here, George Pettingill! Go on, get out! I'll put you out!"

"Don't you dare touch me, you filthy old harridan! I'll — I'll have you fired! You'll lose this soft job — and all the small change you pick up and make away with, and all the food you steal! You don't like that idea, do you! You know when you're onto a good thing!"

"I work here because there's nobody else *will* work for her! Nobody! She can't get anybody else because they won't come! And she has to pay me plenty to make *me* stay!" the woman retorted. "You can't fire me! And she won't! She doesn't dare to! She wouldn't ever dare to! She's the one knows the good thing!"

"Get out of my way!"

"If you hit me with that cane, I'll tell her, and that'll cook *your* goose! You'll see! I'll tell her things she doesn't know about you — "

There was a loud crashing sound, as if a table and a lamp had been pushed over and smashed to the floor, and Asey jumped toward the back steps.

Then he stopped as the voices went right on yelling, as if nothing at all unusual had happened.

"If you don't get straight out of this house, George Pettingill, then *I* will! I'll go — and then the two of you can fight all day long, and all night long if you want to! *And* get all your own meals and wash up your own dishes — and throw them at each other like you always do! And when she sees what you just went and smashed, you'll catch it! You'll catch it good! I'll leave you to it! *I'll go!*"

Asey darted back to the shadow of the drying yard wall as three doors slammed in rapid succession and footsteps suddenly sounded somewhere near the back door.

From the wild intensity of the woman's voice, and from that curious, high-pitched drone — not to mention what she'd actually said — he hardly expected to see what employment agency advertisements referred to as a high-type, refined cook-general.

But he wasn't prepared for the witchlike character with the stringy gray hair who emerged on the back stoop, and stood there.

This was Crazy Mary — no, it was Crazy Martha. He searched his memory for the rest of her name while she carefully pinned a pink crocheted shawl around her thin shoulders, and adjusted a frayed yellow straw hat on which three plumelike green feathers stood bolt upright. Her feet were encased in old-fashioned, high-lace white kid boots, with heels so run over that it seemed impossible that she could manage to walk in them. And she was wearing at least three cotton print dresses of different lengths and styles and colors, and in varying stages of decay. Her basic idea, Asey decided, must be that if part of one dress was missing or worn out, why part of another did just as well. In passing, he wondered if Crazy Martha's layers might possibly have been a source of inspiration to Muriel Babcock.

It wasn't Blodgett, he thought, as he watched her apply lipstick with all the purposeful nonchalance of a Hollywood film star. Nor Brackett. Nor Baxter. She was the one whose husband had been killed in an accident at the old Weesit grade crossing years ago, and ever since then she'd been what Jennie always charitably described as a mite touched in the head, poor thing. She lived in a shack over by the swamp — now what in thunder *was* her last name?

It came to him as she minced past, and he tipped his cap and greeted her politely.

"How do you do, Mrs. Bangs."

"How do," she returned. Her gray eyes had a wild look in them, no doubt about it, and her face hadn't been washed in months. Nor had she. "You're a Mayo. You can't deny it."

"That's right. Asey Mayo. I was aimin'," he said in a low, confidential voice, "to call on George Pettingill. He to home?"

"We don't like to have him here." She lowered her voice,

too. "But he comes just the same. He's a dreadful man. Always after money."

She suddenly thrust her face quite close to Asey's, and peered at him, and he backed against the latticework until he could feel it giving behind him.

"I don't like George." Asey tried not to look at her teeth. "I really don't want to see him very much. But I got to."

And that, he thought, was all true enough.

"George's no good. Him and his sister, they fight like cats and dogs. She never gave him that money to go away and start business in the city because he got girls into trouble, like folks say. It was because he fought so with her, she was scared of him, and he stole money from her all the time. He only comes to see her when he wants more money. How's skunks over your way?"

Her swift transition caught Asey off balance.

"Uh — seems to be plenty of 'em," he said, and wondered if skunks were in her mind a logical follow-up to the topic of George Pettingill.

"I'll have to come over and catch me some," she said. "I like skunk stew."

Asey swallowed. "Wa-el," he said, "it ought to be tasty."

"I'll bring you a tinful. You watch out for him." She waggled a dirty forefinger under his nose. "You watch out for George. He's a dreadful man. He hits people. He tried to hit me just now. He hits his sister when she won't give him money. Always after money, all the time! If you catch any skunks, you keep 'em for me."

With that admonition, she swung off down the garden

path at a rate of speed Asey wouldn't have believed possible in those pointed boots and with those run-over heels.

It didn't occur to him until he was quietly opening the back screen door that he hadn't even heard a footfall after she was a yard away from him.

As he stepped into the kitchen, it occurred to him that she probably did catch skunks. And it didn't surprise him in the least.

He noted that the kitchen, in direct contrast with its care-taker, was spotlessly clean. But almost nothing short of acute starvation would have induced him to eat one of the small chocolate cakes lying on a plate on the center table. Crazy Martha could be one of the world's best cooks, but you couldn't escape the association of ideas!

Skunk stew.

"Wow!" he said softly to himself. "Wow!"

Half a dozen doors led out of the kitchen, but he ignored them. Directly ahead of him was a large dining room, and George Pettingill was in a room beyond that. Asey could hear sounds of him stirring around.

As he tiptoed across the worn green Axminster rug, he glanced at the bric-a-brac covering every available inch of flat surface in the dining room, and at the glass-fronted closets stuffed full of hand-painted china and heavy cut glass. Somehow even Muriel Babcock's home managed to achieve the same general over-all effect of clutter that had existed in the museum.

He continued his stealthy progress a few feet along a wide hall, and then at the doorway to what was apparently a com-bination library and office, Asey paused.

George Pettingill, still wearing the tan raincoat and the brown felt hat, was on his knees in front of an open, old-fashioned iron safe. The Turkey carpet on either side of him was littered with heaps of papers and documents and folders, and he was busily engaged in pulling out still more, and tossing them on top of the others.

The missing cane was lying across the arms of an over-stuffed chair, and against a large brown fringed leather pillow whose hand-painted decoration brought a smile to Asey's lips. It was a pretty terrible but only too easily recognizable version of Quanomet's famous bay view. And just in case anyone should have any doubts as to the identity of the scene, the artist had thoughtfully thrown in a broad hint.

"Welcome," it said in flowing capitals around the border of the picture, "to Picturesque Quanomet, Cape Cod, Mass."

Along with the portable Geiger counter, Asey added the painted leather pillow to his mental list. He would never rest entirely happy until he'd presented that pillow to Buff Orpington as a memento of his vacation in the pea-green folder. Provided, of course, that Buff ever chose to stop running and return to the fold!

It was almost a wrench to tear himself away from contemplating View One, and to turn his attention to the crook-necked cane.

But it was the missing cane, all right. After the length of time he'd stared at it back in the cemetery, Asey practically knew by heart every variation of the pattern of the grain, and just where the silver name band was tarnished the most.

He continued to lounge quietly in the doorway, watching George Pettingill jerking papers out of the safe, and wondering just where to start in on the fellow. A bungling approach, he suspected, could easily turn George into a first-degree problem child.

You could put all the faith in the world in Crazy Martha's opinion of the man, if you wanted to. Jennie surely would, he knew. Jennie claimed that children and queers could never be fooled in their estimates of character because they never got distracted by any side issues. They went straight to the point.

Or you could figure it fancylike. Perhaps George had once caught Crazy Martha filching some of Muriel's small change, as he'd insinuated during their set-to. And perhaps she was just queer enough and warped enough to switch the situation and claim that George was always after money, and stole from his sister. Cummings had a two-dollar word for that sort of thing, where a person completely erased his own crimes from his mind, and honestly convinced himself that they were the work of some other party.

Still and all, that conversation he'd overheard had hardly made George out a very lovable character! And he'd obviously tried to hit Martha. Asey didn't think she'd made that part up, in view of the crash he'd heard. That episode must have occurred in one of the rooms leading off the kitchen, because he personally hadn't noticed any rubble strewn around anywhere. He'd look into the matter later, if he thought of it —

"Put up your hands!"

George Pettingill had swung around suddenly and was

facing him, and Asey found himself looking into the barrel of a Colt automatic.

And, for the first time, he had a good look at the man. Thick black eyebrows, close-set black eyes, full lips, a pudgy chin.

He recognized that face! And mentally congratulated himself for having dallied so up till now.

Because this was now going to be a whole lot simpler than he'd anticipated!

"Put up your —"

"Tch, tch, Mr. Pettingill!" Asey said reproachfully, but he didn't move. "Lay your little pistol down. You didn't have any pistol in your hand last time you called on Bill Porter about advertisin', did you? Leastways, I don't recall that you did. I'd of said the last thing in the world you wanted to do was to brandish guns viciouslike at any of us fellers at Porter Motors. You thought we was such fine folks, an' you hoped so much to do business with us. In a big way."

The gun slid from George's hand, which seemed to have become limp and puttylike, and Asey scooped the weapon up before it hit the rug.

"There, now, that's better," he said. "Trouble with a feller gettin' a gun in his hand is so often he sneezes or something, an' it turns out he plugs somebody, to his ever-lastin' regret. You know, you still don't look like you remembered who I was — oh, you do? P'raps these clothes I got on was what threw you off at first. You only seen me in my city clothes before."

"I — I only thought I heard someone, and the — the pistol

was right here in the safe so naturally I grabbed it! I didn't think it would be you!"

"Course not, why should you?" Asey said soothingly. "Now most usually I remember faces fine, but I don't always remember the names that go along with 'em. Now I seen it, I remember your face. You're one of the lads that wants to revolutionize our advertisin'. You was goin' to fix it so's we'd be sellin' Porters like they was some new pill guaranteed to cure colds in three minutes or your money back. I s'pose you just wanted to check up on your copy, huh, an' that's why you went an' stole my Porter?"

George gulped audibly. "*Yours?*"

"Uh-huh. Mine. Why?"

George was too completely flustered to do more than stammer helplessly. But he finally managed to make Asey understand that he thought he was taking his sister Muriel's new car.

"She said she — she was going to buy a new Porter coupé," he added lamely.

"Oh? An' if she said she was goin' to buy herself a new yacht," Asey remarked, "I s'pose you'd of set off on a nice cruise in the first new forty-footer you stumbled on, huh? Stuff an' nonsense! You wanted to get away from that cemetery in an awful hurry, so you went an' swiped the first car handy, an' it happened to be mine. Isn't that right? Isn't that the truth?"

"I dud — I dud-don't know what you're talking about!" George protested.

"May I suggest for your own future good, Mr. Pettingill," Asey said crisply, and every trace of drawl or of Cape accent had abruptly disappeared from his voice, "that you speak the truth? In full? It's not my intention to point your pistol at you, or to dangle the Porter Motors advertising account in front of you."

Not much, he thought to himself. Not much!

"Or even," he went on smoothly, "to mention the extent of our many affiliations in various fields."

He paused for a moment to let that one sink in, and noted with pleasure that George was looking good and racked, as if both his arms were being twisted out of their respective sockets at once.

"Or even — what's this piece of paper you're handin' over?" he demanded.

"It's her letter. Muriel's letter. About her intending to get a new Porter. Read it!"

Asey glanced over the indicated paragraph. Then he grinned, tilted his yachting cap back on his head, and perched himself comfortably on the wide arm of a black leather chair.

"I think," he said, "that you an' me now understand each other fine, George — mind if I call you George? Good. Okay, George, I'll swallow the Porter item. She said she was goin' to buy herself one, an' you thought she had, an' so you took mine — but would you have taken it, I wonder, if she was alive?"

"Alive? What do you mean?"

Asey sighed. "An' I thought we had things on such an even keel! George, you know she's been killed. Killed, as murdered."

"No! *No!*"

George certainly sounded as if he were speaking the truth, and he certainly gave every appearance of a man who'd just been rocked to the very core. But monosyllables, Asey thought, could always be made to sound so heartfelt. And he'd personally never run across anyone engaged in George's trade who couldn't manage to look shattered to pieces when the occasion demanded it.

"Wh-what happened?" George went on. "Wh-what —"

"We'll get to that," Asey said. "S'pose you tell me first how you happen to have Davis Williams's cane?"

George said simply that he'd found it. "I knew it was Dave's. I've seen him carry it often enough — and it has his name on that silver band. So I picked it up. I — I practically tripped on it in the woods, over by the old cemetery."

"I can't tell you how happy I am, George," Asey said, "to have you reach them woods first. What was you doin' over there, exactly?"

George drew a long breath and said it was a little difficult to explain that.

"Uh-huh, I sort of sensed it might be," Asey returned. "But plunge in, George. Let's have the whole story. Uh — take it slow."

"As a matter of fact, I came to Quanomet today for a very definite purpose." George's stammer all but vanished when he took plenty of time speaking, Asey noticed. "I came here to contact a member of my organization. His name is Orpington. John Orpington. Perhaps you may remember him as Flash Orpington, the great half-back."

Asey smiled.

"That," he said, "is goin' to be a very tough one to sell me, George. Because Buff Orpington didn't know he was comin' to Quanomet until somebody passed him over his ticket. Uh-huh," he added as George stared at him in wide-eyed amazement, "old Yogi Mayo knows all, hears all an' sees all. You'd be surprised at the little tidbits of information that fall into my lap. Anyway, if Buff himself didn't know he was comin' here, how did *you* know it, George? Use your ouija board, or just consult the stars?"

"I found out purely by chance. Last night at the club, I ran into an old college classmate of mine who'd just returned from Weesit," George said. "He casually mentioned that he'd happened to bump into Buff while he was changing to the New York train, and Buff was waiting for the Cape bus. He told me Buff said he was on his way to Quanomet. And of course you can check up on that very easily by asking Buff if he remembers running into Harold Gregory yesterday."

"An' how did you come here?" Asey inquired. "By plane?"

George nodded. "I phoned the charter service last night and arranged for a plane to fly me up early this morning. We landed over at the Weesit field beyond the Country Club."

"Seems to me," Asey drawled, "like you made considerable of an effort to contact somebody you only finished firin' yesterday mornin'."

That flustered George sufficiently to start him stammering again.

"Whoa up!" Asey said at last. "Take it easy. You probably had your reasons. Just sum 'em up."

"Through a series of regrettable errors on the part of some of our office personnel," George said slowly and with deep earnestness, "Buff was informed that his services were no longer required. Unfortunately, I advised him to that effect myself. When, however, the situation became clarified later by the discovery of these deplorable staff errors, I deemed it only fitting and proper, and my particular duty, to rectify the unhappy condition in person, and with all possible celerity."

"With kindest personal regards," Asey said, "believe me to be yours most sincerely."

"Wh-wh-*what?*"

Asey chuckled.

"Business language," he said, "is so useful, ain't it? Covers things up like a nice big warm fleecy blanket. What you really mean, I surmise, is that you blew your top an' fired Buff in a hasty moment, an' then you repented awful fast an' furious when some big account or other said he'd work with Buff Orpington, thanks, or Pettingill, Whatever and Company could go climb the nearest tree or two. That about the size of it?"

"Well," George said, "well, yes. As a matter of fact, it was 'Lively.'"

"Gasoline?" Asey asked. "Perfume? Soap? Or maybe girdles?"

"Pet-food. Dogs love 'Lively,' cats love 'Lively,' white mice love it — "

"An' hamsters cry for it. I see. Wa-el, now we got all that

cleared up, what was you doin' over at the cemetery? Or better still, s'pose you pick up the ball at the Weesit Airport, an' bat it around from there."

First, George said, he'd tried unsuccessfully to phone his sister. Then, when he'd learned at the airport that pageant rehearsals were going on at the Quanomet ball park, he'd hired a car to drive him there.

"I knew Muriel would surely be at the rehearsal, and I thought she probably was the best person to help me locate Buff," George went on. "If she couldn't find out with whom he was staying — if it wasn't with anyone we know — I thought she might tell me about those places that rent rooms, so that I could check around and find him. But I couldn't even find *her* at that infernal rehearsal!"

He went into some detail about his various attempts to unearth his sister in the crowd, and Asey gathered that he'd been caught up in the vortex of moving groups in much the same fashion that Buff had been.

"Everyone had just seen her!" George said plaintively. "Just a minute before. Just a second before. But no one knew where she *was!* And then someone told me she'd gone to the old cemetery — "

"Hold it! Who told you that?"

"Some pageant character or other. Someone with a beard." Asey sighed.

"I know. A *shaggy* beard. Whenever you use that word 'beard' in my presence, George, always remember to stick *shaggy* in front of it. This is Shaggy Beard Day on the Mayo calendar."

"But it wasn't shaggy," George said. "It was too small for

the fellow and it kept falling off — he was someone out of the Civil War episode, I think. He had on a — what do you call it, a forage cap? Anyway, it wasn't a shaggy beard. It was quite short, and trimmed. I've seen pictures of General Grant that — what did you say?"

"I said all the time, new trends keep croppin' up," Asey told him. "At this point, an unshaggy beard is almost what you might call futuramic. Why'd General Grant think your sister'd gone to the old cemetery?"

"He said he thought he'd heard her tell someone so."

"Not," Asey said critically, "what I'd call very definite information, George!"

"Well, since it was the only information I could get about her, I got a lift over there — "

"Who with?"

"The Harriman boy's parents," George said promptly. "I forget their name."

"Not Harriman, by any chance?" Asey suggested.

"No. It's Lamb, I think. I forget who Helen Harriman married last year," George said, "but he has sandy hair and wears glasses. So they drove me over to the cemetery. At least, they dropped me off at the entrance because they were in a hurry to get home before it rained."

Asey looked at him thoughtfully. No one could claim that George hadn't neatly managed to document himself every step of the way, so far. His story was all so checkable. It was all so very natural, too.

Except for a few little things that struck a false note.

He hadn't shown the slightest curiosity about his sister's

murder. He hadn't displayed anything akin to sorrow. Even perfunctory sorrow.

"An' neither you," Asey said, "nor General Grant, nor the Harriman boy's sort of anonymous parents — not one of you thought there was anything the slightest bit funny about your sister's goin' to the old cemetery? None of you seen anything odd about it?"

"Good God, no!" George said. "Muriel spends as much time in cemeteries and museums as anywhere else. One summer nobody ever found her anywhere except in holes, digging for old Indian relics. Muriel can be almost anywhere. Everyone knows that. Well, anyway, that's the reason I was over there. I was hunting her."

"An' where was you when it rained?"

"Under the trees," George said. "Later on, when it stopped, I saw someone — "

"With a shaggy beard," Asey interrupted. "I know. I felt in my bones that the man with the shaggy beard was due to pop up about now!"

"No, I saw Buff Orpington!"

"Now here," Asey said, "here is where I think perhaps you just possibly may get stuck, George. You flew here to find Buff. You braved the pageant rehearsal to find your sister to help you find him. You got lifted to the cemetery to find her to help you find him. An' then, George, then you found Buff! There he *was*. Now why in time didn't you march straight to him? If he was practically your main object in life, why'd you lurk around in those woods? An' don't say you didn't! Because I had you spotted, you know. I watched you till I was cross-eyed!"

George looked down at the rug.

"Well," he said, "well, I — well, people came. Dr. Cummings, and you — although I didn't know that it was you, then. I didn't recognize you. I'd only seen you dressed in — in dark clothes."

"You mean, George," Asey asked solicitously, "that you was just shy?"

"Well, I — I didn't want to say to Buff what I had to say to him before a lot of people."

"The throngs scared you, huh? Tch, tch! I see. So you just lurked in the woods instead."

"I was only waiting there until I could get Buff alone! And then he ran away, and you ran after him. And I waited," George said, "and waited. But Buff didn't come back. So I left. Oh — and around then it began to pour once again, so I waited underneath a pine tree until the worst of it was over. Then I started to walk back to the ball park — that was when I found Dave Williams's cane lying on the ground, and picked it up."

At least the time sequence there was okay, Asey thought. It was after the start of the second downpour, during the time when he was knocked out, that the diploma had been tampered with, and the cane removed.

"Then I caught sight of the Porter," George continued, "and assumed it was Muriel's — naturally I thought it was hers! After all, she's the only person around here who can afford to own Porters! So I — "

"So you just picked it up to keep the cane company," Asey said. "Uh-huh. What takin' ways you an' Buff have, George!

An' were you aimin' to leave your sister there in the cemetery?"

That was far from his conception of an ideal sticker, Asey admitted to himself. But it was the sort of wife-beater question he'd been wanting to throw at George's feet, and it ought to give the fellow a little hurdle to jump over. If George said yes, then he as good as admitted to having known way back at that point that Muriel was dead. If George said no — well, George hardly could say no, all things being considered!

George fooled him.

"I didn't give a good God damn about my sister!" he said explosively.

"Oh? An' just such a short time before," Asey remarked, "you was all but breakin' your neck to locate her. Huh! What caused the change of heart, George? What was the reason for all the sudden anger?"

"There — there wasn't anything sudden ab-about it!" George's stammer had been more or less under control for a while, but now it was cropping out with renewed vigor. "Muriel and I have hated each other all our lives! I was angry then because *she* could afford to have a new Porter coupé and I couldn't!"

He was so childishly petulant and so grimly serious about it that Asey looked at him sharply and wondered if probably that sort of thing hadn't been going on over a period of years. He could almost hear George plaintively wailing that Muriel had a pony, and *he* didn't. That Muriel had a new bike, and *he* didn't. And so on.

"Yet for all your hatin' her," he said, "she was the first

person you thought of turnin' to for help in findin' Buff Orpington!"

"Well, why not?" George retorted with some truculence. "Why not? I certainly didn't want to go around b-broadcasting the fact that I was ready to eat a p-peck of dirt in order to get back somebody I'd fired! Muriel's knowing didn't matter any! Even if I bothered telling her *why* I wanted Buff, she wouldn't have understood — or c-cared! The only thing she's thought about all summer is this d-damned pup-pageant! How she's loved telling people how much she knows about this b-bloody town! She's never b-been so important in all her life before! She's been God! She's known everything. And she's told everybody ab-about it — and they've had to listen to her!"

Now, Asey thought, he was beginning to sound more like the George Pettingill he'd first overheard out there by the drying yard. Once the fellow started to let himself go a little on the topic of his sister, a fishwife streak seemed to emerge.

"I wonder, George," he said gently, "who inherits your sister's money?"

George's face turned a dull red. His hands were trembling, and Asey suspected that it required real will power on his part to control them enough to gesture toward the litter of papers on the Turkey carpet.

"Her will's around here somewhere," he said. "At least it ought to be. I can't find it, but I know it must be here — unless that d-damned fool's in the process of changing the d-damned thing once more!"

"Oh?" Asey said. "Oh. So that's what you was tryin' to

find, huh? That's what you was pawin' around so energetic for!"

George's lips set in a stubborn line, and he stared fixedly down at the rug.

"Or p'raps, knowin' that she was a will-changer," Asey went on, "you was just tryin' to pick out the will that suited you best, with some underlyin' notion of seein' to it that there wasn't any others but it? Or would it be more convenient for you, I wonder, if there just wasn't any will to be found at all? Uh-huh, I wonder maybe if in your case, you wouldn't probably profit by her dyin' intestate?"

George was obviously seething mad, but he still managed not to burst out with anything.

"Maybe it was just a note that you was huntin'?" Asey suggested. "You probably owe her quite a lot of money, don't you? Leastways I've heard that you did. Kind of acted as your banker, didn't she?"

"It's none of your damned business! For all I know" — George's voice rose until he was yelling almost as loudly as he'd yelled at Martha — "she's left all her money to her pet fund for creating the Muriel Babcock Historical Museum out of that damned junk shop of hers across the way in the old grammar school! Or this brand-new fund she's just dreamed up to p-perpetuate this damned p-pageant year after year after year — the Muriel Babcock Memorial Pageant Fund, for God's sakes!"

"Oh?"

And what golden opportunities, Asey thought, what platinum opportunities such a fund would present to Aunt Maude Henning!

"Or maybe the Muriel Babcock Historical Fund — that gem was to keep the Quanomet Historical and Antiquities Society well-fed and happy into eternity! Or the Muriel Babcock Fund for the Preservation of Old Cape Cod Cemeteries and Quanomet Indian Relics — for all *I* know, she may have been in that mood where she decides that she'll just leave everything to Crazy Martha Bangs!"

"It isn't nice manners, George," Asey said, "to scream so loud you scar the guest's eardrums. The point is, you ain't been able to put your finger on her current will, an' you're scared stiff maybe you happen to get left out. Who did you see in the woods while you was lurkin' around in the cemetery?"

"Nobody."

"Come on, George," Asey said wearily. "Tell me all about that man with the shaggy beard."

"I never saw anyone with a shaggy beard — or any other kind of beard! I told you so!"

"Never even caught a peek of Maude Henning, I s'pose?"

"No!"

"Course," Asey said, "there's one great advantage in stickin' to your guns like that. If you claim you didn't see nobody, why nobody can claim they seen you. It's always a smart angle."

"What b-business is it of yours to ask me all these questions, and jape and t-taunt — "

"Whoa up, George!" Asey interrupted. "Didn't I remember to tell you that your sister'd been murdered? Did I forget that little news item?"

"No, you said so. But it's still no business of yours to pry—"

"Okay, George." Asey got to his feet. "You have it your way. So I got no right to butt into your affairs an' ask you personal questions of an insinuatin' nature—do you cherish any sentimental feelin's about 'Welcome to Picturesque Quanomet'?" he added as he reached over and picked up Davis Williams's cane from the overstuffed chair. "I mean this arty leather job here."

George surveyed the decorated pillow with extreme distaste.

"That was Muriel's Christmas present to her father when she was eleven. She painted it. It's the first thing I intend to destroy in this house, now that it's mine."

"In that case, I'll save you the bother, an' take it off your hands." Asey tucked it under his arm and paid no attention to George's stumbling protest. "Now come along, chum. Time for us to get goin'."

"Bub-but what—"

The rest of his sentence was one long stammer.

"Like you pointed out," Asey said, "this ain't my bailiwick. So I'm goin' to cart you over to Lieutenant Hanson, whose business it is—don't look so flustered, George. I like to hope the cops'll treat you as gentle as I have, an' I wouldn't let myself brood about them rubber hose yarns, if I was you. Only right here an' now, I'll make you a little bet. I bet you they'll find your sister's will. Or wills. Hanson sets a lot of store by a good will, an' he's uncanny about ferretin' 'em out. Tears down houses if he has to. He always says he don't know anything that provides stronger motivation than somebody's will, unless maybe it's two or three of 'em. Come on."

"B-but —"

"Now don't get fractious an' tryin', George! I can always order you to stick up your hands, an' prod you dramatic all the way with your own little pistol — but what's the use? You might as well come along amiable, an' not look any sillier than you have to. Save up all your righteous indignation for Hanson. He's a patient man. He'll listen — probably he'll even urge you to get hold of your lawyer quick, an' get yourself some sound advice, too. He really prefers to have murder suspects know just exactly what they're in for. Saves 'em a lot of anguish."

All of that percolated pretty successfully, Asey decided. George was obviously progressing from his state of seething anger to a state of melancholy and deep self-pity. In short, George was finally beginning to catch onto himself.

"B-but — but all the publicity! All the —"

"Shucks, don't worry none about *that!*" Asey broke in briskly. "If you're innocent, why it ought to be worth a million dollars to Pettingill, Watrous an' Company. Maybe more. You can assess it better'n I can. Come, George, let's get goin'!"

With infinite reluctance and a certain amount of unhappy stammering under his breath, George preceded Asey along the hall to the front door, and opened it.

"Just hop right into the car," Asey said, "an' I'll have you in Hanson's hands in a jiffy. You'll like Hanson, once you get to understand his little quirks an' —"

He stopped short.

"The — the Porter isn't here!" George said. "Your Porter's *gone!*"

"So," Asey agreed, "so it seems. Sort of looks like those gremlins whisked Everybody's Model away once again, don't it?"

"But — but I left it right there in the driveway!"

Asey nodded. "I know. Huh! I guess somebody swiped it while I was out back, while you an' Crazy Martha was busy screechin' at each other — sure, George, I heard all of that encounter! Wa-el, as Jennie always says every time she misplaces something, I guess maybe I got something else to hand that'll do me just as good. I got a spare, George, that'll do us. Hike along down to the corner."

Halfway down the block, he stopped and held out the leather pillow toward George.

"B-but *I* don't want that thing! Why — "

"Just hold it a sec," Asey said, "while I peel off my jacket. Looks like the day was really goin' to turn out like the radio predicted early this mornin', after all — hot, sultry, an' sticky, the fellow said. Uh — give this left sleeve of mine a little hitch, will you, George? I seem to be stuck."

George obediently gave the sleeve a twist.

"Thanks. Yessir, I love that weather boy," Asey went on chattily. "Another excessively hot an' uncomfortably humid day, he said, with clear skies mostly, an' no expected sign of any precipitation in most sections to any extent, probably. Or words to that effect. Uh — how can you stand wearin' that raincoat, an' not melt away into a thin trickle, George? Thanks, I'll take the pillow now. I was practically roastin'."

"I'm not too warm — is *that* your spare car?" George asked hurriedly. "That old coupé?"

"Uh-huh. Get in — no, on second thought," Asey said, "s'pose you wait a minute, George. S'pose you hold this work of art again. Uh — I want to fix them papers on the shelf behind the seat so's they don't keep fallin' down all the time."

That was a flimsy excuse for stalling, he thought, but George didn't appear to see anything wrong with it.

"Isn't this Clifton Bird's car?" he wanted to know. "Those papers look like those d-damned genealogical charts that he and Muriel used to p-pore over."

"Yup." Asey knelt on the seat and began to pile the charts and papers in neat heaps. "Got another hand? Then reach over an' grab hold of this briefcase, will you? Looks like I got to repack from scratch here."

"Didn't Muriel hound *him!*" There was almost a gloating note in George's voice. "She made his life hell!"

"Oh? What for?"

Asey paused long enough to turn and look searchingly at George, and made sure of what he'd been wanting to confirm.

"Muriel had d-designs on him." George gave an unpleasant little giggle. "They had a lot of common interests in old historic Quanomet, you know. They were k-kindred spirits."

To Asey's annoyance, he giggled again, and kept on giggling.

"Meetin' of scholarly minds, I s'pose," he said as he turned back to the papers. "An' that reminds me of something I meant to find out — how old is Bird, anyhow? Fifty-nine or sixty-ish?"

George shook his head. "He's only forty-eight or so. When Muriel learned that, she redoubled her efforts. But thank God, she d-didn't manage to hook him — I can't stand that little b-bore! He thought he knew almost as much as she thought she did, and he was just as d-damned eager to tell you all about it, too! What do you want this ghastly pillow for, anyway?"

"As a memento." Asey mopped his forehead with his shirt sleeve. "Golly, how you can stand that raincoat's more'n I can understand. Okay, get in — no, there's one thing more. Go take a gander at that right rear tire, will you, before we set out? See if it still looks soft. I don't think Bird takes what you might call a lovin' interest in the upkeep of this vehicle."

While George was leaning over and quite seriously investigating the tire situation, Asey slid out from the front seat and walked quietly up behind him, and stood there.

"Looks dubious, but I guess it's okay," he said, and then he put his right hand behind his back. "I guess that'll get us as far as the cemetery — hop in, George! We mustn't waste any more time!"

George turned back to the door, and Asey started around the rear of the car toward the opposite door.

He couldn't keep from grinning broadly.

After all, there'd had to be some reason for George stubbornly keeping on that heavy raincoat, what with the perspiration streaming down his face, and the sun beating down like a broiler in full flame!

And the answer to why he hadn't taken it off began to be apparent when he'd first held the pillow, and the bulge in his raincoat pocket became noticeable. When he'd held both the pillow and the briefcase, that clinched things. George wasn't taking off that coat because he had something stowed in his coat pocket from which he didn't wish to be parted for one moment.

Asey paused behind the car to finish stuffing inside his shirt the fruits of the impromptu pocket-picking which he'd just staged.

One rolled-up paper — will size, and definitely something that could have been inside the diploma.

Also one beard — genuinely shaggy.

Asey was whistling blithely as he got in behind the wheel. And then his Porter went whizzing past.

"D-did you see that?" George stammered. "A m-man with a bub-beard was d-driving!"

vii

▼▼▼▼▼▼▼▼▼▼▼▼▼▼▼▼▼▼▼▼▼▼▼▼▼▼▼▼▼▼▼▼▼▼▼▼

WHEN Asey didn't at once answer, George repeated his question.

"Yes, George, I seen him," Asey said very patiently. "I also noted the beard. Huh. What's that poem that Doc Cummings's so fond of quotin' — something about how he never nursed a dear gazelle that right away it didn't fall on the rug, butter side downwards!"

There was something faintly supercilious about the way George stared at him. "I know quite a lot of p-poetry, but I'm sure *I* never heard of any such p-poem! Look, why didn't you follow him? Why don't you? You've been talking about men with beards, and there's your stolen car being driven by a man with a b — "

"Yes, George," Asey interrupted. "I know. I didn't try to whip off after him because even if Clifton Bird was drivin' my Porter in his own inimitable an' inept fashion, I couldn't overtake him in this thing. Not unless he wanted me to. Wa-el, let's face it. Let's pick up the gazelle an' wipe the butter spots off the carpet. George, do you by any rare chance happen to have any part in this pageant, as an actin' part?"

George said yes, certainly. Muriel had absolutely insisted on his being in it. Muriel had made his life miserable until he promised he'd portray Lord Andrews in the War of 1812 scene. Muriel felt that he ought to since their mother was a direct descendant of Lord Andrews. In case Asey didn't know it, he went on, Lord Andrews was the British admiral who'd attempted to capture Quanomet in 1812, and who had actually made a landing on Quanomet Point.

"Where the embattled farmers an' intrepid fishermen gallantly repulsed the invading force with gusto, like the bronze marker says. An' did your ancestor Lord Andrews have a beard?"

George nodded. "Muriel said it would be provided as a part of my costume, but I brought along an old one I once had for a college show. It fitted me very well and I thought someone could trim it down a bit. I've got it right here in my pocket. The — "

An expression of bewilderment came over his face as he pawed around with increasing agitation in the pocket of his raincoat.

"Okay." Asey pulled the shaggy beard out from inside his shirt. "Here you are. An' I s'pose this rolled-up paper is just your briefin' on how to be a proper pageant admiral?"

"That's a new idea I had for p-possible P-porter copy," George said with pride. "I b-blocked it out coming over on the p-plane this morning, and developed it as much as I could. It was b-bumpy."

Asey unrolled the paper and read just enough of it to confirm that George was telling the truth, and then he leaned over and stuffed it back into George's pocket.

"It's rather an unusual approach, and I feel it p-presents new angles — ".

The rest of his new angles were drowned out as Asey started the car. Lucky for him, he thought, that his Cousin Jennie wasn't present. She could soar to heights with cracks about the brainy Codfish Sherlock at this point.

And well she might!

He chose to return to the cemetery by way of the town instead of cutting across lots and using back roads, the way he'd driven over to the museum with Clifton Bird. He intended to ask the traffic cop at the Four Corners light if he'd seen the Porter, and to tell him to pick it up if it should cross his ken. There's been just about enough, Asey decided, of people bouncing that car from hand to hand as if it were a community-owned volley ball.

George was stammering on about his new and unusual approach to Porter advertising, which he somewhat optimistically expected Asey to relay to Bill Porter as soon as he could, and Asey said uh-huh at intervals without paying any particular attention.

He couldn't satisfactorily explain to himself his tendency to feel that George had told a straight story, or as reasonably straight a story as people were ordinarily able to tell. When you came down to brass tacks, the average person couldn't describe how they'd mailed a letter and bought a bottle of aspirin without hemming and hawing, and backtracking half a dozen times.

George was at least consistent in his callous attitude and general lack of sympathy about his sister's untimely end. He hated Muriel and he made no bones about it. He was equally frank about business. To keep his pet-food account, he'd admittedly eat crow.

All in all, Asey decided, his original estimate of George as not a lovable character was sound.

But you couldn't hold that against him in this business. You couldn't hold his utter lack of imagination against him, either.

That utter unimaginativeness was where he differed so from — say — Aunt Maude Henning. When her intuition told her that she couldn't stall any longer, she quit fencing and answered questions. Only the net result was rather like finding that you had a Ping-pong ball in your hand instead of the rear molar you thought you'd been extracting. Aunt Maude had imagination, and so she tailored her story. Probably it was straight in its basic essentials, but she'd told only what she wished, and Asey felt rather sure that she'd deliberately kept a lot back.

At least she'd kept back the pink glass egg.

And the only hitch there was why she should want to kill Muriel for a pink glass egg!

As far as imagination was concerned, little Mr. Bird was still another kettle of fish. Once started, he'd gone into voluminous detail without any attempt at flights of fancy. Bird wasn't, Asey suspected, the sort who'd be content to say he was fine, thanks, if you stopped him casually on the street and asked how he was. Bird would probably sum up the situation with scholarly precision, from the little pain just in back of his right ear to the splinter that had been in his left thumb last week.

All that Fire Society stuff was, in a manner of speaking,

just another pink glass egg. Muriel's thwarting him about his assembling the genealogical data for membership requirements hardly constituted an iron-clad motive for murder. Muriel had after all only delayed the process and not stopped it in its tracks. As for George's giggly innuendoes about Bird and Muriel, Asey discounted them. That was more in the nature of a commentary on George.

If any of Muriel's projected memorial funds actually had been set up, and if any individuals directly benefited from them, a different light would naturally be cast on a lot of things. Maude Henning, for example, might be tied up with that pageant fund. Perhaps so tied up that the pink egg would roll itself out of the picture and back under the glass display case as an item of historic consequence only. He'd have to ask Jennie about the Historical and Antiquities Society, and all the others George had mentioned.

And *had* Jennie once told him, long ago, that Thamozene Sturdy was involved with the antiquities outfit? Or was he confusing it with the museum, where Bird said the Sturdy family papers were kept?

Asey found himself devoutly wishing that the name Thamozene wouldn't keep cropping up. Or else that Muriel might have been found in front of some tombstone that bore another name. Because the temptation to try and connect the graveyard Thamozene with Whistler's Mother was almost irresistible.

And almost completely idiotic!

For if Muriel had been lying in front of the stone belonging to Thamozene Winter's brother George, you certainly wouldn't strain any sinews trying to hook him up to George

Pettingill. Or George Anybody. You simply wouldn't give it all a second thought.

But the name Thamozene was unusual, and caught your attention. And two Thamozenes presented all the fascination of a fresh paint job. You couldn't quite keep your fingers from pointing out in that direction.

Right now, however, wasn't the time for him to get distracted by assorted Thamozenes, Asey thought. Right now his only preoccupation ought to be with the assorted chores at hand.

Like George.

He wasn't going to turn George over to Hanson in the same spirit in which he'd marched the fellow out of Muriel's house such a short time ago.

But he greatly doubted if that would make much difference to Hanson, or if Hanson would ever be content to accept George merely as Muriel's next of kin with whom he'd ultimately have to confer anyway.

Hanson would unquestionably pounce on George and gnaw on him at length and with relish. Hanson was a sucker for simple frameworks. He'd smack his lips over a brother who might have killed his half sister about something good and basic, like money.

Asey knew from experience that there wouldn't be any use in suggesting to him that if George didn't stand to gain by his sister's death, he'd have been foolish to kill her just from spite.

Because Hanson would only retort that plenty of murders were committed out of sheer spite, that George couldn't begin to substantiate any of his cemetery narrative, and that the shaggy beard and the rolled-up paper probably had been deftly planted in that raincoat pocket as an exceedingly clever blind.

Wa-el, of course, there was always the chance Hanson could be right.

Perhaps they had been.

"Uh-huh," he said aloud, as he realized that George had stopped talking. "Uh-huh. Yup."

As he stopped for the traffic lights at the Quanomet Four Corners, he heard his name yelled out, and turned to find Dr. Cummings beckoning to him from the gas station on his right.

"Asey! Asey — hey, pull in here! Listen, what've you been up to?" he went on as Asey swung in off the highway. "Twice your Porter's passed me, but you wouldn't stop when I tooted at you! And about twenty minutes ago I saw you parked in front of that hamburg place on the shore road, that Juke Box outfit, but I couldn't find you — "

"Who was drivin' my car?" Asey interrupted.

"Who? Why, I assumed that you were, of course! And now you turn up in this jalopy of Bird's — oh, hullo, George, I didn't notice you before. Asey, what've you been doing?"

"First you tell me what's been goin' on over at the cemetery, Doc. How are things there?"

"I haven't managed to get back over there yet," Cummings said. "I called my office from Maude Henning's and found some calls I had to attend to — one was an emergency job for Thamozene Sturdy. She got a nasty cut on her left palm while she was opening up a Mason jar of preserved peaches. I asked her all about Orpington, and apparently everything he told us is true."

"Did you tell her about Muriel?" Asey asked.

"Funny thing," Cummings said, "but she already knew. Seems she'd been putting flowers on the grave of some ancestor in the old cemetery, and all of a sudden she looked over to see two cops herding a group of men out of the woods, so naturally she investigated — she's a busybody of the first water, you know! And in the process she found out about Muriel before the cops shooed her away. *That* was really why she was so anxious to get her hand sewed up, don't you see?"

Asey shook his head. "No, I don't."

"Why, she'd left the pageant in a huff, and after she discovered Muriel was out of the picture, she couldn't wait to get on her costume and whip back. So — "

"But I thought," Asey said, "it was Maude Henning that Thamozene was sore at!"

"She told me she considered things on her way back from the cemetery, and she decided it was all Muriel's fault, and that she should have known from the first that Muriel was only causing trouble, as usual," Cummings said. "She told me all about it — it was one of those Muriel-said-that-Maude-said issues. Casting aspersions on the Sturdy family, and so forth. So when she got home, Thamozene phoned Maude and asked her point-blank about the situation, and found it *was* Muriel's work. So she'd put on her sunbonnet, and was all set to go over to the rehearsal when that jar-top incident intervened. The preserved peaches were intended as a snack for Buff — where *is* that fellow, anyway?"

Asey shrugged.

"Who knows? Doc, what was all that about the cops herdin' a group of men out of the woods?"

"Oh, yes. I meant to go back to them — look, Maude Henning kept insisting all the way home that she really *had* seen a man with a shaggy beard, and — "

"S'pose, Doc," Asey broke in, "that we don't discuss shaggy beards at this point. Right now I'm kind of allergic to the topic of beards!"

"But how can I tell you about this group of men with*out* mentioning beards?" Cummings retorted. "Because Thamozene Sturdy said that they *all* wore beards, every last one of 'em. All six!"

Asey leaned back and chuckled.

"I told 'em to grab anybody they seen with a beard, an' so they're obeyin' orders — huh, I wonder if we'll find they been scoopin' up everyone with a trace of five o'clock shadow! Anyway, it explains things. Jennie just didn't notice the cops' car, an' Muriel was there all the time, like I suspected. An' the cops was off collectin' stray pageant characters — at least, I presume that they *was* pageant characters, wasn't they?"

"Well, I asked Thamozene that, and she said there weren't six characters like that around in the show up to the time *she* left, but of course you couldn't guess what might have been added since then. Anyway, it proves — "

"It proves," Asey said, "that beards is rife in Picturesque Quanomet. Doc, s'pose you take George here over to Hanson for me, will you? An' if Hanson hasn't come, tell the cops to set up a prisoner stockade an' add him to their little bearded group — "

"Oho!" Cummings said. "Oho! I see, now! Tan raincoat and brown felt hat! Hm!"

"Just so. George, you pop along with the doc, an' tell Hanson the same yarn you told me, from tryin' to rescue 'Lively' by way of Buff clear to Crazy Martha. An' just to make sure they reach Hanson intact, the doc'll take care of that rolled-up paper, an' your beard — "

"Beard?" Cummings broke in eagerly. "Does George have a beard, *too*?"

"Everybody's got a beard," Asey said. "George here, he's got an admiral's beard. You tell Hanson that Jennie's caught one real beard, an' so far I only got two falsies to the coppers' six. But I hope to work up to somethin' really big, like the House of David ball team. I'll be over shortly. I just want to chat with the traffic cop an' — "

"Wait." Cummings put a restraining hand on Asey's arm. "I have to say that I honestly do believe all of Maude's story after talking with her. But listen, there's something else. Bobby Pouter — by George, he's a bright youngster! Know why he sat quietly in your car through the storms, and never batted an eyelid when he learned about Muriel, and so on? It seems that he wants a — "

"A Geiger counter. A portable Geiger counter. An'," Asey said, "he's doin' his best to be a good boy so's he'll get it for his birthday."

"Sometimes I ask myself why I try to help you by saving up tidbits for you!" Cummings said irritably. "You just always seem to know 'em anyway! Would there be any use in adding that all the way home, Bobby kept asking Aunt Maude what she dropped out of my car, back in the cemetery? She kept insisting that she didn't drop anything — but I suppose *you* know that she really did?"

Asey grinned. "Don't be surprised, Doc, when you find Clifton Bird over to the cemetery lookin' like Bobo the Dog-Faced Boy," Asey said, "an' Jennie all done up like a pioneer woman without a covered wagon. Makes for kind of a side-show touch, an' — "

"Stop it! *What?* What did Maude drop?"

"An egg," Asey told him with a grin. "A pink glass egg, of course. What else? You two get started, Doc. I'll be along as soon as I have a little chat with the traffic cop yonder."

But the Four Corners cop was nowhere to be found. A quick poll of the gas station attendants showed one in favor of his probably being home to lunch, and three who thought he might possibly be found at the public parking lot on the shore road.

"On a day like this," one of the latter added, "he likes to check up on the parking there. Gives him a chance to cool off with a swim, see?"

"Thanks," Asey said, and decided to give up his idea of locating the Porter in what had originally seemed the easy way. He wasn't going to waste time tracking down this local cop when Hanson's boys were available, and handier.

He'd just let Hanson take over the job of retrieving Everybody's Model, he thought as he climbed into Bird's car and set off for the cemetery. Knowing Cummings's ordinary pace, he rather suspected he might arrive there long before the doctor and George did.

He was speeding along the shore road when he noticed the garish, billboard-size signs of the Juke Box, the hamburg joint which Cummings had mentioned, and where he said he'd seen the Porter parked.

On impulse, Asey stopped and backed up toward an empty space by the chrome-striped front door. Perhaps there might be someone around who'd be able to tell him something about the man currently driving the Porter.

For any pertinent information, he thought, he'd willingly give two portable Geiger counters, absolutely free and without cost.

In fact, he'd happily pass out a gross of Geiger counters to anyone who'd dare to be different for a change, and swear that the driver was not a man with a shaggy beard!

As the coupé's rear tires came to rest against the concrete parking curb, the brown leather pillow jolted off the shelf behind the seat, and fell down on the car floor. Asey replaced it, and snapped off the ignition, and turned to find the door beside him suddenly being wrenched open by a very blond and very beautiful girl who nearly pulled him bodily out of the car as she embraced him with warmth and enthusiasm.

"Clifton, darling! You — oh. Oh, I'm so terribly sorry!"

"Uh — not at all," Asey said politely, and told himself she really did have on a bathing suit of sorts. It just happened to match her tanned skin with such alarming exactness that at first glance you couldn't quite figure out where it began and where she left off.

"But I'm simply scarlet with embarrassment, really I am! I thought you were Clifton Bird! After all, it's his *car!*"

"Uh-huh."

She could be one of those models who draped themselves against custom Porters at auto shows, Asey thought, only usually they were swathed from head to foot in sables. He wondered idly how Jennie would describe that bathing suit, and surmised she'd come out flat-footed and succinctly call it a diaper.

"*I* thought," she went on brightly, "that you were Clifton, and that he'd managed to get off his beard!"

"Oh," Asey said. "Oh. So you're the one who insisted on stickin' that thing on him, are you?"

She pouted very prettily. "*I* didn't insist! He wanted me to!"

"You're Miss — " he searched his memory. "Miss Spirit of Quanomet. Miss — Miss Poole. That's it!"

And it was more and more apparent, as Bird had diffidently suggested, that she wasn't quite what the founding fathers probably had in the back of their minds as the Quanomet Spirit.

"Yes, I'm Linda Poole — oh! If you know me, perhaps you're hunting for me? Are you? Did the Forty-niners send you? I was beginning to be afraid they'd gone to the wrong place — I simply couldn't bear it if they got lost *again!* They just won't learn their way around town, and it's so desperately simple! Think of anyone getting lost in Quanomet, really!"

Lost Forty-niners?

Asey considered the matter briefly, and then began to grin.

"How many are missin'?" he inquired. "Forty-niners, that is?"

"Why, all of them! All six!"

"Wa-el," Asey said cheerfully, "it's real nice of you to clear up that bearded sextet for me — they all *are* bearded, I s'pose?"

"They're simply darling beards! I really worked my fingers to the bone on them! I *slaved!*"

Something in her voice insinuated that she'd drudged for years in the scullery's meanest work, like Cinderella amid her ashes, and Asey nearly found himself patting her on the back and telling her she was a brave girl.

But he restrained himself.

"Uh — they're something new in the pageant, huh, these Forty-niners?"

He discovered to his sudden surprise that he'd somehow moved over, and that Miss Poole was sitting chummily beside him in the car.

"My dear, they're these six ducky boys from the Noko-wasset House who've just taken over this week — they're the new orchestra, you know. The old one simply *stank!* But utter corn! And — d'you have a cigarette? Oh, thanks just loads! And what a sweet lighter — I always *yearned* for one of those thin platinum things!"

"I'm afraid," Asey said untruthfully, "that it's just common ordinary ole tin. An' how do they work into the pageant?"

"Well, Maude Henning and I both felt we really needed a sort of *break* before the Civil War — a sort of light touch. Something really gay. So *she* thought of Forty-niners, and I thought of the boys — we're just going to sing 'Oh, Susannah!' Without any hot licks or anything, of course. Just straight. And those dear ducks said they'd do it for me, but only if I'd be in the scene with them. So we finally worked that angle out."

"I s'pose," Asey couldn't resist the opportunity, "that you pan gold?"

"Oh, no! No, I just sort of float around in the background. Highly symbolic, of course. I represent the goal men really were aspiring to when they went through all those terrible hardships and privations, and so on. There's a lovely program note Dave wrote explaining it, so people won't just think that I'm the gold at the end of the rainbow, or anything."

"I see."

He'd give all the portable Geiger counters on the market, Asey thought, to hear what Dr. Cummings would have remarked at that point.

"My costume's really sweet — I had it on this morning, but when it got so cold and started simply pouring and all, I just slipped into this old thing."

"Something really warm, as you might say." Asey had a little trouble keeping the corners of his mouth from turning up into a grin. "Uh-huh. I wonder, Miss Poole, if you happened to notice — "

"Why, that's Dave's cane up on the shelf behind your head!" she interrupted suddenly. "That's the one we — I mean, the one he — why, *where* did you find that? Or did Clifton find it? Or," she paused, "or who?"

Asey turned around and pretended to view the cane for the first time.

"That? I just thought it was Bird's cane," he remarked.

"It isn't! It's Dave Williams's, and we forgot — " She stopped short, and then flashed him a gay smile. "Probably Clifton found it around somewhere. Probably at the pageant rehearsal. Probably he's just keeping it until he sees Dave again." She reached up for it. "I'll just save him the trouble and give it back to Dave this afternoon, myself. I know

Clifton'll be glad not to have something *else* to think about, poor little man! Maude's simply showered him with so many details! Why — why, what are you doing? You're not taking that cane *away* from me, are you?"

"Uh-huh, an' puttin' it right back up on the shelf," Asey said. "If Bird found it, we'll let Bird give it back to the owner. After all, I've only borrowed this car of his, you know, an' I'm sort of responsible for the things in it. P'raps it *is* your friend's cane — "

"You can see that it is! There's his name, right on that band!"

The dulcet overtones were rapidly receding from her voice. In another sentence or two, Asey thought, she ought to be sounding downright sharp.

"So 'tis," he said. "Davis Williams, plain as day. Huh. Well, maybe Bird wants it for a pageant prop. Must be some good reason why he's got it here in the car. Now, Miss Poole, I wonder if you seen — "

"Did anyone ever tell you," she interrupted, and the dulcet tones were back in full force, "that you're absolutely *just* like Gary Cooper? Around the mouth, that is? Just then, when you were being so terribly firm with me, all I could think of was Gary Cooper. But of course simply everyone's told you that — haven't they?"

"No," Asey said, "it's something I been spared, to date. Course, if you really *know* where Dave Williams lost his cane, an' all about it, I s'pose maybe you *could* have it, perhaps."

"Aren't you sweet! Dave didn't really lose it, exactly," she said. "I mean, he *forgot* it. The poor dear's worked *so* hard on the pageant, he's simply a — a bundle of nerves. You know. *Tense.* And this morning he said to me if he didn't get away from that utter madhouse of a rehearsal, he'd simply break! He couldn't stand it another minute. He just *had* to get away."

"Wanted a little peace an' quiet, huh?" Asey suggested, and nearly added aloud that the desire seemed to be a family trait.

"Exactly! So he and I took a little walk, just to relax — really, just getting away from that howling mob was such a relief!"

"But then he went an' forgot his cane over by the cemetery woods, huh?"

The Spirit of Quanomet, he observed with pleasure, floated right into that one.

She nodded.

"Yes, and I suppose that's where Clifton must have found it — at least, I hope he did! I mean, I hope *he* found it! Because sometimes people — well, they don't always under-*stand!*"

Asey conceded the truth of that statement.

"Clifton has a *sort* of artistic temperament, in a way," she went on, "and he'd understand that Dave simply had to get away from people sometimes. But Maude Henning, sweet as she *is* — I mean, if she knew that Dave and I had taken a few minutes off to walk in the woods and relax, there's just the possibility that she might think we'd been — well, not *shirking* our work, but not working as hard as we might!"

"Layin' down on the job, like," Asey said. "Uh-huh. I see."

"And of course if Muriel Babcock *ever* knew!"

She sighed deeply, and then twisted her lovely features into an expression of extreme pain.

"I s'pose she'd think you was shirkin' your pageant work, too?" Asey asked blandly.

"Oh, no, she wouldn't care about that part! She'd just simply make poor Dave's life miserable! She's the most jealous," she paused thoughtfully, "thing!"

All the time, Asey thought to himself a little wearily, new trends! Why in thunder should Muriel have been jealous about Davis Williams?

"I don't really know Muriel Babcock," he said, "but I understand that on the whole, she's kind of tryin'."

"Trying! My dear, that woman simply needs fumigating!"

"I gather," Asey said, "that you don't like her?"

Miss Poole looked shocked.

"But I love her! I've known Muriel for ages! She's the most intelligent *thing!* But of course she's just simply *so* misled about Dave's interest in her! Don't you really think," she said earnestly, "that sometimes those frightfully intelligent women who aren't very good-looking and just let themselves go and don't bother about clothes and all are actually on the dull side? I mean, wouldn't you honestly think she'd have the intelligence to realize his interest in her was *purely* intellectual?"

"An' is it?" Asey inquired.

"But my dear man, what *else?*" She stared at him in wide-eyed amazement. "I mean, if you'd ever taken *half* a look at Muriel, you'd know it couldn't be anything else! Everyone knows it couldn't be anything else — except Muriel! Really, she's got poor Dave *down* — she's simply being a millstone around his neck, that's all! He's utterly despondent about her. Utterly frustrated! But he has to keep her pacified, and all, or else she simply *won't* help!"

"With the pageant?" Asey was beginning to feel a little punch-drunk.

"No, no, with his new novel! She's got all that wonderful material he wants for this new novel he's going to write about the Cape! But every time she sees him with me, or anybody, she just gets so terribly jealous she simply refuses to help! That's why we were so frightfully careful not to let anyone see us leaving the rehearsal this morning. I mean together. That would have been simply *fatal,* Dave said!"

"I see," Asey said, "what he meant."

"But when it looked as if there were going to be such a simply terrific storm, of course we *rushed* back. And we hurried and tore so, Dave somehow just *forgot* his cane, and — well," she said gaily, and flashed her brightest smile, "now I can just take the old cane back, and — "

"Did you get caught in the rain?"

Asey thwarted her gesture toward the cane merely by leaning back against the seat.

"Oh, *that's* why I had to change that sweet costume! We got drenched! Utterly drenched! So if Dave gets his cane back, don't you see," she returned to the topic with the simple persistency of a child, "everything'll be *so* much simpler for everybody! Then it won't matter who found it, or if anyone noticed our coming back to the rehearsal together, and Dave not having the cane when we did, and all. Because of course if he has it, he can just always show it to people and say that they were terribly, terribly mistaken. About *every*thing!"

The logic of it seemed startlingly clear to her.

Considerably clearer, Asey thought, than it did to him.

But at least her motivation was perfectly obvious.

And at least she'd established how Davis Williams's cane had entered the scene. He'd left it there, and someone had picked it up.

Hanson would say it was too easy. But it was probably the truth. While she might possibly possess more imagination in some fields than Maude Henning and all the others combined, Asey guessed that the Spirit of Quanomet wasn't capable of embroidering very much unless she had something good and tangible to start with.

The details of this cane episode, he decided, could best be worked out with Davis Williams himself. All he really cared about was the time element. He'd like to find out, if he could, just when the cane had been left in the woods. And just how long it had been lying there for anyone to pick up before the first storm broke.

Miss Poole had been edging over toward him, inch by inch, and now her right arm was starting to move up to the shelf, and toward the cane.

"Now you simply *must* tell me all about the Forty-niners!" she said eagerly. "I know that's why you came here to find me, but we've just had such fun talking, I completely forgot to ask you what happened — where *are* those darling boys?"

"They got detained," Asey informed her honestly. "An' I meant to ask you — what in time are you meetin' 'em here for?"

"Oh, there was such a mob over at the ball field, and all the lunch arrangements were so terribly mixed up because of the rain — practically all of the box lunches got simply flooded, and that enormous coffee thing we borrowed from the Red Cross wouldn't work, and so on," she said. "So I thought it all over seriously, and decided the really wise thing was to meet the boys over here, and rehearse in *comfort* — don't you think that was wise?"

"Uh-huh." Asey noted that she nearly had the cane within her grasp. "An' then you could always relax with a swim or something."

"That's just what I thought! I suppose that little slave driver of a manager at the Nokowasset House went and made the boys play on the terrace after they got through in the dining room — they were afraid of that! But they'll be along soon, won't they? Did they tell you when they could come?"

Asey shook his head. "No, they didn't. Say, did you happen to see a Porter parked around here earlier?"

"Oh, that simply *divine* car! Yes — and the *sweetest* man driving it!"

"You know him?"

"Not *yet!* But he's too sweet! And *such* a car!" She rolled her eyes ecstatically. "But such a car! Didn't you adore it?"

"Wa-el," Asey said, "the fellow caught my eye because he was wearin' a beard."

He might just as well get that beard settled right at the start, he thought.

"A beard?" she said. "Oh, no! He didn't have a beard! He wears glasses, though. Quite thick glasses with those wide rims. And of course he's quite old. That is, he's an older man. He must be twenty-seven or twenty-eight, at least. But I *like* older men," she added quickly. "They're always so terribly stimulating, I think. I mean, you can *talk* with them. Really talk. Just the way you and I've been talking."

No beard, but thick glasses with those wide rims!

Would that be Buff Orpington?

"Wa-el, older men have their good points," he said judicially. "But that man drivin' the Porter wasn't dressed up to it, was he? With a flashy car like that, you'd sort of expect something fancier than just old flannel shorts an' a faded blue shirt."

"With a car like that," she returned, "who really cares what he wears? Actually, I never noticed! But of course he was just driving away when I came. Only I don't think clothes make the man, do you? Although it's always marvelous to *see* a well-dressed man — "

Could it possibly have been Buff Orpington?

And if so, why?

While Asey turned that one over in his mind, Miss Poole ran on lightheartedly about well-dressed men, older men, and those ducky boys from the Nokowasset House who dressed but so superbly.

She had a good grip on the cane, now, and was facing the awkward problem of trying to ease it along the shelf behind his head. Asey let her work away at the maneuver without interfering or even paying any attention. If she thought she was going to slide that cane down and make off with it, well and good. Let her dream on.

Could it have been Buff?

With wide-rimmed glasses, yes.

With a beard, no.

But maybe with a beard, too. Why not? If everyone else

in Picturesque Quanomet had a beard, Buff could have acquired one.

"I always feel that older men really understand me — could I have another cigarette, please? Because they *know* so much, and are so ma*ture* — "

She broke off as a beachwagon slewed into a parking space beyond them, and a quick smile of genuine delight appeared on her face.

She even let go of the cane, and withdrew her hand from the shelf.

But as a slim girl in blue shorts and a blue denim shirt got out of the beachwagon, her smile faded.

By the time the girl walked over toward them, Miss Poole had assumed an expression of artificial politeness which reminded Asey of the way Jennie always looked when unwanted and uninvited company appeared without warning at the front door.

"Hel*lo*, Kay darling!" she said brightly. "What a *sweet* bracelet! Is it new?"

"Hi, Glamour-puss. I only want to tell Mr. Bird that the programs have arrived in all their glory — oh, I thought you'd snared Clifton Bird in there, Linda." She paused and frankly stared at Asey, and then she drew a long breath. "I know you're Asey Mayo. I'm Kay Pouter."

Asey got out of the car and walked around to her.

"It's been my aim," he said, "to get to you sooner or later."

"It's been my aim," she returned, "to get to you sooner. Aunt Maude tells me I picked the wrong card, but I want credit for trying — oh-oh!"

She was looking at the cane which Linda Poole had quickly

snatched down from the shelf the instant Asey left the car.

"Oh-*oh!*" she said again, and looked very thoughtfully at Linda.

Then she placed the tips of two fingers against her lips and let out with a piercing whistle which startled even Asey with its volume.

A door of the beachwagon she'd just left swung open, and a tall, good-looking man with iron-gray hair emerged in a most leisurely fashion. He wore spotless white flannels and a white shirt, and a plaid silk scarf was knotted Ascot-style under his open collar.

As he strolled over toward them Asey suddenly recalled Cummings's comment about Davis Williams's always reminding him of an amiable St. Bernard.

And one swift look at the rapt expression on Linda's face was enough to substantiate the rest of the doctor's remarks about Williams's charm.

"Mr. Mayo, this is my father," Kay said, "as you probably have guessed. Pappy, talk quick!"

"My dear," he said pleasantly, "I *do* hope you're not trying to manufacture any more mountains out of the veriest molehills! Glad to meet you, Mayo — always wanted to. Linda, lamb, what a fetching suit! Really, Kay, what makes you feel the constant need for drama? Why in the world should I, as you tensely suggest, talk quick?"

"Look, my fine-feathered parent, that's *your* cane there!"

"So it is. But — "

"Your own little walking stick," Kay went on. "And I *told* you what Maude wormed out of Cummings — that a cane was what killed her. And when Buff Orpington told me about it, I *felt* he was describing your cane, even though he didn't know it and hadn't even noticed the name on the band. Now, *face* things! There's Muriel. Here's Asey Mayo. And here's *your* cane!"

"My dear, I told you all about it!" Dave Williams said patiently. "I simply had to leave that madhouse of a rehearsal before I went berserk. I love my good sister and your good aunt, but I could not have her tell me another thing to do. I love the excellent Clifton, but I could not have him ask me one more idiotic question. I like to think that I'm a reasonable man, but there are limitations to human endurance. I reached them. So I left. I — "

"Pappy — "

"My dear, do let me tell Mayo all about it, since you seem to feel it's of such desperate significance. I quit that rehearsal. That chaos. That imbroglio. That Donnybrook Fair. That — "

"Here, Roget!" Kay said. "Here, Roget! Come to Pappy, nice thesaurus!"

"Sometimes," Dave Williams said pensively, "I feel that I should have been permitted to spank you a great deal more than I did, my dear. Very well, I'll trim my narrative down. I quit that rehearsal cold. I walked right out on my appointed tasks. I took a good walk, a refreshing and invigorating walk. I carried my cane, yes. I always carry my cane. It's a matter of common knowledge. I bought that cane with the first money I ever earned, the proceeds of the first story I ever sold. When I was writing that, I remember promising myself — "

"Let's not," Kay interrupted, "get into how you firmly

fixed the foot on the first rung of the ladder of success, my pet. Our Mr. Mayo hasn't got all day. Besides, I suspect he wants facts. What did you *do* with that cane on your nice refreshing walk?"

"I killed a snake," he said simply.

Kay looked at Asey, and then she bit her lip.

"I killed a snake," he repeated. "And at that precise point, the heavens looked as if they were about to descend bodily. And, dude that I am, I had on my new doeskin pants, and the last ones shrank when rained upon. So I didn't pause to retrieve my cane. I raced back to the rehearsal and the shelter of the dressing tent. After, of course, carefully marking the spot where the cane was. Between two tall pines, and just beyond a very large rock. A puddingstone, with a small cedar growing beside it."

"Your besetting fault," Kay said, "has always been that tendency to overdo local color. Mayo'll know if there's puddingstone around!"

"I know puddingstone when I see it," Dave Williams said. "Anyway, it was my intention to return at some later time and recover my cane. But rain intervened, and pageant chores intervened. Now, I ask you — is there anything in that simple recital which necessitates your putting on such a tragic face?"

"Yes, Pappy," Kay said.

"What, specifically?"

"Specifically," she said, "I think that Linda killed your snake first."

Asey grinned.

But Dave Williams wasn't a whit abashed.

"There's a perfectly logical explanation for poor Muriel's

unfortunate end, and I've told you so repeatedly, it seems to me, for the last half hour. I was at her house last night, and I overheard her quarreling with that poor demented woman who works for her — Muriel had found her stealing money again."

"The whole trouble there," Kay said as he paused, "was that Muriel never *could* make change — and you know it! I never believed any of her stories about Crazy Martha stealing money! It was all Muriel's bad arithmetic!"

"Whether she stole it or whether she didn't, my dear, is of no moment. The fact remains that Muriel had accused her, and that the woman was in a towering rage — a murderous rage! And I like to think that it was she who lured Muriel to the cemetery this morning, with the very simple motive of getting revenge. After all, Muriel said yesterday that there were things happening which she couldn't explain or understand — obviously! That poor deluded woman probably — "

"That poor deluded woman," Kay interrupted rather hotly, "didn't own *your* cane!"

"She simply picked it up, that's all!" Linda Poole said suddenly. "She just picked it up in the woods over there by the cemetery. Because she was *there!* We saw her!"

viii

"DIDN'T we, Dave?" she went on.

The faintest of sighs escaped from Dave Williams's lips. He looked quickly from Kay to Asey, and there was a twinkle in his eyes.

"Didn't we see her there?" Linda persisted.

"I suspected all along," Kay said, "that the snake had been killed long before we got here, Pappy. Have you got a nickel?"

"Yes, my dear," he said. "Just about! But no one can say I didn't do my best! It wasn't too bad, was it, Mayo? On the whole?"

"As snakes go," Asey told him, "it was pretty good. Only if I was your editor, I'd suggest your cuttin' out items like doeskins an' puddingstones an' such, an' maybe just sayin' instead that it's awful sort of awkward havin' to carry a cane when you're runnin' like mad for shelter."

Kay laughed.

"I thought of that, too," she said, "but I decided to let well enough alone. I wasn't being figurative about the nickel, Pappy. If you'll give me one, Linda and I'll go toy with the juke box, and leave you and Asey to settle the snake bite. I think you'll make better time that way."

Dave Williams looked after her appreciatively as she propelled a somewhat unwilling and reluctant Linda inside the little restaurant.

"My daughter," he said, "is an extraordinarily tactful girl, I sometimes think, for one who can be so exceedingly outspoken. What can I tell you? Shoot."

"The Spirit of Quanomet," Asey said, "has already obliged with the details of the general framework, as you might say. But can you tell me how long before the first storm broke did you abandon the cane? Or puttin' it another way, where'd the first storm catch you two?"

"Just getting back to the ball park," he said promptly. "That would make it — let me think, now. We really rushed back. Oh, I'd say it was fifteen or twenty minutes before the storm broke that we decided to leave. Those doeskins were true, by the way — I didn't want to get 'em wet. And I thought of the cane after we'd taken about a dozen steps, but it was so dark by then that it didn't seem sensible to go back and waste time groping around for it. I really intended to pick it up later — I'm very fond of that cane. And I know exactly where it was, if the information would be of any use to you in figuring out who might have ultimately picked it up. I can't describe the place, but I could draw you a picture, or lead you to the spot."

"An' you really seen Crazy Martha there?"

Dave nodded.

"Frankly, she was another reason for our hustling away. We hoped she hadn't seen us. Crazy Martha has a marked inclination to chat with everyone she meets, you know, and she likes to tell where she's been and whom she's seen lately. Linda was a bit unhappy about that angle. For my part," he added honestly, "I particularly didn't want her to chat with Muriel. You see, I'm trying to block out this historical novel of the Cape, and Muriel has all the material, and — er — I wonder how I can explain to you about her, and — er — "

"Linda told me," Asey said. "I gather you been tried by Muriel."

"She's driven me crazy, she's driven my sister crazy, she's driven Kay crazy — I think she's even had Bobby on the ropes! She's hung around the house, she's followed me all over the place — she's haunted me! Every time I've shaved, I've had to ask myself if it was my chin or hers that I was shaving! If there'd been any earthly way of getting at that material otherwise, I assure you I'd have taken it. I've had some weird experiences in preparing material for books, in my day, but I've never run into anything like Muriel — and I hope I never do again!"

He stood there expectantly, looking at Asey.

"Well, what else?" he asked. "What else do you want to know about?"

"Nothin'," Asey said reflectively.

"No comment? You don't really think the rational explanation for all this is that poor deluded woman? She really *was* in a rage at Muriel last night, you know. And she *was* there in the cemetery today — and I like to think she was the only other human being besides myself who knew where my cane was!"

"Wa-el," Asey said, "I grant you she'd be an awful convenient sort of solution. It's always sort of comfortin' to tell yourself that murders only get committed by folks that ain't entirely rational, like. Only," he grinned, "she hasn't got a beard."

"But you don't put any stock in that crackbrained notion of Maude's that this is all the work of some bearded saboteur?"

"If you'll sort of think back to the start," Asey said, "you'll see someone planned — "

"We need another nickel, Pappy." Kay appeared beside them.

"You can come out now," he said amiably. "We're through. Where's Linda?"

"Phoning the Nokowasset House about the Forty-niners. Banjo-on-her-knee seems to have lost her faithful posse, and she's carrying on quite a discussion with the Nokowasset manager — and if you recall that prim little fellow with the pince-nez, you'll see why she's having such difficulties. They speak a different language entirely, and — "

"Kay," Dave interrupted, "I've just had the hell of an idea, and I'm going back to the studio — "

"You're going back to the rehearsal and help your poor sister!"

"My dear, I'm going back to the studio — look, you know where the sea captain and the girl — "

"No, Pappy, and I don't want to hear about 'em, either! And no — don't ask me! You can't drop me off at the ball park and take the beachwagon, because I need it! And if I drop you off at the studio, you'll have to be called for, and — "

Asey waited patiently while the drop-off situation became more and more involved.

"Look," he said finally, "let's settle this! S'pose you take Bird's car wherever you want to go, Mr. Williams, an' then Mrs. Pouter can leave me at the cemetery — I been meanin' to get back there for hours. Then my Cousin Jennie can drive Bird to your studio an' pick his car up, or you can return it to him yourself. There! Oh, first I'll take your cane out, an' my leather pillow. I mustn't get parted from Picturesque Quanomet!"

Bird's papers and charts fell down again when he removed the pillow, and Dave laughed.

"I've never seen Clifton's car that papers weren't falling all over it — is that Linda coming? Well, suppose I just fix the rest of those papers later!"

He drove away in Bird's coupé just as Linda came out the door of the Juke Box.

"Pappy just about beat that, didn't he?" Kay inquired in a low voice.

Asey chuckled. "You mean that was all a stall for him to get away from her?"

"Mostly, I suspect — have you any more business to transact with her? Then start over toward the beachwagon, quick — I'll take the pillow. Yes, I suspect that Linda tries him in some ways more than Muriel. And now she's learned from me who you really are, and that the cigarette lighter probably *is* platinum, and that you own a Porter Coupé de Ville, I wonder if perhaps you also hadn't better jump!"

Asey slid in behind the wheel of the beachwagon.

"P'raps," he agreed, "we'd better!"

At the end of the shore road, he suddenly pulled up and stopped.

"What's wrong?" Kay asked curiously. "You look so worried!"

"There's something I'm tryin' to connect in my mind," he said, "an' I can't quite make it. While I think it out, s'pose you clear up a few odds an' ends for me. First off, tell me about Muriel. She's really been harryin' your pappy, huh?"

"It's been simply hell on toast," Kay said. "For him and all of us. She's been on his neck morning, noon and night for weeks, ever since he got the idea of this Cape book. Well, let's face it — no female over the age of eleven months ever looked at Father without breathing heavily and sighing. They always have and they always will — and he *is* charming! If he loses his teeth and acquires a paunch, I'm sure they'll probably still pant — when he autographs books in department stores, they rush up from the silk slip sale in the basement and buy books instead. Cooing! We accept it as a matter of course. Mother did. I do. But Aunt Maude never has, poor dear!"

"Oho!" Asey said. "Could be that was what she was holdin' back from me so strenuous? About your father an' Muriel?"

Kay grinned.

"She said she was so afraid she'd break down and really tell you what she thought about Muriel, she had to keep pinching herself. She yearned to tell you everything, but she didn't want to bring in Father. And I see her point, don't you? Unless you knew Father, and knew Muriel, it wouldn't sound very sensible."

"Did your Aunt Maude swipe the pink glass egg from Muriel's museum?" Asey asked out of a clear sky.

"Dear God, no!" Kay said. "Whatever made you think that?"

"Sure?"

"Positive. We fought the battle of the pink egg and lost. Muriel wouldn't let us use it for publicity pictures, and that was that."

There was no doubt in Asey's mind but that she was telling him the truth.

Only he wondered if perhaps Aunt Maude wasn't maybe still holding a little something back!

"Now," he said, "we come to the fascinatin' topic of Buff Orpington. I gather you seen him lately — just where'd you run into him?"

"I didn't. He practically ran into me on the new highway behind the cemetery — oh, hours and hours ago! Before the second rain. He said you'd ordered him to run, and he was running. So," Kay said, "I picked him up."

"An' you run together, huh?"

"You have to remember," she said, "that I was wildly hunting for Aunt Maude, at that point. I'd rushed away from the ball park when I saw her car leave — I was never more torn to pieces! I had to leave Bobby there because I couldn't find him, and I really was terribly worried about something happening to her! And of course I missed her at the start because it simply never occurred to me to drive through that cemetery short cut! She never used it in her life — she loathes cemeteries! Anyway, Buff and I hunted Aunt Maude from pillar to post. And back. I still wasn't happy about Bobby, but Buff and I felt he was safe with you."

"An' so Buff told you all that'd happened to him, an' then you both connected with Aunt Maude after Cummings brought her home," Asey said. "An' she'd pumped *him* dry.

So you put it all together, an' that's how you got such a sterlin' picture of what was goin' on. Uh-huh, I see. Now, here's the sixty-four-dollar question for you — where's Buff now?"

Kay shook her head.

"I don't know — truly, I don't! I haven't the faintest idea!"

"What happened to him?" Asey demanded. "Did he just decide to start runnin' again?"

"Practically. Well, yes."

Asey looked at her quizzically.

"I know it sounds crazy!" she said defensively. "But as Buff kept muttering to himself, this is Picturesque Quanomet! We were on Main Street, going into the post office — I was checking up on a missing costume that was supposed to be sent special delivery. And all of a sudden, Buff looked out the window and said 'By George!' And he ran out, and ran around the corner. And by the time I got there, he'd completely disappeared!"

"An' he never come back? He — say, would that be a box of lunch there on the back seat?"

"It would be Bobby's emergency rations that we never got to," Kay said. "Somewhere in the smoke and flame of battle, we had a pick-up meal at home — good Lord, d'you mean you haven't *eaten?* Here, let me get it for you! But don't expect any de luxe Blue Plate Special! It's probably very much on the stale side!"

"I'm starvin'," Asey said. "Go on about Buff."

"Well, he simply disappeared from human sight, and apparently forever and ever. I hunted around for him, and peered into assorted stores, but I finally had to leave — they were panting for that costume. Frankly, I can't guess why you seem so pleased! Does any of this saga of Buff make sense to you, or are you just terribly fond of dried-up ham sandwiches and animal crackers?"

"Both," Asey told her with his mouth full. "Huh! What I'm guessin' is that he looked out the window an' saw George Pettingill in my Porter, an' decided to follow him up—yessir, I bet it was Buff that swiped the car from in front of Muriel's!"

"I wondered why you were touring in that thing of Clifton's," Kay said. "Has your car really been stolen or borrowed again? But why would Buff take it?"

"Maybe he's just got into the habit," Asey said. "Maybe he feels sort of responsible on account of him bein' the original pincher. Maybe he just *felt* like chasin' after George—who knows? Who can tell? Course, it seems like Buff had ought to have seen that driveway sign with Muriel's name on it, an' maybe done a little investigatin' first. But on the other hand, maybe he sneaked up on the Porter from the rear or something, an' never noticed. That's as good a guess as I can muster up about it all, anyway—tell me, does Buff have a beard?"

Kay looked a little puzzled.

"While it's not a topic on which I'm personally informed to any extent," she said, "I assume he probably requires the use of a razor from time to time—if you don't mind my saying so, what a strange thing to ask me! I mean, Buff is a pleasant soul, and lots more fun than I'd remembered his being, and I like him. But I hardly know very much about the state of his beard!"

Asey grinned.

"I meant beard," he said, "as a pageant or false job."

"Oh. Oh, yes. He has a beard. I'm sorry, I just didn't understand what you were driving at!"

"Uh — did you feel maybe he might get lonesome in Picturesque Quanomet if he was beardless?" Asey wanted to know.

"Aunt Maude thrust it on him, as a matter of fact," Kay said. "You see, we never really did know whether or not George Pettingill would ever manage to get here in time for the performance tomorrow night. Muriel said that he would, but we'd learned not to place too much faith in some of her assertions. And when I first saw Buff this morning, it occurred to me he'd be a wonderful spare in case George didn't come. I said as much to Clifton Bird. And then at lunch, Aunt Maude pointed her finger at Buff, and announced that *he* was going to be Lord Andrews in the War of 1812 scene. Oh — now I've got to tell you all about *him,* and Muriel insisting that George play him — "

"I know," Asey said. "George told me."

"How merciful! Well, Aunt Maude felt that even though George would unquestionably be here because of Muriel, he probably wouldn't care to cavort about in a pageant under the circumstances. So she promptly elected Buff. Created him an admiral on the spot, and presented him with a spare beard she providently had on hand."

"I meant to ask you," Asey said. "Is this problem of Muriel goin' to affect the over-all pageant situation at all?"

A little smile hovered around Kay's lips.

"I wondered about that, myself, and I asked Aunt Maude at once if we canceled, or postponed, or what. She searched her soul for about three quarters of a second, and then said in a voice vibrant with sorrow that she felt sure dear Muriel would wish us all to carry on as if absolutely nothing had happened. She added she thought dear Muriel's sad loss might possibly prove to be just the very spur we needed."

"What's the literal translation of that?" Asey inquired. "Did she mean that everybody ought to smile real brave through their tears, an' put 'Quanomet Through the Ages' over with a bang? Or that dear Muriel's sad loss was the pageant's gain?"

"Both, very likely. She never came right out with the crass statement that the publicity wouldn't hurt one bit," Kay said, "but she whipped off a sadly refined little press release at once, and telephoned it to the Boston papers. Then she changed into a somber black dress and memorized three sentences about our sad loss that would fit almost anything anyone could possibly say to her about Muriel. And then she inserted a few careful words of eulogy and bereavement into her opening speech of welcome."

"Forehanded, ain't she?" Asey commented.

"The situation," Kay said, "is well in hand — look, all this maundering around isn't *getting* you anywhere, and I somehow have the strangest sense of detaining you. And keeping you from important things — don't you want to get on, and be up and doing?"

"I *am* doin'," Asey said gently.

"Oh?"

"Uh-huh. Among other things, I've figured out what probably must have happened to my car," he said, "an' I think it sort of mattered who took it — wa-el, I s'pose we might as well go whole-hog, an' assume that Buff went an' put his admiral's beard on, an' that he was the man that George an' I seen in the Porter. Only why in time *should* he put it on, anyway?"

There was something almost a little smug and superior about Kay's smile.

"Women always try on hats," she said. "Everyone knows that. But when you've stood around on the fringes of pageants as long as I have, you'll know that *men* always try on beards. They cannot resist them! I rather marveled at Buff's not demanding a mirror at once when Aunt Maude gave him that beard. He showed incredible restraint. But probably he finally succumbed, and stuck it on, and — duck! Duck *quick!*" she added. "*Duck!*"

Asey obediently ducked down out of sight.

"All right, you can get up now," Kay said after a car sped past them. "That was Linda Poole's gray convertible, and I thought you'd better be safely out of her sight. It's only fair to warn you that she's taken a strong fancy to your cigarette lighter, and I don't think at the moment you probably want to waste your time keeping her at bay. She — ah, I thought so! She's going over to the Nokowasset House to find out in person about those orchestra boys — see? There she goes, off on the turn!"

"Nokowasset," Asey said thoughtfully. "Huh."

"There really was a Nokowasset, wasn't there? An Indian Chief?"

"Uh-huh. Head of the Quanomet Tribe. Nokowasset! If I rolled that name over my tongue once since we been sittin' here, I bet I rolled it fifty million times! *Why* can't I get

Nokowasset out of my mind? It didn't plague me none when the Spirit of Quanomet first brought it up."

"Probably," Kay said, "because you've been staring straight at it for the last fifteen minutes! It's that barny-looking, gray-shingled job ahead, sticking out of the sand dunes — but *you* certainly know that dreary old pile!"

"If you want to know the truth," Asey said, "I really wasn't lookin' at it. Course I know it, but it somehow never entered my head that you might be talkin' about the *old* Nokowasset! I don't get over to this neck of the woods once in a dog's age, but I had an idea that old place either fell apart or else closed down years an' years ago!"

Kay said that the Navy had given it such a beating during the war, when it was used as a barracks, that no one had ever expected it to reopen.

"But there it *is,* still going strong! Same porches, same lines of green rockers — and the rockers all filled with the same sort of women who always fill rockers to the utmost! Whenever I go there, I always wonder if they take those women in with the rockers every September, and put 'em all in storage together, and then dust 'em off every spring and put 'em back in the same rockers — oh, where are we going?" she added as Asey started up the beachwagon. "Over to the cemetery?"

He shook his head.

"I finally got it," he said. "What I been tryin' to connect up, I mean. It wasn't Linda Poole's talkin' about the Nokowasset. It was *your* talkin' about it, an' the fellow with the pince-nez. Those pince-nez did it. See?"

"I certainly don't see! When did I ever — oh, yes. I *did* mention them. I said Linda was speaking on the phone with that prim little fellow with the pince-nez. So," Kay said, "what?"

"Back when I run into my Cousin Jennie," Asey said, "she told me she'd tracked down the person that was responsible for harryin' your Aunt Maude. Said he was a foreigner, named Tanik or Tonic. At least, she said, *that* was what the clerk with the pince-nez told her. I went flippin' off before I could ask her what clerk, or where. An' then you talked about this Nokowasset fellow with the pince-nez. An' I finally managed to make connections."

"Jennie *really* tracked down whoever was harrying Aunt Maude?" Kay said. "But — well, does it matter any, now? After Muriel?"

Asey smiled.

"If you think back, I s'pose maybe you can assume that the same person who harried her was also harryin' Clifton Bird, an' Muriel. So — "

"So," Kay picked him up excitedly, "if Jennie really found out who was after Aunt Maude, then you've found out *who?*"

"Wa-el, maybe that's bein' pretty optimistic," Asey said. "Let's be conservative an' admit we're playin' a long shot. I think somebody harried all three for the same reason. He got everyone an' everything worked up an' confused — sort of reminds me of the old-fashioned pea-and-shell game, where the fellow used to twiddle three walnut shells around quick, an' give you the privilege of payin' to guess which shell the pea would be under. Only *he* knew all the time which one he intended to pick. See?"

"Sort of," she said hesitantly. "Only — "

"Jennie said that the 'clerk' told her the name," Asey went

on. "That sounds like a hotel. An' his pince-nez don't sound much like a grocery store clerk, say. An' while we got beards around by the score, this is all the pince-nez that's come to light. So let's turn here, an' sally into the old Nokowasset House, an' ask the man with the pince-nez for Mr. Tonic. An' never say I ever claimed it was anything but a long shot!"

"I *like* it!" Kay pointed to a gray convertible. "There's Linda's car — and there she is, talking with a bellhop. Drive over to the other parking space, and she won't notice us. Isn't this a barn of a place? And all those dreary miles of covered porches!"

"Last time I was here," Asey said reminiscently, "there was three pictures of Calvin Coolidge in the main lobby, an' rubber plants all around."

Kay's laugh was almost a chortle.

"Grab that empty space," she said. "Oh, wouldn't it be wonderful if there *should* turn out to be a Mr. Tonic? Or am I being like Father, and just wistfully hoping it isn't anyone we *know?*"

Asey understood the reason for Kay's chortle when they entered the lobby.

There were still three pictures of Calvin Coolidge hanging on the unpainted pine walls!

There were rubber plants, too. And wicker chairs, and straw mats. And golden-oak letter boxes, and frosted glass around the old-fashioned cigar case at the main and only desk. And the same bulbous water cooler he'd seen on his last visit.

And there, emerging from a door labeled "Manager's Office," was a bald man with pince-nez.

"Buffum," Kay said suddenly. "That's his name. I just remembered. Oh, go ask — and I don't mind telling you if there *is* a Mr. Tonic, I shall probably scream with pleasure. And then faint!"

"So," Asey said, "will I."

He strode over toward the desk.

"Mr. Buffum," he began, and then stopped. Nobody was ever named Mr. Tonic!

"Yes, sir, what may I do for you, sir?"

Asey drew a long breath and politely asked for Mr. Tonic. And Mr. Buffum took the request in his stride.

"Ah — er — Mr. Ten Eyck?" He pronounced the name very clearly and distinctly, and then turned and surveyed the key rack behind the desk. "Yes, sir. Certainly. He's in. I'll have a boy call him."

"I mean," Asey said hurriedly, "Mr. Tonic with the beard."

A look of pain crossed Mr. Buffum's face.

"Yes, sir. Quite. Mr. Ten Eyck. Oh, how do you do, Mrs. Pouter? I didn't realize that you were with this gentleman. And how is Bobby? Getting his portable Geiger counter for his birthday, I hope? He told me all about that Geiger counter when he was here for Billy West's party."

"How Bobby disseminates his propaganda!" Kay said. "Everywhere I go, someone else tells me about that thing! I do hope he behaved himself at the party."

"Oh, beautifully! I'll send for Mr. Ten Eyck at once — oh, did you know that he won our bridge tournament last night? Perhaps while you're waiting for him, you might care to look at the very interesting caricature of him done by another of our guests. It's over on the bulletin board by the dining room door. I'll ring for the boy."

Kay and Asey crossed the lobby to the bulletin board in nothing flat.

"Wa-el," Asey said as he looked at the caricature, "we couldn't ever miss it, could we? Now *there* is my conception of a good, shaggy-type beard! Golly, he looks like a cabbage that's sprouted fur!"

"It's a sinister beard!" Kay said. "*He*'s sinister! He looks like someone who might drop in to borrow a cup of arsenic. What nasty slit-eyes!"

"There is kind of a touch of the Dragon Lady about 'em," Asey agreed. "Huh. Tonic. Ten Eyck. It couldn't happen anywheres else but Picturesque Quanomet! Let's go camp among the rubber plants an' see what new trends crop up next!"

After ten minutes of impatient waiting, Asey got to his feet.

"Another brain wave," he said in response to Kay's question. "Who was Muriel's lawyer?"

"Someone in New York. I don't know who. But Mayo in the village might be able to tell you. He always did little odds and ends of legal work for her — is he a relation of yours? Isaiah Mayo."

"If he isn't a cousin," Asey said, "he will be. I'm goin' to phone him from that booth in the corner. I'd ought to be able to see Tonic when he comes, but if I should miss him, yell."

A quarter of an hour passed before he returned.

"Where in time *is* that fellow? Nope, it wasn't a fruitful conversation, in spite of him turnin' out to be a genuine third cousin. He's one of the cautious Mayos that guards his tongue. Muriel hasn't asked his advice or spoken to him of any new wills lately, but of course he couldn't say that didn't mean she hadn't had a dozen drawn up. I managed to lure him into admittin' she couldn't get out of leavin' a lot to George Pettingill. Something about a family trust — say, you go coo at Pince-nez, will you? See if you can't find out what's holdin' things up."

Kay reported when she came back from interviewing Mr. Buffum that Mr. Ten Eyck certainly was in the hotel somewhere, and that two bellboys were hunting for him. Most assiduously.

"And Mr. Buffum also says," she added, "that Rome wasn't built in a day. It's dreadful waiting like this, isn't it? I don't dare let myself think he might have gone! Buffum's so positive he's here!"

"I wish," Asey said, "that we could get some local color on the fellow. You acquainted with anybody stayin' here, like any of the rockin' chair brigade out on the porch?"

"Why didn't I think of that!" Kay said. "I know at least three of Aunt Maude's cronies. Let me see what I can do. Maybe I can extract — oh, you'd better sit behind that palm tree so Linda won't spot you if she should pop in. I'd really regret your losing that lighter. I'll pump the girls and be back in a flash."

Her return to the lobby lacked the buoyancy and the bounce of her departure.

She looked distressed and depressed and disheartened, and her feet dragged.

"I know," she said before Asey had a chance to utter a word. "I know. I can see the clock! And it's the longest thirty-three minutes *I* ever put in — haven't they found any trace of him at all?"

"Mr. Buffum's doin' his very best, sir. He's told me so five times. How'd you make out?"

Kay sighed, and sank wearily into one of the wicker chairs. Then she straightened up quickly.

"Wicker fools you so, doesn't it? It's so unpliant! Listen — and I hope I can remember it all. I'm groggy with details. Mr. Horatio Ten Eyck has been here roughly three weeks. He's come here every summer that anyone can remember. He used to come with his mother — she was a sweet character, a dear, dear person, and such a *won*derful mother. Lived only for her son. Since her death, he's come alone. He always raises a beard. Raising a beard is his vacation hobby. He works at it the way other men work at their chip shots and their putting. Mr. Ten Eyck likes himself with a beard. Nobody else does, much — where's that, and I quote, cherubic lighter?"

Asey grinned as he held it out for her cigarette.

"Why's outside opinion against the beard?" he inquired.

"Thanks. Well, it's felt he scares children, and that isn't *good* for them. And the beard is so untidy. And Mr. Buffum's confided to a few intimates that he doesn't think it's a nice touch for the Nokowasset lobby to have Ten Eyck sitting around like that. He thinks it looks communistic."

"Offensive to Mr. Coolidge, huh?"

"Definitely," Kay said. "Mr. Ten Eyck is a very friendly man — I think by that they meant he talked to people without being properly introduced. He's unmarried. Forty-ish. He's engaged in the greeting card business. He sends everyone the most wonderful 'Get Well' cards when he hears they're ailing. And very, very funny ones on April Fools' Day — can you gather what I went through to achieve this?"

Asey chuckled.

"Remember *I* been askin' questions of people since almost the dawn's early light! Go on."

"He's a friend of the Harriman boy's family — "

"What *is* their name?" Asey interrupted. "Lamb?"

"No, Guernsey." She paused. "D'you know, Horatio Ten Eyck sounds so overwhelmingly respectable, it worries me! It really throws me. All I can think about is Aunt Maude's original notions that I thought were so foolish and utterly nonsensical and generally wacky. Her suspicions about the subversive element being at work, and boring from within, and all that sort of thing. For the first time, it seems to make some sense to me!"

Asey looked at her reflectively. "How come?"

"Oh, those people are always so — well, so respectable!" Kay said. "I mean, when you read accounts of their trials in the papers, they sound like such nice, normal souls! They remember silly little things so exactly, like their maid's breaking the iron cord on Wednesday the twelfth at nine-thirty, and then they forget important things, like the date when they were entrusted with the secret documents, or the city where they inadvertently misplaced 'em. They think they must have lived in this apartment at that time, because it was when their little girl was having her bite corrected, and wore that horrid plastic thing on her teeth. And — d'you see what I'm driving at?"

"Wa-el," Asey said, "in a sort of way."

"Everything's just so damned innocent — just like the greeting card business! There couldn't be anything *more* innocent, could there?"

Asey conceded the truth of that.

"And traitors and saboteurs," Kay went on, "are always basically Ten Eyck's type. They vacation with their mothers, who live only for them — that's odd grammar, but you know what I mean. They strive to do something spectacularly virile, just to *show* you. Like raising beards. They have a strong sentimental streak. Like the greeting card angle. Psychiatrically speaking, to use one of Pappy's favorite phrases, Ten Eyck's perfect fodder for the subversive crew!"

"Could be," Asey said. "But how'd you hook him up with all this?"

"Oh, suppose that he fell for Aunt Maude's holy purpose — the pageant's holy purpose, that is. Suppose that he really *did* believe what our posters and publicity releases say, about the pageant being America asserting itself, and so on. Suppose that he decided it was a dandy chance for him to mess up a grass root — dear me!" she said with a grin. "I probably sound like something holding forth from a soap box, myself, but this business really worries me! I feel — look, don't you think you could perhaps bully Buffum into scaring up a couple of other bellboys to scour the premises for our Mr. Ten Eyck?"

"I'll try. My foot," he said, "is also tappin' away hard, like yours. An' I'm almost ready to start chewin' my nails!"

Kay walked over and joined him at the desk while Mr. Buffum was promising, with infinite restraint, that he'd see what else could possibly be done to facilitate locating Mr. Ten Eyck.

"Asey, another thing is bothering me," she said as Buffum went into his office. "How could your Cousin Jennie be so positive that he was the one who'd been harrying Aunt Maude?"

"Her prime source of information," Asey told her, "was your son. Bobby claimed this man he'd seen hoverin' around the ball park had a *real* beard, an' — "

"Oooh!" Kay exclaimed with genuine anguish in her voice. "Ooooh! But don't you see — "

She broke off as a man walked up to the desk and stopped expectantly in front of them.

He was short and chubby and round-faced, and he wore pale green rayon slacks and a printed green cotton shirt whose pattern consisted primarily of panting wolves.

His cheeks were amazingly pink, and his forehead was deeply tanned.

"Ten Eyck," he announced, smiling genially. "You the good people who wanted to see me?"

"I'm afraid there's been some mistake," Kay said quickly. "We — we wanted Mr. Ten Eyck with the *beard!*"

"Hah-hah!" Ten Eyck laughed with great joviality. "Hah-hah! I'm your man, but I'm going home tonight, you know! Playtime's over for this year. Have to shave off all that foliage before I get back to civilization and the big city and the daily grind! That's why I kept you good people waiting. Been down in the barbershop getting shorn. Last place in the world the boys thought of looking for me. Now, what can I do for you?"

"Mrs. Henning of the Quanomet pageant," Asey said smoothly, "wondered if you p'raps might be able to act as a substitute for one of the characters that's got taken sick today. She'd noticed your beard, an' admired it, an' thought you'd be just the person to help if you could possibly make it."

"Now, I'm sorry! I'm real sorry! Nothing I'd like better than to be in that pageant! I've been down and watched the rehearsals, and I've gone to Mrs. Henning's splendid little talks to the cast — what a fine, fine thing that show is!" Ten Eyck said earnestly. "If more people stopped and thought more about the history of their home towns, and took time off from their busy lives to really look back at the past, and the wonderful things our ancestors did with so little, why this old world'd be a better place for all of us to live in — excuse me, please."

He drew a pencil and a memorandum book from the pocket of his shirt, and jotted something down.

"Little idea there that I can use in my business," he explained. "If you write 'em right down when you have 'em, then you've *got* 'em, I always say! Now that's mighty nice of Mrs. Henning to think of me, and I appreciate her interest, and you tell her for me how sorry I am I can't make it. But Horatio's got to be back on the job bright and early tomorrow morning — more's the pity!"

"Too bad," Asey said. "I'm sure Mrs. Henning'll be real

disappointed. Say—didn't I see you at the rehearsal this morning?"

"Yes, indeed, I spent the whole morning there! Seeing that I had to miss the big show tomorrow night, I wanted to take in the dress rehearsal," Ten Eyck said. "It's a little rough still. It's still got a few bugs in it, if you'll pardon the expression. But I know all those good people are going to put on a great performance when the time comes, because they've really got their *hearts* in that fine project, and they all—"

"Ho-*ratio!*"

Linda Poole came running across the lobby.

"Horatio, *duck!* You've gone and cut off your lovely, lovely beard!"

Ten Eyck beamed.

Then he shook his finger at her roguishly.

"Linda, you bad girl! You promised old Horatio to have a bite of lunch with him on his last day, and then you went and stood him up! I added an inch to the beard, waiting at the ball field for you!"

"Darling, I was just so frightfully busy that I practically had spots before the eyes! All those dear people are so frantically *helpless* about make-up! I was simply standing on my head—duck, where *were* you?"

"Just where you promised you'd meet me," Ten Eyck said in a reproachful voice. "Right there by the side entrance of the big dressing tent! I sat there with Guernsey until he left, just before the first rain came, and then afterwards I hung around with Davis Williams until after the second storm. You're right about Williams—he's a mighty fine man, and I'm glad I finally got the opportunity of meeting him—"

"But darling, how *pitiful!*" Linda said quickly. "And I was there all the time, working my poor fingers to the very *bone!*"

"I asked everybody where you were," Ten Eyck said, "but nobody seemed to be quite sure — "

"Miss Poole," Asey interrupted suddenly, "hold out your little hot worked-to-the-bone right hand!"

She looked bewildered at his command, but she held it out.

Asey dropped his cigarette lighter into her palm, and then he took Kay by the arm and firmly marched her across the lobby toward the door.

Out on the top step of the porch, she stopped and stared at him.

"Why?" she asked simply.

"She earned it," Asey said. "She provided the finishin' touch to Ten Eyck's story. If Horatio was at the ball field with Guernsey an' your pappy, then he wasn't over at the cemetery. An' it seemed well worth that lighter just to get that straightened out in short order. I'd just about had my fill of the Nokowasset lobby an' the encirclin' gloom. I was tired of the water cooler, an' Mr. Buffum, an' Mr. Coolidge starin' at me from all sides, an' — "

"Asey, look!" Kay pointed toward the sky, now as dark as it had been before the earlier storms. "And the ocean's turned black, too — look at those waves slamming up on the shore! When did all *this* happen? It's going to pour again! It's going to be like those other storms!"

"The way these porches cut out the light," Asey said, "you couldn't ever guess from inside what was goin' on here outside — hustle along!"

"It all looks so exactly the way I feel!" Kay said. "Black and gloomy — I don't know *why* I kept hoping up to the bitter end that the subversive angle might work out! And I still think," she added defensively, "that Ten Eyck *is* the perfect new-style subversive character! Those people don't look like old-fashioned anarchists with bombs in their hip pockets, nowadays, the way Aunt Maude likes to think! They're little people, like Ten Eyck. Thwarted and frustrated by events over which they haven't any control, and — "

As she stopped to get her breath, Asey opened the door of the beachwagon for her.

"If bein' thwarted an' frustrated is the proper basis," he said, "then I'm probably as subversive as anyone you'll ever bump into. I told you it was a long shot we was playin', but I sort of had my hopes, too. I feel let down. I'm low."

Kay looked at him in a puzzled fashion as he backed out of the parking space, and started down toward the shore road.

"You sound it," she remarked. "But of course you're only kidding. *You*'ve got everything all worked out."

"That so, huh?" Asey returned.

"Sherlock, don't try to fool Bobby Pouter's mother! Until I met you, I always thought Aunt Maude won the jackpot for facial control. You can look as if Pappy, or Linda, or Ten Eyck — or anybody, for that matter — was the one thing that mattered in your life. But all the time you're somewhere else, brooding away like crazy. Of course there's something *you*'ve noticed that nobody else has — isn't there? Isn't there something you thought of at once, something that's been occupying the back of your mind while the front of it took on the little problems at hand?"

Asey grinned.

"I don't know," he said, "as I ever been paid a nicer tribute in a more sincere soundin' voice — hang on tight, by the way, I want to make up some of the time we been fritterin' away. Oh, sure. Sure, there was something that hit me in the face, but I'm almost kind of sorry you went an' brought it up. I'd about made up my mind to forget it."

"Tombstones!" Kay said with triumph.

"Huh?"

"Tombstones — and I pin a medal on myself. I've actually made you blink!"

"Whatever made you guess?" Asey demanded. "What made you say that?"

"Because during the Coolidge era," Kay said, "during our long, fruitless fritter, you kept doodling away on the back of that grocery list you took from your pocket. And no matter how you started out your doodles, all forty thousand of 'em turned out to be tombstones in the end! What've *they* got to do with things, besides Buff's finding Muriel in front of a tombstone named Thamozene Winter — oh!" She stopped short. "Oh! *Oh! Thamozene* — are you brooding about Thamozene *Sturdy?* Is that it?"

"If her name was Mary," Asey said with a smile, "or if the tombstone happened to be named Jane, you wouldn't ever think twice about tryin' to make any connections there, would you? No. Look, in passin', I got some things I been savin' to ask Jennie about Thamozene Sturdy, an' there's some others you could most likely tell me about. Just what *was* her part in the pageant, before she got sore an' quit in a huff?"

Kay pursed her lips.

"I practically have to beat my brains out," she said, "to think about anything that happened any farther back than yesterday, and it was a good ten days ago that she left in a cloud of steam. Let's see. Thamozene was in the Indian Treaty scene — she's a direct descendant of the parson's wife who made peace with that Indian squaw. And she was a farmerette — no. She was a Red Cross worker in the World War One group. A knitter. Oh — and then she was a pioneer crossing the prairies."

"An' how do we manage prairies in the confines of Quanomet's ball park?" Asey inquired.

"We indicate. We have two covered wagons departing amid much wild frenzy and tumult," Kay told him. "You know — there were a couple of 'em that left from every Cape Cod town. Anyway, when Thamozene quit, we scurried around and replaced her. Sometime yesterday morning — "

She broke off as the beachwagon left the road and swerved off onto a lane whose existence she had never before noticed.

"Only takin' a short cut," Asey explained. "So?"

"So — uh — so yesterday I helped put gussets in the parson's wife's costume and the Red Cross outfit, so they'd fit Lucy Kenrick, who's roughly twice Thamozene's size. I can't recall if we just omitted a pioneer entirely, or added another one on. But I do remember Thamozene's having some ancestor's blue sunbonnet and calico print dress. Almost exactly like the ones that Jennie hauled out in such a rush this morning — Asey, this storm is going to be a genuine dilly when it hits!"

"Uh-huh. Looks like a real tempest comin' up. Does

Thamozene have anything to do with the Quanomet Historical an' Antiquities club, or whatever that thing is?"

"She's the head, probably. I don't really know," Kay said honestly, "but it's safe to assume she's the head and soul and moving spirit of any antiquities projects afoot. I'm still *so* unhappy about Ten Eyck!" she added. "And yet when you said Bobby told Jennie it was a *real* beard he noticed on the hovering man, I felt qualms. I knew in my heart that Ten Eyck was going to prove a flop!"

"Why?"

Asey remembered the note of anguish in her voice when he'd mentioned that, just before Ten Eyck appeared.

"Because, don't you see, Bobby has a Disguise Kit," she said. "That's what the toy catalogues call a little box full of false noses and toupees and such. It includes a *real* false beard. And — d'you hear that thunder? Listen to it! It's more rumbly than it was this morning!"

"Uh-huh." Asey started to slow down. "Go on."

"Well, to Bobby," Kay explained, "there's simply no such thing as a real or growing beard. He's never actually seen a real one. When Aunt Maude gave Buff his admiral's item, Bobby said, 'What a honey of a *real* beard!' A false beard is a real beard to him — what are you stopping here for? The cemetery lane turn is ahead — oh."

She suddenly spotted by the side of the road the figure which Asey had apparently noticed seconds earlier, even in the increasing darkness.

It was Crazy Martha, still wearing the high white boots and the plumed hat. She was carrying a tin pail in her left hand and a short-handled clam rake in the other.

As the beachwagon came to a stop, she jumped hastily **away** toward the woods, and stood there glaring at them.

Asey leaned past Kay, and waved at her.

"Hi!" He had to raise his voice to make himself heard **over** the thunder. "Goin' after a mess of clams?"

When she didn't answer, he repeated the question.

But she stared at him as if she'd never seen him before **in** her life, and continued to edge away toward the pine trees.

"Or are you goin' after skunks for a stew, maybe?" Asey asked with a grin.

At that, she came up to the door of the beachwagon, and peered inside.

"I'm goin' over to the pond an' get me a nice mess of frogs for supper," she said. "I like a mess of frog legs, Asey Mayo!"

And then before Asey could reply, or stop her, she turned and disappeared into the woods.

"She's so quick!" Kay said. "She moves so quickly — I've already lost sight of her! Going after a mess of frogs — *eeek!* Just plain *eeek* is my only comment! And something tells me that she uses the handle of that clam rake to go after 'em, too! I can practically see her clubbing away at those squirming, wriggling things — *eeek!* Really, I can almost wish you thought Pappy *had* something there in his easy solution of her being your proper and logical quarry! She — can you see the lane up ahead? Why don't you snap on the headlights? Yes, Crazy Martha's certainly on the eerie side, and you can't deny it!"

"I wonder why she'd be headin' for the pond from this direction," Asey said thoughtfully as he started slowly toward the lane entrance. "Seems awful out of her way. She lives clear over on the other side of town, don't she? Near that swamp on the town boundary line?"

Kay shook her head and said that Crazy Martha had moved.

"She changed swamps. One day last month, people noticed her shack over there was empty, and they discovered she'd gone. She now resides in one of the tar-paper-covered huts that the road builders left behind when they finished the new highway. It's very near here, beyond the south swamp — how *can* you see without lights? Have you got cat's eyes? Are — "

A state cop stepped in front of the car and held up his hand as Asey started to turn into the cemetery.

"You can't use this lane. Go around."

"I'm Mayo," Asey said. "I — "

"Yeah, sure. Everybody's Mayo. I know. Go around."

"What d'you mean, everybody's Mayo?" Asey demanded.

"Everybody's pulling that one to get inside here. We had one guy an hour ago said he was Mayo — and ain't he sorry now! Then we had another guy was driving Mayo's fancy Porter that said he — "

"Chum," Asey interrupted, "run back an' fetch Hanson here — no, I guess it'll be quicker an' easier if you just hop in an' drive right along with us!"

"Listen, you can't use this lane, see? You can't even cut through! Go around! You won't get any wetter!"

"*Jump!*" Asey used his quarter-deck voice.

The cop automatically jumped aside, and Asey swung the beachwagon into the lane, just as the first heavy drops of rain began to fall.

"You'll have to give that windshield wiper knob a little

jiggle before it'll work," Kay said. "It's sluggish — *look* at all the cars lined up along here! No wonder they're keeping people out! And did you know that cop's panting along after us, pell-mell?"

"Let him pant. These cars are Hanson an' his cohorts strung out — apparently he brought down his whole crew."

As he vainly hunted for a place in which to park, Asey mentally noted the presence of Jennie's car and Cummings's sedan. There was also a gray car which looked suspiciously like Aunt Maude Henning's.

And there was his own Porter, which probably meant that Buff Orpington had returned to the fold!

"Gang seems to be all here!" he remarked to Kay. "An' look — there's Clifton Bird's coupé! Now I wonder if maybe it could've been your pappy who tried to crash in here by sayin' he was me!"

"How can you ever tell one car from another at this point?" she asked plaintively. "Or anything from *any*thing in this light? I can't!"

"Yup," Asey said, "I bet that your pappy's literary curiosity got the better of him. Doggone this wiper! Try your wiles on it, will you? It's not respondin' to my touch, an' I need to see what I'm doin' to pull out of these ruts, if I can ever find any room!"

Kay leaned over and briskly twisted the wiper knob off, and then on again.

"That'll do it," she said with confidence. "That *always* does it. Bobby taught me the system."

The wiper promptly stopped dead, and refused to function at all.

And then the rain came pelting down with fire-hose intensity.

"You're stymied here!" Kay almost had to yell to make herself heard. "I apparently killed that wiper with my bare hands — listen! Hear that? Hear that rattling on the roof?"

"Hail. Doggone it, I wanted to — " He paused and drew a long breath. "I said, I wanted to get hold of Jennie before Hanson got hold of me! I s'pose she's with all the bunch runnin' for the cars."

"How can you see?"

"I can't really," Asey yelled. "Not now. But I could make out there was a crowd over to the left, an' I could hear cars doors slammin' just now. So I figure they're all runnin' for cover. Well, we'll sit it out!"

He leaned back against the seat and philosophically folded his arms.

After several futile efforts to be audible over the increasing din of the storm, Kay gave up and sat back too, and listened to the sound of the hailstones bouncing off the beachwagon.

The rain seemed even heavier after the hail abruptly stopped. The instant it showed some slight sign of abating, Asey opened the car door.

"You can't go out in that!" Kay said. "You're crazy! You'll only get soaked!"

"But it's clearin'," Asey said. "It's much lighter. See? The skies aren't a quarter as dark as when we come. I think the rain's lettin' up a lot. An' I want to find Jennie — if anyone wants the beachwagon moved out of the lane, tell 'em to go ahead an' move it."

A dozen feet from the car, he stopped.

Then he bent over and picked something up from the ground.

As he stood and looked at what he held in his hand, something in his manner caused Kay to jump out and run over and join him.

"What is it, Asey? What's the matter?"

He held out a sopping piece of blue cloth with long strings.

"Sunbonnet," he said briefly.

"Oh, that's Jennie's! Why, she must have run right past us, and we never even saw her!"

"But — " Asey began, and then broke off as a state cop came hurrying up to him.

"Mr. Mayo!" He was one of the pair who'd first come to the cemetery earlier. "Say — Ted's just found a woman lying over in the woods there! He thinks she's dead. She's been hit over the head just like that other woman was, with a cane or a club. And she's somebody from the pageant, too. She's got on a costume. Sort of a long-skirted dress."

ix

"A CALICO dress?" Asey asked in an even voice, but it made Kay wince.

"I guess so. Sort of a printed thing. Don't you want to come see —"

"Mr. Mayo!"

It was Aunt Maude Henning, her hair awry and her black dress sopping wet, who insinuated herself between Asey and the state trooper.

The latter tried to sidetrack her.

"Look, lady, Mr. Mayo's busy right now! He hasn't any time to —"

But he might as well have attempted to thwart a tidal wave with one finger. Maude Henning had no intention of being diverted.

"Mr. Mayo, I've been waiting around here for hours just to see you! I simply have to tell you everything. I *have* to confess. I must. I can only throw myself on your mercy for what I've done. But I must add I thought I had ample justification at the time, and I still feel that under the circumstances, I did only —"

"See here!" Cummings frankly elbowed his way past both

her and the trooper. "See here, Asey, where've you been? You told me you'd be over here directly when I saw you, and that was hours — "

"Mr. Mayo," Maude Henning interrupted, "I feel that I have the floor — that is, I feel that *I* was talking to you first, and that other issues are currently secondary to what I have to say! So — "

"If," Asey said, "if anybody will let me get a word in edgewise here! Doc, have you seen Jennie?"

"Jennie? No. Not for half an hour or more. Back before the storm broke, and everyone stampeded so madly for the cars — that's her sunbonnet, isn't it?" Cummings adroitly moved his shoulder, and blocked Maude Henning's effort to edge past him. "Listen, Hanson's had a field day with George Pettingill! Trapped him very neatly into admitting he got the lion's share, or at least the major part of Muriel's estate because of some family trust arrangements — oh. So you know that already, do you?"

"Yes, Doc," Asey said patiently. "An' now will you please come — "

"Hanson had another field day with the Nokowasset House orchestra and their beards!" Cummings was obviously too wound-up to notice the expression on Asey's face. "And he's just gone to town on Davis Williams — Williams wormed his way onto the scene by telling a cop he was you. Then he blandly informed Hanson that he'd told *you* everything, and had only come to look around. And Hanson demanded the story at once from him — good God, Asey, d'you realize how many people were wandering around in the vicinity of this place this afternoon?"

"Mr. Mayo!" Maude Henning said before Asey had a chance to answer. "I really do feel that I — "

"Hush, Maude," Cummings said. "I've got important things to catch him up on. Listen, Asey — "

His own diagnosis of how Muriel had met her death, he announced with pride, had been confirmed by Hanson's experts. The process had involved the better part of an hour, and the use of machines and devices whose names he, personally, couldn't even spell, and wouldn't even wish to.

"And what *are* you gripping Jennie's sunbonnet like that for?" he concluded, and then he let out a groan of despair. "Look — *more* hail!"

Asey turned quickly to Kay.

"S'pose," he said, "you take your aunt over to the beach-wagon until this installment of weather gets over. Doc, if you utter one more word, I'll most probably bash you with the nearest blunt instrument. Come along." He beckoned to the trooper. "Show us. Come on, Doc!"

"What's the matter?" Cummings was suddenly filled with contrition. "I didn't understand that anything was as serious as you sound! I'm sorry! I didn't mean to run on and keep you from — "

Asey took him by the arm.

"Okay. Come on. Which way?"

"Over there." The trooper pointed toward the pines. "Hey, what weather! Now it's raining again, and *no* hail — probably snow next! She's kind of a wispy old girl, Mr. Mayo."

"*What?*" Asey stopped stock-still. "Wispy? Did you say *wispy?*"

No one in his right mind ever referred to Jennie Mayo as wispy!

"Well," the trooper said uncomfortably, "you know — frail, sort of. A sweet-looking old lady. Anyone ought to be ashamed of themselves, bashing somebody that looks like their grandmother!"

"Who?" Cummings demanded. "*Who* got bashed?"

"Apparently," Asey said as he started walking, "not who I thought. This still isn't good — but mercifully it isn't Jennie's limp body that we're headin' for!"

"*Jennie?* Jennie's limp body? What utter nonsense!" Cummings said. "Whatever made you think anyone would kill Jennie? What for?"

Asey looked at him, and then he grinned.

"Now you put it that way," he said, "I honestly can't imagine! I can't think of any good reason. But she had on a blue sunbonnet an' a calico dress, an' this sounded an awful lot like Jennie till we come to that word 'wispy'! Now, I wonder — wa-el, let's hustle along, an' then if only we can find Jennie, quick!"

They found her standing with the state trooper beside the limp figure of Thamozene Sturdy.

"Take a look, Doc," Asey said.

But Cummings was already kneeling down.

"I kind of wondered," Asey went on, "an' now I keep right on wonderin' if maybe we aren't p'raps findin' ourselves face to face with what you might call a fatal error! Jennie, I never had a worse moment than when this fellow told me about a woman lyin' here in a calico costume, an' I'd just found your sunbonnet!"

"I think this is dreadful!" Jennie said. "The poor woman — where'd you find it, or what's left of my bonnet? I took it off because it got so darned hot, and then the wind must have taken it and blown it away when I wasn't looking, because all of a sudden I couldn't find it anywhere! I'd hated to have lost that. It belonged to my great-great-grandmother."

"So you wasn't wearin' your sunbonnet, then," Asey said, "but Thamozene Sturdy was wearin' hers — what about it, Doc? Anything you can do?"

"Wait," Cummings said in a puzzled voice as he got to his feet. "That's all I can suggest. Unless you want her moved at once, and I suspect you don't. Jennie, what was Thamozene doing over here, do you know? I never saw her around any-where!"

"Nor did I!" Jennie said. "I didn't know she was within a million miles!"

"She wasn't inside the cemetery decoratin' any more ancestors?" Asey inquired.

"Oh, no — Hanson wasn't letting people in. Course, he wouldn't dare throw me out, because of you, and he didn't say anything about Clifton Bird because he was with me, and Mrs. Henning just wouldn't listen to him," Jennie said. "She didn't pay any attention to him at all. She just brushed him off."

"An' you never caught a glimpse of Thamozene over here?"

Jennie misunderstood his question.

"No, no! I never came trotting over here to see *her,* or anything! I tell you *I* didn't know she was around! The only reason I happen to be over here, and near where she is," she said, "is the rain. When it started to pour, I'd wandered over to the other side of the cemetery, the old part, and I was so far from the car I thought I'd just sit out the rain in the woods, under a good big pine. Then I lost the heel off my shoe, running, so I sat down right where I was — and I must say I never was so wet in my born days as I am this minute! Then when I started back, just now, I saw Ted here, so I came over. No, *I* didn't know she was here, and I can't think of any reason why she *should* be!"

"Except what?" Asey asked as she paused for breath.

"Well, she *is* nosy, you know! And if she'd ever found out about Muriel — "

"She did. She found out when she was grave decoratin'," Asey said. "After you left her then."

"Well, then you don't need to hunt around for any *more* reasons," Jennie said. "She just couldn't keep away, that's all. She wanted to know what was going on, so she was here in the woods watching, because these men of Hanson's would've shooed her away in short order. Asey, I been wanting to see you. I decided if the man with the real beard I found was after Mrs. Henning, and Clifton Bird says someone was after him, *and* after Muriel, why then it was probably all the same person, and you'd ought to go over to the Nokowasset House and look *in*to that Mr. Tonic!"

Asey grinned.

"All five ounces of Mr. Tonic," he said, "has just been poured out with care. Okay. When it rained, you run into the woods around here, an' then you lost a heel an' stopped cold. Thamozene was most likely in the woods here, watchin' what was goin' on. An' the light was mighty poor. An' she was wearin' her sunbonnet. An' somebody bashed her instead of — hey! Just where d'you think *you're* goin' to?" he added as Jennie started away.

"Oh, dear!" she said. "Did I do *that* again?"

Cummings and Asey and the two troopers stared at her.

"Do what again?" Asey demanded.

"I've been starting off on the wrong foot and turning the wrong way ever since I came here!" she said, as if that made the matter entirely clear to everyone. "I'm just all twisted up. It's that old stone that's twisted me so!"

"Hold it!" Asey grabbed her arm as she started away again. "You're not goin' anywheres — *what* stone?"

"You know I don't like this sort of thing much," Jennie said apologetically. "I mean, bodies. So I'm just going back and wait inside of the car. I don't think this rain's *ever* going to let up much more, and I can't get any wetter than I already — "

"*What stone?*"

"Goodness gracious, Asey Mayo, don't roar at me so! You're yelling loud enough to wake up the dead in their — " Jennie broke off, and then she added in a low, awed whisper, "Did *she* move, then? It — it looked to me like Thamozene *moved!*"

"Yes, she moved," Cummings said. "Why not? She isn't dead. Just knocked out, the same way Asey got knocked out earlier, that's all. And for all her fragile appearance, she's as tough as he is, if not tougher."

Jennie sat down abruptly on the pine needles.

Then she as abruptly rose.

"Well, for goodness' sakes!" She turned to the trooper

named Ted. "And there you went and let me think that she'd been killed, and I went and said all those nice sympathetic things about her!"

"Honest, I only said I thought she *looked* like she was dead!"

"Well, for goodness' sakes," Jennie said with asperity, "then why don't some of you do something about the poor woman? What're you just all standing here for, doing absolutely nothing?"

"Calm down," Asey said. "We're doin' a lot. We're standin' by, hopefully anticipatin' that she may be able to present us with some enlightenin' statement — only if the fellow that biffed her was as efficient as when he biffed me, I don't think she's goin' to come to mumblin' any exact description of him, any more'n I did!"

"She's a mighty lucky woman, that's all!" Jennie observed sagely. "Mighty, mighty lucky — when you think how close she came to *being* killed!"

"An' you," Asey said, "are an even luckier woman, because whoever went for her really intended to kill *you* — golly, don't you realize that?"

"Well, I certainly don't know," Jennie said indignantly, "why anyone *should*! Should *try* to, I mean!"

"Neither," Asey returned, "do I. Not yet. An' it's what's worryin' me most, too. Let's get back to the stone that twisted you. What stone?"

"Why, I just naturally started off in the other direction when I first came over here," Jennie said. "That's all! *I* don't know why I had it in my mind all the time that that Thamozene Winter stone was over on the other side of the cemetery. I mean, over in the newer part instead of the old part, where it is! Remember when I traced the Winters and the Mayos, Asey, two years ago? I wasted more darn time over here! I had to cut grass and untangle berry vines and scrape off more moss before I tracked down that stone of great-great-grandfather — "

"No genealogy!" Asey said. "I remember the time you had. An' so you just thought that Thamozene Winter stone was somewheres else other than where it actually is?"

He tried to keep from sounding as disappointed as he actually felt.

Because what he'd been hoping she'd say was something about the weeping willow decoration at the head of that stone, the weeping willow that had first caught his attention because all the surrounding stones were decorated with skulls and crossbones. Kay Pouter hadn't noticed, over at the Noko-wasset House, but his grocery list doodlings that turned out to be tombstones were all embellished with vigorously weeping willows!

But his puzzling about the decoration of the stone was one thing.

And Jennie's being puzzled about the situation of the stone was something else entirely!

"Certainly I thought it was somewhere else!" Jennie said tartly. "I keep telling you and telling you, that's what's got me all twisted up! That's why I was way over in the old part of the cemetery when I got caught in the rain. Because if Thamozene Winter's stone is where it *is*, then there must be another stone somewhere with a name almost exactly *like* it, Asey! Otherwise I'd never in this world get so twisted up!

So I was walking up and down lots to see if I couldn't *find* that other and get things straightened out in my mind. See?"

"I get the general idea," Asey told her. "Only why hunt in the old part if you had a notion that she was over in the newer part?"

"Because there's *so* many names I might have mixed her up with!" Jennie said. "There's Winner, and Wing, and Winn. And so many funny old names that end in *zene*. And almost all of the Winters are buried there. I just meant to work my way over to the new part, lot by lot. I was going to *scour*. I was just bothered enough so I decided I'd make sure!"

"Leavin' no stone unturned in your — is she finally comin' to, Doc? Good."

It was Asey's impression, as he watched Thamozene Sturdy open her eyes and look interestedly around, that she'd withstood the biffing process considerably better than he had himself. She sat up at once, and would have risen to her feet if Cummings hadn't stopped her.

And she looked delighted when the doctor told her what had occurred.

"Gracious! I can't think of any Sturdy woman in our whole family who ever had that happen to her before!" she observed. "Tell me more about it!"

"S'pose you tell us," Asey said.

But she hadn't seen who hit her, or known what hit her, or heard anyone. She'd just been standing there in the woods, she said, watching all the activity in the cemetery. She'd seen Jennie run, and disappear among the trees quite near her. That was all she remembered.

As an afterthought, she added that she'd just started to run when everything went blank. She didn't like being alone in storms — Sturdy women never did — and she'd suddenly taken it into her head to catch up with Jennie, and to join her.

"That does it!" Cummings said. "Someone obviously mistook her for Jennie. Someone was going after Jennie, and Thamozene intervened. God knows the figures certainly are different, but in that light, the sunbonnet was probably all the fellow had for identification — or all he ever thought he needed. After all, if you were pursuing one pioneer woman, you'd hardly expect a duplicate to pop up in your path — Didn't you see anyone, Thamozene? No men with beards? Shaggy beards?"

She shook her head.

"Didn't *any* strange characters wander into your ken?" Cummings persisted.

"Not a single soul," she said. "No one but Crazy Martha Bangs."

"When?" Asey asked quickly.

"Oh, long before I was hit! Five or ten minutes before."

"Was Crazy Martha goin' after a mess of frog legs?" Asey asked. "With a pail an' a clam rake? Uh-huh. Then you seen her right after Kay an' I did. Did she have anything to say?"

"Well," Thamozene said reluctantly, "well — you know how she is! She's *queer!* And think — she already *knew* all about Muriel! I started to tell her, but she already knew!"

"How'd she find out?" Cummings demanded.

"She always seems to know about everything that's going on!" There was the faintest note of envy in Thamozene's voice. "She said very seriously that it was all George Pettingill's work — and why *I* didn't even know George was in town! I told her the police wouldn't allow her to cut across the cemetery, and what do you suppose she said? She said she never *did* walk through. She always circled *around* it very carefully. Because of witches!"

"Witches?" Cummings demanded. "Oh, friends of hers, I assume!"

"She's certainly a queer one!" Thamozene said. "She told me she'd never minded walking through this cemetery until she moved over this way and found out that it had these witches."

"That's nice to know about," Cummings said. "If you just spot where witches hang out, you can always circle — "

"What in time made her think that?" Asey interrupted. "Did she tell you?"

"She said they made a lot of strange noises at night, whirring noises and tapping noises, and that lights flashed off and on. I told her she'd probably just heard parkers, and she said she thought so too, at first. But now she was sure it was witches. She claimed she'd been near enough to see them at work among the graves. Digging, she said!"

"That woman," Cummings remarked, "is even madder than I suspected! She'll have to be looked after — "

"Mrs. Sturdy," Asey said suddenly, "what do you know about old tombstones — like the kind that's in the old cemetery, I mean? With the skull an' crossbones, or the weeping willow decoration at the top?"

As he spoke, he noticed that Jennie was frantically wig-wagging at him, and he began to realize the reason why when

Thamozene beamed happily, and said she hadn't thought about those old stones in years, but gracious, she knew *all* about them and their decorations.

"At least I do about this cemetery's stones! I guess I probably know as much as anybody does, considering there's more Sturdys buried here than anybody else! Now you see — "

And she proceeded to launch briskly into the topic without further ado.

What those tombstone books said, she announced, was mostly a lot of foolishness. Particularly when they claimed that all the stone decorations before a certain date were nothing but skull and crossbones, and that everything after then was nothing but weeping willows. That was sheer nonsense, according to her way of thinking. Because in the Quanomet cemetery, people kept right on having skull and crossbones decorations on their stones long after the books said nobody *did*.

Cummings looked with bewilderment at the rapt expression on Asey's face as she ran on.

Then he looked questioningly at Jennie.

But Jennie merely shrugged and shook her head. She was also clearly bewildered by Asey's deep interest in the subject.

"And it was all because of us Sturdys!" Thamozene went on proudly. "By the way, you know I'm a Sturdy who *married* a Sturdy, don't you? So you see I know everything from *two* sides! Well, old Abijah Sturdy — my grandmother always said they used to call him Methuselah — he was the stonecutter here during the time the books say the decorations changed. And he lived to be a hundred and three, and four months — all the Sturdys were awful long-lived — and he absolutely *refused* to change the skull and crossbones he'd always cut all his life for any of those newfangled, new-style weeping willows! He wouldn't hear of it! He just wouldn't *do* them!"

"See here!" Cummings began as she paused for breath. "See here, I —"

"So whatever those tombstone books say" — she ignored his interruption — "whatever they say about there never being anything but weeping willow decorations after eighteen hundred and — oh, I don't recall the exact date, it's been years since I thought about this! But don't you believe a word about it! In Quanomet, we didn't change. In Quanomet, we kept right on having good old skull and crossbones on our stones for certainly twenty years longer on account of old Abijah being so long-lived!" She bobbed her head in a little nod of smug satisfaction. "It was because of us Sturdys!"

"In some manner obscure to me," Cummings said, "you seem to have made Asey a very happy man, Thamozene! Why, Asey? What *is* all this?"

"I kept feelin' from the first, Doc, that there was somethin' strange about the weeping willow decoration on that Thamozene Winter stone. That's all. An' it seems like I was right."

"But what's it all got to do with Muriel Babcock?" Cummings inquired. "Muriel's our primary problem — not weeping willows!"

Asey grinned.

"Like Mrs. Sturdy just said, weeping willows aren't the norm for this cemetery. So — "

"But I never noticed that!" Jennie broke in. "I never noticed, and I certainly spent enough time here — "

"Uh-huh, you never noticed. But why should you? You was huntin' names, wasn't you? Not decorations. Even if you knew as much about things as Mrs. Sturdy knows, you probably wouldn't ever take any notice of that Thamozene Winter item an' its weeping willows — because when you come here, you'd only just be concerned with your *own* family lots, wouldn't you? You could decorate the graves of your own ancestors till the cows come home without ever once passin' by that particular stone, let alone noticin' it!"

"Well," Jennie said, "for goodness' sakes, Asey, what *of* it?"

"If you read all the tombstone books," he said, "you'd know beyond any shadow of a doubt that weeping willow decorations was right an' proper for stones after a certain date. You wouldn't have any way of findin' out that because old Abijah Sturdy was a stubborn fellow, weeping willows wasn't right for this cemetery. That's just something you couldn't find out from books. An' I don't hardly think it'd occur to anybody to ask around local about it. You just wouldn't ever expect to find people like Mrs. Sturdy knowin' things of a hundred an' twenty or thirty years ago like it was day before yesterday!"

"While you're unquestionably magnificently *right,* as usual," Cummings said, "where does this *get* you? After all, despite old Methuselah's artistic whims, the Thamozene

Winter stone *has* weeping willows! Can't you just assume it's an imported job that the Winters had made in some other place by some other cutter?"

"Sure, you could assume so," Asey said. "An' perhaps somebody hoped you would. But I kind of prefer assumin' that maybe this hooks up with Crazy Martha's witches that dig around in the dead of night. Anyway, now we got this, let's think what we can do with it! Huh. I wonder — "

"Oh, you've got *that* look on your face!" Cummings said in exasperation. "Jennie, do you see it? A lot of nonsense about weeping willows and witches, and he gets *that* look! Asey, break it to me gently — don't tell me you're planning to saw a lady in half *again!*"

"Gracious!" Thamozene gave a little squeal. "Saw a lady in — oh, you're just fooling! I see!"

"Wa-el, Doc, I'm goin' to have a try," Asey said. "The hook-up ain't entirely complete, an' it's goin' to take a mite of co-operation — Mrs. Sturdy, I wonder if maybe you couldn't help. Would — "

"Don't forget," Cummings broke in, "you've got to include Hanson in any mad plans you may be dreaming up!"

"Considerin' Hanson was so busy keepin' out of the rain," Asey said, "that he don't know yet that we nearly had another victim, an' apparently never even noticed our comin' over here, I reckon he'll be obligin'. Mrs. Sturdy, would you do me a favor? Would you pretend to be the official corpse for a short while, just long enough so's folks can see you bein' removed?"

"The *official* corpse? Gracious," Thamozene said, "I don't

know that any Sturdy woman ever pretended to be a corpse! Although there *was* an old family story about one Sturdy — that was Caleb, the son of Jonas — who pretended that he was dead when he was really only wounded at the Battle of Saratoga! But he — "

"That's real nice of you!" Asey said quickly. "An' I sure appreciate it. All you got to do is let yourself be covered up good, an' borne off by seven or eight men. One man could manage you fine, but Jennie's heavy. If anybody pinches you, don't make a sound — remember you're a corpse! You're Jennie!"

"Why?" Cummings demanded.

"Wa-el, somebody wanted to kill Jennie, an' somebody made a real good try, so let's let him think he's been successful," Asey said. "An' then later on while he's preenin' himself, maybe we can saw a lady in half for him, as you like to phrase it. Maybe we can put on a little benefit performance. Like Jennie's reappearin' in the flesh, say. I think it might maybe prove kind of disconcertin' to have Victim Two stroll up to you, alive an' kickin'. At least, I think it'd kind of disconcert me! Now — "

"But see here — can you get away with it?" Cummings interrupted. "Suppose someone knows that he *didn't* succeed in killing her?"

"How could he know? Nobody's seen Jennie since she run off into the woods," Asey said, "at the time everyone else was runnin' for the shelter of the cars. Nobody's been able to see us inside the woods here — otherwise Hanson would have been here hot-foot, long ago. I don't think anyone's dared take a peek. There's too many people around. An' if Victim Two's produced with the proper amount of moanin' an' groanin', I should think that ought to clinch any doubts in anyone's mind. Now — "

"If Thamozene's going to be *me*," Jennie said plaintively, "then what do *I* do?"

"Your heel still off your shoe?" Asey returned.

"Oh, no! I whacked that back on. Why?"

"You an' I are takin' a little walk," Asey said. "Doc, I leave it to you an' the boys here to get Mrs. Sturdy carried away lookin' like our second corpse. Genuine, dyed in the wool, an'," he grinned, "a yard wide. Fix it with Hanson that Victim Two's Jennie. If anyone asks where I am, say I'm currently bowed down with grief, but you expect I'll pull myself together an' return shortly. Thank you, Mrs. Sturdy. I knew I could depend on one of your family. Thank you, boys. Use all your inventive genius, Doc. Come along, Jennie."

She bustled after him as he hurried into the woods.

"Wait for me! I don't understand any of this!" she said. "Where are we going?"

"To the nearest place where you'd ought to be the safest," he said, "an' the last place anybody'd ever think of your bein' if they ever decided to look. We're goin' to Crazy Martha's hut, an' you're goin' to *stay* there!"

"Asey Mayo, *no!* I *won't!*"

"Look, Jennie, somebody missed you once. You're goin' to be careful no matter *how* silly you think it is!"

"But what on earth does anyone want to kill *me* for, for goodness' sakes?"

"Because you know something," Asey told her. "An' I

suspect it's pretty much the same thing Muriel Babcock knew, an' what I think she got killed for knowin'."

"But what?" Jennie asked irritably. "Because I'm sure *I* don't know I know it!"

"Somebody else knows you do, though. Somehow you've let 'em discover that you know."

"For goodness' sakes, Asey, what is it?"

"It's still got to be proved," he said, "an' probably I got to prove it the hard way unless I can manage to pin you down. But I think your wrong-footed feelin' about the Thamozene Winter stone was probably sound as all get out. Just as my feelin' about the weeping willow bein' wrong turned out to be sound. Can you still use a gun?"

"How can you ask me foolish questions like that!" Jennie said with annoyance. "After the hours and hours that I spent plopping away at those tin cans when I was in the Ladies' Defense League during the war! Honestly!"

"Okay. Then you take George Pettingill's little pistol," he said. "Here. Tuck this into your bodice. Just in case."

"And what're you going to do while you leave me at this — this awful place?"

"Chores. Assorted chores. From checkin' up on Crazy Martha's witches," he said, "to acquirin' a fresh sunbonnet for you from somebody in the pageant. An' then — look, Jennie, s'pose you tackle it this way. S'pose, instead of your figurin' what's *like* the Thamozene Winter stone, you switch your point of view around. Figure out instead why that stone is in the newer part of the cemetery. An' then I won't have to comb that place with a fine-tooth comb, an' scour Muriel

Babcock's museum clutter, an' the Lord only knows what else! Why is that stone in the newer part?"

"But it isn't! You know perfectly well it isn't! You've *seen* it where it is!"

"Listen," Asey said wearily, "didn't you pay one whit of attention to what Thamozene Sturdy was sayin'? That Thamozene Winter stone with the weeping willows is nothin' but a fake."

She stopped and stared at him.

"A fake? Asey Mayo, sometimes I think you're stark, staring crazy! Crazier than Martha Bangs! There's nothing *fake* about that stone! It's real!"

Asey sighed.

"Okay," he said. "So I got to do it the hard way! Wa-el, I'll be back for you sometime, after I've plowed through the chores. Meanwhile, you're to stay put at Crazy Martha's, d'you hear? An' just *try* sayin' to yourself over an' over that the weeping willow stone is a forgery, an' why is the *real* one somewheres else? See if maybe you can't perhaps figure — "

"A-sey Ma-yo!" Jennie's voice rose an octave, and she gripped his arm. "A *forgery? That* kind of fake? Well, for goodness' sakes, why didn't you say so? Then I really saw the *real* one, didn't I? What I remembered was the *real* stone!"

"That's right," Asey said patiently. "Now — what's the real one doin' somewheres else, do you s'pose? What'd be the reason for it?"

"Well, I couldn't ever be *sure* about the reason why!" she said. "All you can ever do is *guess* why somebody isn't buried where you think they probably ought to be. Because if there are any sort of records, they're awful casual — sometimes there's gaps of years. But I think I could make a *guess,* because it's something I've found happening twice before, when *I* lost somebody out of a family."

"Jennie, get *to* it!"

"Well, I lost Marilla Mayo, you know, and finally located her with the Tubmans. And Eunice Howes turned up with Mayos clear over in Weesit! I just stumbled on 'em by chance. And I *guessed* the reason why they were somewhere else, and *not* with their husbands or parents. But for goodness' sakes, I don't think I could ever *prove* — "

"Jennie," Asey said, "*why?*"

"Well, I guess that their children probably just moved 'em later on!" she said. "Because those two I lost turned up in their children's lots, even though they'd died when the children were little! Years before! Their fathers had married again, see, and *I* decided the children hadn't liked their stepmothers. So when they got the chance, later, they moved their own mother to their lots. And if that isn't the answer to Thamozene Winter, Asey, there's probably some reason just as simple to guess!"

The sun was out again and shining brightly when Asey returned to the cemetery some forty minutes later.

Cummings greeted him by the cluster of parked cars.

"We removed Thamozene in the ambulance," he announced, "and she's now waiting further instructions over at my house. It was a very successful act. Hanson looked bereft, and I dabbed at my eyes with my handkerchief, and Jennie would have been proud at the grief she aroused — hm. Your line's forming!"

"Line?"

"All those people hovering at a respectful distance." Cummings gestured toward them. "Your being the bereaved family of Victim Two has touched people deeply. They want to *tell* you things. Little omissions and amendments. They can't wait. They've already told me at least twice apiece —"

"Mr. Mayo!" Aunt Maude Henning appeared and warmly gripped his hand. "What can I say? What can I *say?*"

"S'pose," Asey suggested, "you tell me why you stole the pink glass egg."

"I *tried* to tell you — I intended to tell you before you went off to the woods just now on your sad, sad errand! I stole it this morning because I simply could not bear to lose the publicity I knew it would bring us. I had it in the sleeve of my pink lace this morning, but after I found out about poor Muriel, something compelled me to throw it away! I had to! I was afraid of your finding out that I'd taken it, and the notoriety — oh, how can I tell you how ashamed I am! What can I *say?*"

"He knows all about it anyway," Cummings said. "Let Clifton Bird have a crack at him, Maude. Bird's got something on his conscience, too."

What was visible of Bird's face behind the shaggy beard was very pink indeed.

"It's — er — about Miss Babcock," he said. "Er — we touched briefly on the subject, but I — er didn't go into it. When I first came to town, she — er — formed rather an attachment to me, as you might say. And I'm afraid that possibly I did not act — er — as she anticipated. But I certainly didn't," he added in a rush of words, "want to marry her in the least!"

"So?" Asey inquired.

Bird looked perplexed. "Why, I — er — I'd kept something back from you, and I felt that you should be informed. I thought you ought to know!"

George Pettingill felt Asey should know that he'd known all the time that he would inherit the greater part of Muriel's estate, actually, and managed to work in a plug for Pettingill, Watrous and Company. Davis Williams pressed into his hand a diagram of the exact spot where his cane had been left, and begged Asey to see for himself what the rain had done to his doeskins.

Buff Orpington just shook his head.

"I can hardly look you in the face!" he said. "Kay says you know everything up to the post office, and you guessed right about that. I saw George in your Porter, and I ripped after him. He had no business with your car that I could think of, and I felt vaguely responsible for it since *I* stole it first. Just for the record, I then had a brain wave and proceeded to check the artist."

"Artist?" Asey said. "*What* artist?"

"The one with the beard I saw doing the ants-and-molasses picture this morning. That consumed quite a bit of time," Buff said. "He's a real artist, it's a real beard, and at the time of the first storm he was eating his lunch at the place where he boards. Fun, fun, *fun* in Picturesque Quanomet! And since we're on the topic of your car, I — well, it — er — "

"What's the matter now?" Asey inquired.

"Well," Buff said with a grin, "since Aunt Thamozene

has all my worldly wealth, I couldn't buy any gas. I just managed to get back here and park when the last drop went. I dare say you can always borrow a cupful from a cop, but I thought you should be warned that you can't just jump in and drive off — "

"Asey!" Cummings reappeared, consulting his watch. "I've got to start thinking about my patients — let me talk with him alone a moment, will you, Buff? Look, Asey, just when *do* you plan to stage your presentation of sawing a lady in half? Tomorrow, perhaps? Or the next day? When?"

"Wa-el," Asey said, "I ran into Hanson comin' back just now, an' things are under way. He's riggin' up some cock-an'-bull yarn so's to keep everybody here until six."

Cummings stared at him, and then hurriedly consulted his watch again.

"In an *hour?*"

"Uh-huh."

"Asey, are you crazy? You haven't even found out a *motive* yet! Or," he added quickly, "*have* you?"

"Sure. One forged tombstone named Thamozene Winter — "

"One *what?*"

"You heard — golly, Doc, didn't *you* listen to that tombstone decoration recital, either?" Asey asked. "Anyhow, we got that forgery. An' then we got one *real* tombstone named Thamozene Winter."

"You're crazy!" Cummings said flatly.

"Nope. The real Thamozene Winter stone is in a lot belongin' to the Lombard family, in the newer part of the cemetery. In a quiet way, I just checked up on it, myself.

Jennie an' Crazy Martha didn't have any idea what the lot name might be, but they got together on the location, an' I walked right smack into it."

"If you don't mind my saying so," Cummings observed, "this sounds strangely *like* Crazy Martha! Did she tell you all about her friends the witches, too?"

"Yup."

"Asey, stop grinning like a Cheshire cat — remember you're supposed to be in mourning for Jennie! And tell me *why,*" the doctor said, "anyone would want to *forge* a tombstone? *Why?* Particularly if there was a *real* one, anyway?"

"It's kind of ironical," Asey said. "They didn't hunt the real stone hard enough to find it, so they forged one — but they had a perfectly genuine one sittin' here all the time. Only trouble was, Thamozene Winter's daughter moved her mother at some later date to her own lot, in the newer part. So — "

"*Why?*"

Asey shrugged. "I'm kind of partial to Jennie's simple guess of stepmother trouble — I had Hanson take a quick look, an' Thamozene Winter's husband *did* marry again. But the why of the movin' don't matter, Doc. The point is, Thamozene Winter finally got buried in a place you wouldn't ever think of huntin' for her. Because the newer part probably wasn't even thought of when she died."

"Of course," Cummings said, "if I ask you silly questions about motivation, I suppose I deserve silly answers! A forged tombstone and a real one — of all the mad nonsense! And see here — you haven't even found what was rolled up inside Muriel Babcock's diploma yet!"

"But I will. An' then I got to pick up a fresh sunbonnet," Asey said, "an' check things a mite more. An' that part's just been made easier for me, too. Oh — Buff says my car's out of gas, so tell Clifton Bird I'm borrowin' his again, will you? It's handiest. An' — let's see. I got to pick up Whistler's Mother, too."

"Thamozene Sturdy? What for?"

"I don't think," Asey said, "any Sturdy woman ever seen a lady sawed in half before, an' I feel we owe it to her for takin' that crack meant for Jennie. I'll be seein' you in an hour!"

"If you can ever put this together by six," Cummings said, "I'll — I'll — "

"It's an awful wise time," Asey said, "for you to be speechless, Doc! Because when the Congregational Church clock strikes six, Jennie's goin' to put on her benefit performance. For the benefit of everybody here, she's goin' to emerge from the woods behind Thamozene Winter's weeping willow stone, see? With her calico dress all ironed out, an' a fresh sunbonnet on. An' we'll see if maybe I'm not right about who gets sawed in half at sight of her headin' towards 'em!"

As the last stroke of six died away, Jennie appeared on schedule.

It was Clifton Bird who screamed at the sight of her, and covered his face with his hands.

Then, in an amazing burst of speed, he started to run.

In a flash, Buff Orpington was after him, and brought him down half a dozen lots away.

"You needn't have worried one bit, Doc," Asey said to Cummings. "Hanson's spare crew's strewn around the woods waitin'. Bird hasn't been out of their sight for more'n an hour. Wa-el, he sawed real satisfactory, didn't he? I only wish he'd given Jennie the chance to speak her little piece about the futility of forgin' ancestors on Cape Cod!"

It was around half-past eight that night when Asey climbed into the grandstand of the Quanomet ball park and was guided to the top tier by Jennie's strident hoo-hoos and Bobby Pouter's shrill yells.

"We're here, Asey! Hoo-hoo! Here we all are!"

"I see you. Present, Mr. Orpington." He passed the brown leather pillow to Buff, who was sitting between Kay and Bobby. "It's your official memento of Picturesque Quanomet," he added. "I hadn't time to give it to you earlier. An' how's the dress rehearsal progressin'?"

"The loud-speaker system has bugs," Kay told him, "and the floodlights are balking, so there's been a slight delay in starting. And Bobby's torn his Pilgrim Lad pants and has to sit quietly because mother forgot her needle and thread. Otherwise everything's fine — before the band starts again, will you run through things for us? We've pieced it together, but we still have gaps — and *did* he confess?"

"He didn't have much choice," Asey said. "We had everything, from the dagger he claimed someone tried to stab him with this mornin' to the papers he'd taken from Muriel's diploma, an' all that truckle from his car — I sure appreciated your runnin' out of gas, Buff! I'd wondered how I could ease his car an' papers away, an' take a good look at 'em!"

"You'd had his car for so long!" Kay said. "And with all those things *in* it! It must have driven him crazy!"

"Not at first," Asey said. "He'd very carefully showed me those papers to prove how innocent they was — he drove *me* stark crazy with genealogy! When he realized I hadn't caught onto anything, I think he relaxed. But after I packed him off with Jennie, an' he never seen his car again until your pappy turned up in it, I think he worried plenty. Because Muriel's papers from the diploma was right there on the shelf, rolled up neat among his charts."

"How'd you begin to suspect him?" Buff asked. "When?"

"Oh," Asey said, "back when I thought what a fine time for a bearded man with an alibi for his beard to show up, an' see how things was workin' out. An' Bird arrived on the scene. But I couldn't bring myself to believe he'd kill Muriel for thwartin' his efforts to get into the Quanomet Fire Society, even if it was his greatest desire in life."

"But didn't he?" Jennie demanded.

"Nope, he killed her because she promised to expose his tombstone forgin', an' show him up for a fraud. Muriel'd spotted the forged stone, an' apparently knew about the real one. Bein' her, she'd written out a scholarly an' kind of long-winded exposé about it — an' was unwise enough to inform him a couple of days ago that she meant to tell the world. Wa-el," Asey said, "it's one thing not to get into a little club. But it's something else again to have someone promise to broadcast far an' wide your forgin' efforts to get in. That was the big thing — her promise of exposure."

"Why was she so venomous about it?" Buff wanted to know. "She could just have *told* him she knew, which would have been enough to stop him!"

"Muriel once coveted little Mr. Bird," Asey said, "an' he

wasn't havin' any of her. So she was payin' him back. Anyway, when he come here to live, he couldn't locate any data on his key ancestor that he needed to get into the Fire Society. So he decided to forge some material about Thamozene Winter. An' he got so carried away in the process he even got her made a forged tombstone — he wouldn't tell us where he got it, but I suspect some old Vermont slatecutter made it in good faith, probably under the impression that it was a replacement. The stone was historically accurate accordin' to all the books, but locally all wrong — whee! There go the floodlights!"

"Just a flash in the pan," Kay remarked as the lights promptly went out again. "Look, why was Muriel idiot enough to go with him to the cemetery, as I assume she did?"

"Wa-el, that was where his original harryin' an' confusin' tactics paid off," Asey said. "It was Bird you heard on your balcony, of course — he did all that harryin' of Aunt Maude, dressed up in his beard. He felt safe. He knew how she hated to bring up little problems, an' that your pappy wouldn't bother his head if he could possibly avoid it. Then Bird harried Muriel a bit, an' then he told her *he'd* been terrible harried too, himself."

He paused while the band burst out into a tentative fanfare.

"This mornin'," he continued, "Muriel went to him in anguish because someone — which was Bird — had tried to stab her durin' all that rehearsal confusion. But Bird was in so much more anguish about *his* presumed stabbin', he disarmed her completely. She fell right in with his frenzied suggestion that they go right off to the village an' tell the local cop — an' Bird took the short cut through the cemetery. An' the weather provided him with such a lovely opportunity — "

"But his car wasn't parked there!" Buff interrupted.

"Nope. He drew up out on the highway, an' said he didn't want to alarm her none, but he thought he'd just caught a glimpse of a man in the cemetery who looked like the fellow he'd seen just before he was attacked, an' why didn't they sneak back an' see if maybe they couldn't identify him. So they circled back, an' Bird stumbled on your pappy's cane — I suspect till then he really meant to use his own dagger on her, but he couldn't resist that cane!"

"Why'd he wait till he got *into* the cemetery?" Jennie asked. "Why didn't he kill her there in the woods?"

"She was so excited an' jumpy, he told us, that she walked jerky — he didn't get a good chance. Anyway, Buff interrupted before he could get the papers out of her diploma — "

"What on earth were they in there for, anyway?" Kay demanded. "Why did she put 'em in that?"

"She was so proud of her exposure handiwork," Asey said, "she couldn't resist showin' the papers to him, an' she stuffed 'em into that diploma because it was handy, I s'pose, an' she was carryin' it with her. Anyway, Bird was the fellow I watched so long, an' the one who biffed me — an' then he went off an' got Linda Poole to stick on that beard, which was smart of him, an' — "

"But look," Buff said, "if you forge, you can *un*forge! Why didn't he?"

"In theory, you could," Asey said. "Only when the new highway got finished, everyone suddenly started usin' that cemetery lane as a short cut, an' it became awful kind of public. He couldn't dispose of the old original stone, even after Muriel told him it existed, an' he couldn't remove the new fake — he was handicapped by the lane bein' used so much, an' by the mechanics of the removal process. An' after all, Muriel *knew*! Crazy Martha knew, too, only she summed up his work of gettin' that stone set up as witches at work. Funny thing, the imponderables you run into, like Martha seein' him when she went out huntin' skunks for stews, an' Thamozene Sturdy an' her stonecuttin' ancestor, an' Jennie rememberin' a name — "

The floodlights came on suddenly, and a wavering spotlight finally focused on Aunt Maude Henning in the pink lace dress with the leg-of-mutton sleeves.

"Hurry up before that loud-speaker comes on!" Kay said. "What about that business of Jennie?"

"She started off toward the real Thamozene Winter stone the minute she come to the cemetery with Bird," Asey said, "an' she was a marked girl from then on. He waited until the storm to get her, an' then he whipped back to the shelter of the cars, not knowin' he'd got Whistler's Mother by mistake — "

A deafening roar came from the loud-speaker system, and Aunt Maude's voice boomed out like a bass drum.

" — deeply regretful of this sad tragedy which has so marred — "

The loud-speakers abruptly broke off.

"That's the part about poor Muriel," Kay said. "I told you she wrote it in this afternoon — whatever *is* all that confusion in the aisle?"

"That's Cummings," Asey said with a chuckle. "What in time have you got there, Doc?"

"You ought to know — it's yours!" he said irritably. "I went to your house to find you, and there was a man wandering around with a Geiger counter for you, and he insisted that I sign for it and take it — he said you'd phoned for it. *What* d'you want with a portable Geiger counter? And listen, Asey — I've thought up a superb title for all this. 'Diplomatic Corpse'! It's a pun, see? Diploma — diplo*matic!*"

"Give that Geiger counter to Bobby an' sit down," Asey said. "I got a better title. My choice is 'Bird in Hand.' I think — "

In one triumphant moment, the floodlights and the spotlight suddenly focused, the loud-speakers came on normally, and the band struck up its fanfare.

"So welcome," Aunt Maude Henning said brightly, "welcome, all, to Picturesque Quanomet!"